Parlance
at
Pemberley

WORKS BY THIS AUTHOR

Writing as S.M. Klassen

Continuations of Jane Austen's *Pride and Prejudice*
in Chronological Order:

What Really Happened Before Mr. Darcy's Wedding

Mary, Mary, Not So Ordinary •

Mary, Mary, Oh So Contrary •

Mary, Mary, How Extraordinary •

Mayhem at the Minster ◊

Parlance at Pemberley ◊

Villainy in Vienna –or– Scull-duggery in Sanditon ◊

• The Adventures of Miss Mary Bennet

◊ Above-Stairs/Below-Stairs Mysteries, continuing
The Adventures of Miss Mary Bennet

Writing as Shelly McDunn

City of Dread: A 1919 New Orleans Mystery

A Superior Menace: Continuing the story of Detective Jimmy O'Connor and Lillette Montague from *City of Dread*

Spies, Lies, & Shoo-Fly Pie: A Pennsylvania Dutch Mystery

Readers' Reviews for S.M. Klassen's *What Really Happened Before Mr. Darcy's Wedding* (a prequel to *Mary, Mary, Not So Ordinary*)

"There are sinister plots afoot...lots of letter writing, exchanges of recipes, insights into other characters in the P&P universe, as well as a batch of new ones for us to get to know. And a to be continued!!! Can't wait for the next installment. A great read!!!"

"Excellent read."

"I am so glad that another book in this excellent series has been released.... I have enjoyed all five books so far...truly the best P&P follow on stories I have read. I only hope that there will be more before too long, please."

"A most entertaining book."

(Translated from German) - "Written in a wonderful mix of narrative and letter form, it portrays the actions, thoughts, intrigues, and sensitivities of many actors of pride and prejudice....
But the best thing about the book is the humor
with which S.M. Klassen tells the events and draws the people.
I often laughed while reading....
Hopefully S.M. Klassen will write a lot of books!"

Readers' and Expert Reviewers' praise for
Mary, Mary, Not So Ordinary

"Brava!" "Loved this book!" "I couldn't put it down!" "Delightful!"
"A fun read." "Honors the Austen tradition." "I'm a fan for sure."

"Didn't want it to end."

"*Mary, Mary, Not So Ordinary* is a delightful continuation of Jane Austen's Pride and Prejudice...a wonderful, witty, and very readable piece of fiction...one need not be a fan of *Pride and Prejudice* to enjoy this work...."

"...readers who can't get enough of Mr. Darcy will be pleased they don't have to wait long to see more of him here –
even though this is Mary's story."

Readers' Reviews for *Mary, Mary, Oh So Contrary*

"Who would have thought that Mary, the quiet, pious sister could be so much fun! Have added this author to my favorites and can't wait for the next to come out."

"Epic!! In one word, this series is Epic!"

"Throughout the novel, Klassen beautifully portrays the tension that these two independent-minded women encounter when dealing with...female role models..."

Readers' Reviews for *Mary, Mary, Oh So Contrary*, continued

"I love the way the book is written and the story is great, so hope there is a number 3."

"Enjoyed the portrayal of this forgotten sister who originally was characterized as zealous moralist."

"I love Mary Bennet as portrayed in this book...she's my absolute favorite Bennet sister."

Readers' Reviews for *Mary, Mary, How Extraordinary*

"I loved this entire series." "More please!" "Fabulous series."

"Upbeat and a well-paced plot make these three novels very enjoyable."

"Another excellent outing with this author's third book in series. Well written and characters stay true to cannon. Absolutely delightful. Can't wait for number 4."

"Thoroughly enjoyed this book. So well written!!"

Readers' Reviews for *Mayhem at the Minster*

"Very Special - I rarely give five stars, but IMO this variation is deserving of the highest rating. Number four of the excellent "Mary, Mary" series, combines mystery, romance, and relationships for a very satisfying read. New and old characters, an evil plot, and persons and places of historic interest mesh together for a book that I could not put down."

"Excellent story - I love this series- Lots of action, clean, and funny. If you like Mary Bennet, as I do, this is a must read."

"Couldn't put it down!! - I love this series, one of my favorites."

"Fun interesting read - The author continues to write intriguing books about Mary Bennet and her adventures with Georgiana Darcy. Almost all of the wonderful characters from Austen's P&P are included."

"Delightful Read - The adventures of the new and improved Mary Bennet continue. Well written with a light playful tone and lots of regency era detail both fashion and historical."

"Mayhem, mystery, murder, and Mary Bennet Ashton - What a fitting sequel to the other Mary Bennet stories.... This one was great."

"Great Regency Details - ...the author really hit her stride with this one! The plot is involved and engaging...relationship between the servants is rich and complex also...a good read with a cup of tea."

Readers' Reviews for *Parlance at Pemberley*

"Have thoroughly enjoyed all the books in this series. The author knows how to write an engaging plot and develop well written characters. She keeps your attention at all times, and has obviously done her homework in terms of period research. Am looking forward to the next.... An outstanding writer."

"Loved it. I happened upon the *Mary, Mary* trilogy several years ago. Loved them so well that I bought *Mayhem at the Minster* and have really been waiting for the next book. While all have had romance, adventure, and some angst, the main driving force behind this series is the friendship between Mary and Georgiana. These ladies along with their maids seem to stumble upon trouble wherever they go. Cannot wait for *Villainy in Vienna*."

"I thoroughly enjoyed all the books on my favorite Mary Bennet. Loved it... when is the next release???"

"Really enjoyed each of these books. A lovely release from the realities of life."

"Excellent."

"At last, another story in this excellent series. Can't wait for the next one to be released."

Readers' Reviews for *Villainy in Vienna -or- Scul-duggery in Sanditon*

"5.0 out of 5 stars another great addition to the series: I normally lose interest in series that have so many books in them, but that's not the case here! I love the continued stories and adventures. The plots don't seem reused or dull. Looking forward to the next installment!

"5.0 out of 5 stars Another excellent entry! This is quite as good as any of the others. I devoured it in a day or so, and my only complaint is that it's ended! S.M. Klassen is a wonderful writer, capturing the humor that makes Jane Austen's works such good reads, and is meticulous in researching the time period and locations portrayed. With intriguing mysteries, beloved characters, and plenty of humor, Klassen's *Mary, Mary* and Above-Stairs/Below-Stairs Mystery series are a delight, and I eagerly anticipate each one!"

"5.0 out of 5 stars Dear SM Klassen, Thank You! My sister discovered this book series and we have both fallen in love with the characters adapted from P&P! We were so excited to see the new book finally released and I look forward to more! There's such a sweetness in reading how domestic our favorite couples are and I love how the author incorporates history into the story. My classical musical tastes have grown thanks to the author!"

Readers' Reviews for *Villainy in Vienna*
-or- Scul-duggery in Sanditon, continued

"5.0 out of 5 stars Great read with historical embellishments.
I am so looking forward to sequels!

"She has brought life to these characters. I hope she plans on several more books."

"5.0 out of 5 stars Excellent Regency period research and a whopping good story! I just finished binge-reading all six of S. M. Klassen's *Adventures of Miss Mary Bennet*, and I'm sorry I only have the prequel, *What Really Happened Before Mr. Darcy's Wedding* left to read. Klassen has promised the adventure will continue, so I will try to wait patiently. I read these books on Kindle Unlimited, but I plan to purchase them. I wish there was a box set."

"The books were like being immersed in the Regency period with our favorite *Pride and Prejudice* characters and some great new ones Klassen created. The author's research into the period was phenomenal. I only started reading the footnotes in volume 5 so will now go back and read the footnotes in the first four volumes. They are a treat not to be missed. I went on several exploratory rabbit trails from things mentioned in the footnotes.

For example, if you wonder how well Georgiana Darcy played the piano, listen on You Tube to the piece mentioned in footnote 70 in *Villainy in Vienna*...Clementi's *Piano Sonata Opus 24, No. 2*.

Or look up the fascinating account of the Horse Shoe Brewery Flood in London in October, 1814. Or download the actual diary of John Evelyn mentioned several times in the last two books of the series.

In my opinion, these books are must reads for those who love reading well-researched fiction set in the regency period and/or want to read a delightful imagining of what happens to Jane Austen's characters after *Pride and Prejudice* ends."

"I enjoyed reading this story, the latest in the series. As with all the previous ones, the range of characters and their lives has been very interesting, and, to my mind, fit very nicely as a follow on to *Pride and Prejudice*. Can't say the same for any others I have read! Look forward to the next one."

SELECTED SOURCES

Austen, Jane. *Pride and Prejudice, a novel in three volumes by the author of "Sense and Sensibility."* London: Printed for T. Egerton, Military Library, Whitehall, 1813. www.gutenberg.org/ebooks/1342

Austen, Jane. *Northanger Abbey (written 1803). The novels of Jane Austen*, Vol. 5. New York: The Athenaeum Club, 1892.

Brunton, Mary. *Self-Control: a novel.* G. Ramsay & Co. for Manners and Miller, 1811. www.gutenberg.org/ebooks/41196

Evelyn, John. *The Diary of John Evelyn.* Edited from the original MSS by William Bray, Fellow of the Antiquarian Society, in two volumes. M. Walter Dunne, 1901. www.gutenberg.org/ebooks/41218

Hutton, Catherine. *The Miser Married,* a novel in 3 volumes. Longman, Hurst, Rees, Orme, and Brown, Paternoster Row, 1813. www.archive.org/details/misermarriednoveo1hutt

The Exhibition of the Royal Academy, M.DCCCXIV, the forty-sixth. Printed by B. McMillan, Bow Street, Covent Garden, Printer to the Royal Academy. "Catalog of the offerings at this year's Exhibition of the Royal Academy. Portraits of Luke Kenny, aged 96, and Kate his wife, aged 88, who have lived in the woods upwards of 50 years, and brought up a family of eight children in the hut represented, which they erect in various parts of the wood, in which case they may have the occasion to follow their employment, being that of burning charcoal." www.royalacademy.org.uk/art-artists/exhibition-catalogue/ra-sec-vol46-1814

"On the power of music upon animals." *La Belle Assemblée, or, Bell's Court and Fashionable Magazine,* J. Bell, London, Vol. 3, July 1 to December 31, 1807, p. 38. archive.org/details/belleassembleoroounkngoog/page/n10/mode/2up

"Parlance, n2." And "Parley: 2a." Oxford English Dictionary (OED), 3rd edition, June 2005.

White, Willow. "Feminist Sensibilities: The Feud of Elizabeth Inchbald and Mary Wollstonecraft." *Eighteenth-Century Studies*, vol. 55 no. 3, 2022, p. 299-315. *Project MUSE*, https://dx.doi.org/10.1353/ecs.2022.0019.

SELECTED CHARACTERS

*Taken from Jane Austen's *Pride and Prejudice,* with grateful acknowledgment. All others created or added to the tale by S.M. Klassen.

Ashton, Major (Christopher): officer in Col Fitzwilliam's regiment; (married Mary Bennet)
**Bennet, Mr & Mrs*: of Longbourn in Hertfordshire; 5 daughters: *Jane; Elizabeth (Lizzy); Mary; Catherine (Kitty); Lydia*
**Bingley, Mr (Charles)*: now at Beechwood, (married Jane Bennet)
**Bingley, Caroline*: Charles Bingley's unmarried sister
Bingley, Eliza: the Bingleys' daughter, born February 1814
Bonnie Morgan (formerly Georgy): the Ashtons' spaniel puppy
Castlereagh, Lord (1769-1822): British foreign secretary *1812-1822*
Chadwick, Mrs: the Ashtons' housekeeper in London
Chandler, Mr (James): eloped with *Miss Anne de Bourgh
Chandler, Anne (nee de Bourgh): only daughter of Lady Catherine de Bourgh; eloped with James Chandler June 1814
**Collins, Mr*: cousin to the Bennet family and heir to Longbourn, the Bennet family home; vicar at Hunsford Parish in Kent
**Collins, Charlotte (née Lucas)*: daughter of Lord & Lady Lucas, Lucas Lodge in Meryton, married the Reverend Mr. Collins
**Darcy, Mr (Fitzwilliam)*: of Pemberley (married Elizabeth Bennet)
**Darcy, Georgiana*: Darcy's younger sister/friend of Mary Bennet
Darcy, Gregory: the Darcys' son, born June 1814
**de Bourgh, Lady Catherine*: Darcy & Col. Fitzwilliam's maternal aunt; from Rosings in Kent; daughter: Anne
Egerton, Thomas (c. 1784-1830): Mary Bennet's (fictional) publisher
Exeter, Lord: society gossip, possibly engaged to Caroline Bingley
Evelyn, John (1620-1706): writer, diarist, etc. (taken from history)
**Fitzwilliam, Colonel (Richard)*: 1st cousin to Darcy, second son of Lord and Lady Matlock of Devonham
Fletcher, Mr: butler at the Ashtons' house on Hertford-street
Greene, Mr: steward at Pemberley
Harriet Turner: lady's maid to Jane Bingley (née Bennet)
**Hurst, Louisa and Mr*: Charles Bingley's sister & brother-in-law
Hutton, Catherine (1756-1846): English novelist/letter-writer
Lord Harold (Harry): colleague of Maj Ashton & Col Fitzwilliam
Lucy Pearl: lady's maid to Georgiana Darcy

SELECTED CHARACTERS, continued

(*Taken from Jane Austen's *Pride and Prejudice,* with respect and gratitude. All others created or added to the tale by S.M. Klassen.)

Matlock, Lord & Lady: (Earl & Countess of Devonham);
Col Fitzwilliam's parents/maternal aunt & uncle to the Darcys
Molly Turner: lady's maid to Mary Ashton (née Bennet)
Penrose, Mrs: London Society hostess
**Reynolds, Mrs*: housekeeper at Pemberley
Westmacott, C M (c. 1788-1868): British journalist/alleged blackmailer
**Wickham, George*: son of elder Darcy's steward (married Lydia Bennet)

Parlance at Pemberley

A Regency Era Above-Stairs/Below-Stairs Mystery
...The Adventures of Miss Mary Bennet continue
and the characters from Jane Austen's
Pride and Prejudice live on.

S.M. Klassen

HOBBINS & DONAVON PRESS
Second Edition

Parlance at Pemberley is a work of fiction, and the views expressed herein are the sole responsibility of the author. Likewise, certain characters, places, and incidents are the product of the author's imagination, and any resemblance to actual persons, living or dead, or actual events, is entirely coincidental.

First edition 2021

Second edition 2026 published by Hobbins & Donavon Press

ISBN Paperback: 978-1-967523-02-3
ISBN E-Book: 978-1-967523-03-0

"...For if it be true, as a celebrated writer has maintained,
that no young lady can be justified in falling in love
before the gentleman's love is declared,
it must be very improper that a young lady should
dream of a gentleman before the gentleman is
first known to have dreamed of her."

— Jane Austen, *Northanger Abbey*

PROLOGUE

(A Letter from Molly Turner to Mrs. Turner)

Pemberley
6 September 1814

Dear Mum,

I know Mrs. Perkins will be reading this to you, so first I will say thank you to her, then tell you a little about our time in the north country.

For their stay in York last month, Mr. and Mrs. Ashton took a house on Grape-street, where everything is hundreds of years old. Many streets there are too narrow for normal carriages, and are paved with uneven bricks or stones so we had to be careful not to stumble. There is a lane not far from the house where the upper floors of the buildings lean so far forwards that Lucy and I were scared to walk under them.

The way people talk is so strange, it made us wonder if we were still in England, and at first were afraid to go out on errands by ourselves. But, just as my mistress thought, we soon began to understand enough to buy a length of ribbon. Everywhere we went we saw hawkers pushing their carts full of pots and pans, fruits and vegetables, yards of true Indian muslin, or old clothes. One day, Lucy and I walked to the edge of the city, where there is a crumbling old wall. They say people used to walk on top of it, all the way round town, but some parts aren't safe anymore. There's also a really big church, called a minster, that I will say more about on my next visit. In the end, I liked York very well and so did Lucy.

There is to be a wedding here and then a ball. I've been asked to make the bridal dress for Miss Anne de Bourgh of Rosings Park (though she's Mrs. Chandler now, something I can explain to you in person). The dress will have hundreds of pearls sewn in, so Lucy has been helping me.

I made the sleeve covers you suggested for my mistress and have not had to clean as many ink stains from the dresses she wears while writing. Her latest novel is based on our adventures in York, and parts of the story give me the shakes.[1]

I'm getting better with pens and ink, and don't think I need to write this letter over even though I did have to cross out a few things. (Mrs. Ashton gave me a book that has the spelling of thousands of words, and I use it all the time.)

We're not going back to London until after the wedding ball, which makes me happy because when we leave here I'll miss Lucy something awful.

Your loving daughter,
Molly Turner

---

1 The novel Molly refers to is tentatively called *The Bell Tower* and is based on the adventures described in *Mayhem at the Minster*.

Parlance: **2.** Speaking, speech; *esp*. debate, discussion, parley. Now *rare*. (*Oxford English Dictionary, 3rd edition, 2005.*)

Parley: 2a: A meeting between opposing sides in a dispute; ... a conference with an enemy, under truce, for discussing the mutual arrangement of matters such as terms for an armistice, ... a discussion of terms. (*Oxford English Dictionary, 3rd edition, 2005.*)

THE FIRST PART

CHAPTER ONE

Pemberley, in Derbyshire

September 1814

~ I ~

Elizabeth Darcy (née Bennet) was in her morning room with baby Gregory's cradle at her side. In her hand was a quill pen, poised above a list of names as she stared absently through an open window.

She was composing a list of prospective guests for a ball at Pemberley to celebrate the marriage of Anne de Bourgh to Mr. James Chandler. The two had eloped to Scotland three months earlier, directly after which Lady Catherine de Bourgh irrevocably disinherited her daughter and vowed never to see her again.

It was Elizabeth's plan to reunite Anne and her mother at Pemberley—a parlance of sorts—where the two could meet on neutral ground. She secretly hoped it would also lead to peace between Darcy and his aunt, for he had never forgiven Lady Catherine for the vituperative stance she had taken against Elizabeth upon learning that there might be a connection between them.[2]

Lady Catherine agreed to come to Pemberley, but only on condition that the miscreant couple agree to a sanctioned wedding ceremony in the family chapel. To further complicate matters she insisted that Mr. Collins, the clergyman at Hunsford under her patronage who would one day inherit the Bennet family home and all its contents, was to be the officiant.

"You seem lost in thought, Lizzy." Darcy had entered the room without her knowing and was bending over the cradle. "Gregory is such a good sleeper in the daytime."

Her proud smile mirrored her husband's. "Even when the dogs bark at the red squirrels, or deer. If you recall, Jane and Charles whispered and tiptoed around Eliza for months."[3]

Darcy straightened. "They still do."

"We have been fortunate so far." She reached over to tuck in the baby's blanket. "At first, I imagined we would cover every door inside the house with baize and have straw laid on the drive."

Darcy moved a chair close to the cradle and sat down. "Have you been adding to the guest list, or taking from it?"

"Adding." She motioned at the littered desktop. "But now I must turn my attention to the more immediate concern of accommodation. With Anne and James moving into the lake house—" she caught his eye "—I can put Mamma and Papa in the blue apartment, as it is farthest from Lady Catherine. But if Aunt and Uncle Gardiner bring the children, it might be a better location for them."

"Pemberley seems to grow smaller by the day." Darcy grinned as he gently rocked the cradle. "But you needn't do this yourself, Lizzy. Mrs. Reynolds can assign the rooms."

"She has offered, but I thought it best if I saw to a few of our

---

[2] Darcy proposed to Elizabeth (the second time) on 6 October 1812, after which Lady Catherine vowed never to set foot inside his house whilst polluted by such a wife, but currently that very lady was residing in a stately set of rooms at Pemberley.

[3] Eliza Bingley was born in February last, Gregory Darcy a few months later, in June.

guests personally." Elizabeth placed her pen upon the handsome silver caddy her husband had recently given her. "Do you think the cottage by the chapel could be made habitable for Mr. Collins? Georgiana and Mary walked by it yesterday but did not go inside for fear an animal might have taken up residence. They report at least one broken window."

"I will speak with Mr. Greene about it today. Are we expecting Mrs. Collins as well?"

Elizabeth shrugged. "According to Mamma's latest information, Charlotte is *not* coming."

"Cousin Richard and I can view the house when we're out riding. What day does the good reverend hope to arrive?"

"We have yet to be informed, but I hope it is within a fortnight. Neither the wedding day nor the ball can be decided upon until he has provided adequate counsel to the 'fallen couple'." She made a wry face. "Papa has promised to send word the moment my cousin departs from Lucas Lodge, whilst Mamma refuses to set forth from Longbourn until Mr. Collins is no longer in Hertfordshire."

"It is all a bit confusing." Darcy peered once more into the cradle. "I had better go or Richard will leave without me."

"Who else is to join you?"

"Georgiana, and possibly Harry. Christopher claims he prefers to read this morning—no doubt anticipating our father-in-law's arrival."

She looked up at him, her eyes dancing. "And what are you reading?"

"*A General History of the Stage.*"

"Have you not already read it?"

"I'm doing so again, for greater comprehension. Your father and I never had the opportunity to discuss it properly."

"I see." Elizabeth was smiling when she opened a letter addressed to her from his Aunt Matlock, finding a note to Darcy tucked inside. "Wait, if you please, Fitzwilliam. Here is something for you."

Darcy opened the folded sheet. "It is from Uncle Matlock.[4] He

[4] Lord and Lady Matlock are Colonel Richard Fitzwilliam's parents, aunt and uncle to Georgiana and Fitzwilliam Darcy. Lord Matlock is brother to Lady Catherine and Lady Anne, the Darcys' deceased mother.

regrets they are unable to accept our invitation, having been asked by Lord Castlereagh to assist with the treaty negotiations at the conference in Vienna."

Elizabeth looked up from his aunt's letter. "And *she* will not allow him to travel so far without her."

"It is typical of them."

"But disappointing! How long is the conference to last?"

Darcy shrugged. "It could take weeks for the representatives of so many countries to decide how to redistribute the lands seized by Napoleon, and how to proceed with the immense burden of reconstruction."[5]

Elizabeth read on. "Meanwhile, Lord Arthur and Lady Arabel will be in residence at Devonham. Your aunt suggests we invite them in their stead." She took a deep breath before making a note on her list, drawing a line through Aunt and Uncle Matlock's names. "Do you suppose Lord Castlereagh will want Harry as well? If so, he may have to leave before the ball, and Georgiana will not be pleased."

"It would please *me* no end," said Darcy firmly. "Ever since his show of bravery on their return from York, she is far too at ease in his company."

Elizabeth put a question mark beside Lord Harold's name. "I cannot believe he has done anything to deserve such unfair treatment by his uncle."

"The truth regarding his past is thickly veiled, in part because he will not speak about it."

"Jane thinks Harry remains silent to protect another's reputation. In which case his reticence is quite noble."

Darcy nodded. "I must forever be grateful for his recent heroism, but, should he go to Vienna or not, I feel very strongly that it would be best if he were far away from Pemberley."

[5] Darcy could not have guessed the congress would last until the coming June.

~ II ~

At the same time Elizabeth and Mr. Darcy were together in the morning room, Mary Ashton (née Bennet) and her husband of three months, Major Christopher Ashton, were in their suite of rooms. It had been dubbed the Shakespeare apartment by Elizabeth, who, in company with her sister Jane, had discovered furnishings from the Bard of Avon's era in one of Pemberley's attics. With great delight they had selected the pieces and chosen where to place them.

Christopher, comfortably seated at the window facing the deer park, suddenly laughed.

Mary, in the chair opposite his, looked up from the book she was reading. "Dare I assume that is a comedy?"

He nodded. "It's from the set of Henry Fielding's works you found in York—a play called *The Modern Husband*, in which a man sells his wife for money, then sues for damages once he decides the amount isn't enough to keep him in comfort."

"How interesting. Do you hope to do anything similar?"

"Only the highest of offers could tempt me," he teased.

Mary turned her attention back to a rare botanical text from the Middle Ages in the hopes of finding descriptions of poisonous plants.[6]

A few minutes later there was a soft knock at the door and Molly appeared. "I'm sorry to disturb you, madam, but Lady Catherine sent me. She is waiting for you in the library."

Reluctantly, Mary set the book aside. "Which means you are free to do as you like for the next few hours."

"Thank you, madam." Molly smiled. "Lucy and I can use that time to finish Mrs. Chandler's gown."[7] Following a brief curtsey, she left the room with a light step.

Mary was conscious of her husband's curious glance. "It is earlier than the time we agreed upon, but I dare not raise Lady Catherine's ire."

Christopher nodded. "I have noticed her temper is not the best of late. Last evening, when I observed how pleasant it would be to

---

[6] The book, taken from Pemberley's library, was a work by Hildegard von Bingen, translated into English.

[7] Molly refers to her close friend, Lucy Pearl, Miss Darcy's abigail.

attend a wedding, having such fond memories of our own, she lifted her lorgnette and said she recalled thinking me impertinent."

"Did she? When was this?"

"Last evening."

"I meant when did she think you impertinent?"

"Ah." He grinned. "She referred to the time Richard and I visited Rosings, many months ago now. I remember quite fondly how vexed you could be with me, and how delightful it was to hear you and Georgiana play duets in the evenings after dinner." He paused. "None of us ate well at those meals, and the music helped me turn a deaf ear to hunger. Later, we would sneak down to the kitchen and raid the larder."

Mary laughed. "Ever since the carriage accident there are memories others have that I do not, but leaving Lady Catherine's dinner table hungry is something I recall with clarity. It was not many days into the visit before Molly and Lucy started to bring a tray to our rooms after we retired."

"How clandestine. Do you recall any of the copious advice we were given?"

"I know I asked Molly to add green sage to the closets, but don't recall the reason to do so." Mary stood up and stretched.

"Well, I hope Darcy's aunt has something useful for you today." He rose and kissed her cheek.

"She has certainly helped me to better understand the unfathomable rules of society." Mary hesitated. "One of my greatest fears now is I will not prove worthy in the eyes of your friends in town."

"Don't be ridiculous, my dear." He followed her to the door. "You know I have no friends in town."

"Very amusing." She glanced at the mantel clock. "Are you riding with the others?"

"Not this morning. I still ache from yesterday's exertions."

She rested a hand on his chest. "It must have been the archery competition. Should I send for the physician?"

"No, but I appreciate your concern. It is simply the lot of one entering his dotage."

Mary smiled gently and stood on tiptoe to kiss his cheek.

Near the end of the corridor Mary came across the two maids on their way to the sewing room. "How are you progressing with the gowns?" She referred to the four that Molly had volunteered to make for the upcoming ball, in addition to Mrs. Chandler's bridal dress.

"Very well, madam," answered Molly. "Before long we'll be asking if you prefer lace, embroidery, inlaid pearls, or ribbons for the trimming."

"You do know the seamstress here has offered to help?" asked Mary.

Molly nodded. "She does fine work on the seams, and we enjoy her company. There's also my sister Harriet who is fast with a needle, but I wouldn't let her do the fancy work. That is, if Mrs. Bingley wouldn't mind her coming to the sewing room in her free time."

Mary had to smile. "As one of the dresses you are making is for her, I dare say she will be more than happy to send Harriet to you any time you wish."

~ III ~

Darcy was correct in supposing his cousin, Colonel Richard Fitzwilliam, might leave him behind, as the other three in the riding party were already mounted on their horses when he entered the stable courtyard.

As they trotted through the deer park, Darcy managed to hide his satisfaction when Lord Harold told them he would be leaving on the morrow. "Lord Castlereagh sent orders for me to go to Vienna."

Georgiana was not unaware of Harry's reputation, nor of her brother's opinion. But, as she told Mary, she chose to judge him based on the behaviour she observed personally, which of late had placed him in a very fine light, as did the foreign secretary's evident confidence in his abilities and discretion.

Gently tugging on the reins, Colonel Fitzwilliam brought his horse closer to Lord Harold's. "Tell me more about this congress."

"I understand it is to be a meeting of various heads of state to discuss long-term peace. Anything else would be conjecture," replied the younger man. "Though, as I am no diplomat I wonder why I've been asked to attend."

"Might it be due to the anarchist plot you foiled?" interposed Georgiana.[8]

Darcy caught his cousin's eye and at the same time his sister, with a singular look of mischief, squared her shoulders and challenged the three men to a gallop.

Colonel Fitzwilliam, who shared in her guardianship, saw that Darcy was about to object and waved his concerns aside. "My horse could use a good run, and Georgiana is an extremely accomplished rider, as well you know."

Darcy shrugged, agreed to the plan with all the appearance of good grace, and on the count of three their horses were given free rein.

The course was well known to the riders, who expertly jumped a low hedge, a stone fence, and finally a narrow stream. They were all laughing when Darcy and the colonel each claimed to be the winner, having crossed the boundary simultaneously.

After giving their horses time to take their fill from the stream the four riders continued at a slower pace and soon reached the lake, stopping under the shade of beech trees planted many generations ago near the shoreline. They were all surprised when Samson, one of Darcy's prized spaniels, jumped into the water to retrieve a stick thrown by an unseen hand.

Seconds later the Chandlers appeared round the bend, Anne's contented smile growing wider when she saw them. "Are you stopping long?" Her clear voice reflected the confidence she had gained since becoming Mrs. Chandler.

The colonel shook his head. "Fitzwilliam and I must view the chapel cottage to see if it can be made habitable for Mr. Collins."

"What a fine idea." Anne's return glance was mischievous, for she had spent countless long evenings at Rosings in the company of the reverend. She looked up at Georgiana. "Would you care to join us on our walk?"

Georgiana nodded, twisting in her seat. "Fitzwilliam, would you mind taking Matilda back to the stable?"

Before Darcy could reply, Lord Harold offered to do so. "I should return to the house, for there are letters to write and I must

---

[8] Georgiana is referring to an event described in *Mayhem at the Minster*.

prepare for departure." He dismounted quickly to assist Miss Darcy down from her horse, much to the chagrin of her older brother.

A few minutes later, strolling along the lake path with his wife and Georgiana, James Chandler continued to throw the stick for the eager spaniel. Happily, the ladies were quite fond of dogs and did not object to a bit of splashing on their skirts.

Laughing as she stepped back from a particularly vigorous shake, Georgiana adjusted the angle of her elegant hat. "Speaking of the chapel, has your mother agreed upon a date for the ceremony?"

"Not yet," replied Anne. "We must first submit to Mr. Collins' counsel, and she insists upon having final approval of my gown."

"Might the interval lead to a complete reconciliation?" asked Georgiana as they resumed walking.

Anne did not look hopeful. "Her manner has softened towards me, but she is still angry and refuses to address James directly."

Samson had finally left the stick behind, allowing Mr. Chandler to keep pace with them. "I've decided to view the sessions with Mr. Collins as just punishment for convincing Anne to leave Lord Wickford at the altar."

"His lordship will not be inconvenienced much longer." Anne's smile was mischievous. "I understand he has gone to Bath in search of another bride."

"If so," said Georgiana, returning her smile in kind, "we may learn about the courtship from other sources. Lord Exeter frequently travels to Bath, so I am told."

"I have heard he can be a wealth of information," said Mr. Chandler.

"And frustratingly discreet when he chooses. He is supposedly betrothed to Caroline Bingley, but the current state of affairs is a mystery to us all." Georgiana looked up to observe the angle of the sun. "I suppose it is time we went home."

Reluctantly, they turned their steps away from the lake and Samson ran ahead as soon as the house came into view.

Anne looked up at the line of windows marking the library. "I believe my mother is peering down upon us now. She must still be in conference with Mary." She tipped her parasol back to catch her husband's eye. "We need not hurry. Could we walk in the shrubbery for a time?"

Smiling, Mr. Chandler offered an arm to each of them.

~ IV ~

While her husband was reading contentedly and the others were racing horses and generally enjoying the freedom of being outdoors, Mary had been sitting at a long table in a room that held many fond memories for her (although writing passages as dictated by Lady Catherine could not be considered as such).

"Have you finished?" That lady was peering over her shoulder.

"Nearly." Mary dipped her quill into the inkwell.

"You must have your maid prepare several freshly sharpened quills before our session begins tomorrow. You are not adept." Lady Catherine pointed at the page. "And you have left something out. The scullery maid must *neglect* to straighten her room before sneaking from the house. Such a picture lends reality to the scene."

Mary patiently drew a line and added the requisite words in the margin.

Lady Catherine steepled her hands together as she paced. "We need to name the poison. It will add credibility to the tale—something I fear you are apt to disregard."

"Yes, of course." Mary's eyes followed the spiral stairs up to the gallery surrounding the main level on all four sides. "My recent searches have been fruitless, but I recall seeing a copy of *Species Plantarum* amongst the botanical collection. It might include poisonous plants." She was about to rise from her chair, relieved to move after remaining in one posture for so long, when Lady Catherine lifted a hand to stop her.

"Time is of the essence. You must continue writing; I will find the book." She made the ascent slowly, her soft kid-leather flats making no sound. Upon reaching the upper level, she bent slightly over the balustrade. "Where exactly is the book?"

Mary glanced up and was about to reply when someone touched her shoulder, making her jump. "Lizzy! I did not hear you enter."

Elizabeth put a finger to her lips. "I did not wish to disturb your work." She looked about. "I thought I heard Lady Catherine just now."

"I stand above you—" said Darcy's aunt "—seeking a tome Mrs. Ashton assures me is here, though I see no section devoted to botany."

Mary again tilted her head upwards. "Forgive me. Those books are on the other side of the gallery—directly opposite from where you stand."

Lady Catherine went directly to the section Mary indicated. "On which shelf is the book to be found?" She had taken out her lorgnette to peer at those on the shelf before her.

Mary, still looking up, thought for a moment. "Perhaps on the shelf directly above the lowest?" She turned questioning eyes on Elizabeth, who was not fully able to hide her amusement.

"Mary, if Lady Catherine can spare you, I have come to seek your advice."

"What was that?" The great lady was once again leaning over the balustrade.

"I am in need of Mary's assistance, Lady Catherine. I promise not to keep her long."

"You need not shout. I enjoy perfect auditory sense." This was followed by a great sigh. "You may go, Mrs. Ashton, but return promptly. There is more to be done before we are finished for the day."

"May I send a tray for you, some chocolate perhaps?" asked her hostess.

Anyone familiar with the mistress of Rosings Park knew she was quite fond of the hot beverage and could not resist it, no matter the time of day or the weather.

"That will be acceptable." Her ladyship turned to face the books and resumed her search, looking only upon those shelves she had neither to bend down nor look up to see.

When she and Mary were in the anteroom, Elizabeth whispered, "I thought you could use a little diversion. Come, we must go quickly."

Asking no questions, Mary followed her sister to the slightly disorganized morning room. She automatically peeked inside the cradle, only to find it empty.

"Gregory was fussy, so the nursemaid has taken him for a rest. I hope to have him with us at teatime, for he creates a welcome distraction." Elizabeth rang for a maid, then sat down at her desk, motioning for Mary to take the chair beside her. "I have a question for you, since Jane is not here to advise me. As you know, Mamma and Papa will be here for the ball, and possibly for the wedding. The dilemma I face is regarding Aunt and Uncle Philips."[9] She studied her hands. "Mamma has managed to curb some of her own—shall we say exuberance?—when in Fitzwilliam's company, but Aunt Philips...." She made a rueful face.

"I can well imagine just how Lady Catherine will treat our mother, and, given the opportunity, our Aunt Philips." Mary sighed. "I suppose we must be grateful that Kitty cannot travel due to her condition, and that Lydia is safely in the West Indies." With a shrug, she added, "It seems you must choose between vexation and guilt."

Elizabeth laughed. "You sound like Jane."

A housemaid entered then, and her mistress took a moment to request the pot of chocolate before returning to the point. "I had thought of placing Aunt and Uncle Philips near you and Christopher at the table. If you could contrive to keep them entertained at dinner, then continue to do so with the help of Jane when we separate from the gentlemen, we might keep a check on unpleasant scenes."

"You may rely on us." Mary did not remind her sister that Miss Bingley had once openly referred to Mrs. Philips as vulgar.

Elizabeth rested a hand on her forehead. "Oh dear—I forgot about Lord Exeter. He will come to the ball, and, in company with Caroline and Louisa, make snide, thinly veiled remarks, and ask impertinent questions of not only Aunt and Uncle Philips, but Mamma and Papa as well, pretending to be their friend when all the while he plans to spread tales the moment he returns to town." Her look was despairing. "Some days I wonder how Fitzwilliam ever dared propose marriage to me."

It was Mary's turn to laugh. "It would surprise me no end if Mr. Darcy noticed anything amiss should you invite the butcher to dine with Lady Catherine, his happiness is so complete."

---

[9] Mrs. Philips is Mrs. Bennet's sister, and therefore the Bennet daughters' maternal aunt.

"He *has* become tolerant of so much more than I could have foreseen." She took a piece of trimmed foolscap from a drawer. "You've been a great help, Mary. I shall write the invitation to our well-meaning aunt and uncle immediately. Once done, best forgotten, as Mamma says."

Reluctantly, Mary stood up. "Then I shall return to the library."

Elizabeth followed her to the door. "You have kept Lady Catherine pleasantly occupied, which has been extremely helpful. The prevailing atmosphere in the house has improved immeasurably since your return from York—Fitzwilliam commented on it only yesterday. You cannot imagine how wearying were the first few days of her visit. She barely spoke to any of us—especially Anne, and *never* James."

"I am happy to be of use and have decided to see it as a challenge. Just this morning she proposed three additional, disparate, plots!" Mary grinned and started on the way back to the library. Before she could go far, however, she saw her dearest friend hurrying to meet her.

Georgiana, still in her riding costume, took her by the arm. "I just left Anne and James in the shrubbery. Have you finished your session with my aunt?"

"Not yet, but I will within the hour. Elizabeth wished to confer with me about inviting our aunt and uncle Philips, who live in Meryton. She's my mother's sister and he an attorney. Do you recall them?"

"Yes, and they are charming." Georgiana tipped her head to the side. "I see what you are thinking, Mary. They may perhaps not be so refined as Caroline might wish to see amongst her acquaintance, but they are a refreshing change for those of us who are accustomed to—and sometimes grow weary of—overly formal manners."

"You are kind to say so," said Mary affectionately. "How was your ride?"

"It is a lovely morning to be out, but we missed Christopher. Not feeling poorly, is he?"

"He is in perfect health, if a little achy from yesterday's competition. I believe he has chosen to embark on a program of extensive reading in anticipation of my father's visit."

Georgiana made a rueful face. "Harry told us he must leave early tomorrow morning."

Mary nodded thoughtfully. "When Christopher is ordered back to town, I should like to go with him. I could look for a house whilst he is otherwise occupied."

"I dread the day you leave us, Mary."

"Then you must make an extended visit as soon as my sister and your brother can spare you."

"Just as soon as you are settled." Georgiana managed to smile. "Now, I must get out of these clothes, but I promise to come soon to the library and take you away, so you can change." She pointed to an ink stain on her friend's skirt.

Mary looked down with a grimace. "Molly is not going to be happy."

~ V ~

On the shady lane leading to the chapel house, Colonel Fitzwilliam slowed his horse and looked over his shoulder at Darcy. "What has you scowling so?"

"My apologies, Richard. I've been thinking about Harry." Darcy brought his horse alongside the other. "It's a good thing he leaves tomorrow."

"I agree, but you need not worry for Georgiana. She has gained far too much sense to risk her heart—or your good opinion—again."[10]

"It's Harry I don't trust. Has your agent in town learned anything further about him?"

The colonel ducked below a low-hanging elm. "Not even the existence of a kept woman, or a child hidden away in some distant farmhouse." Catching sight of his cousin's glower he shrugged. "We were both thinking it."

For a short while they rode on in silence. "I *could* consult a much-feared man who fills his purse by keeping secrets," added the colonel. "He has no known lineage or outstanding achievements, yet the doors of society hostesses are wide open to

---

[10] Colonel Fitzwilliam is referring to her near elopement with George Wickham, documented in Jane Austen's *Pride and Prejudice*.

him. If there is something in Harry's past, it's possible he would know."

"You would consort with a scoundrel?" Darcy's frown grew deeper.

"Ostensibly, he's a journalist."[11]

They had reached the cottage by then, a relatively plain building in a clearing opposite Pemberley Chapel, which was situated on higher ground.

The colonel dismounted, shading his eyes as he looked up. "There are some broken panes, and missing slates on the roof."

"All easily fixed." Darcy was determinedly optimistic as he jumped down from his horse and led the way inside. The furnishings had been removed, making it easy to determine that the four rooms on each floor were only in need of minor repairs and a good cleaning.

Having finished their tour, the colonel was counting his paces on the ground floor. "The entire house is not much bigger than my set at Albany."

"With the addition of modest furnishings it will be enough for the short time Mr. Collins is here."

The colonel grinned as he stepped into the narrow hall and looked up the stairs. "It certainly doesn't encourage an extended stay."

Darcy, clearly satisfied, followed his cousin out. "The sooner we speak with my steward, the sooner the house will be ready."

Leaning against a windowsill in Mr. Greene's office, Darcy described what he and the colonel thought should be done to the cottage, along with the timing for it.

"I may need to bring in additional workmen," replied his steward with a look of apology.

"Engage as many as you deem necessary." Darcy pushed away from the sill. "You might want to speak with Mrs. Reynolds about the furnishings—there is nothing in the house."

"Everything was removed to prevent rot. If memory serves, it was stored in one of the attics in the west wing." The steward

[11] The blackmailer he refers to is Charles Molloy Westmacott (c. 1788-1868).

followed the two men out. "How soon do you expect Mr. Collins?"

"Any time now, and we may have as little as two days' notice," responded Darcy grimly, explaining how he had sent one of his own carriages to bring the reverend from Lucas Lodge to Pemberley, ensuring that the man did not arrive without warning.

"Then I will start the work immediately," said Mr. Greene.

Outside, the colonel matched Darcy's slow pace as they walked across the courtyard to enter through the conservatory. "It will be a good day when this wedding finally takes place." He pushed aside a palm frond. "I'm surprised Chandler willingly agreed to remain in the house a single night, given the steely eyes our aunt rests upon him at every opportunity."

"He showed not only sense, but courage, by asking to be moved," responded Darcy with a lift of his brow.

The colonel laughed. "My respect for our cousin's husband increases each day."

"Anne too, who defied Aunt Catherine when she demanded they have separate quarters until after the wedding." Darcy sighed, shaking his head. "Lizzy had good reason to fear her plans for reconciliation would fail."

Colonel Fitzwilliam showed his surprise. "So, it was Elizabeth's idea for this meeting? A parley of sorts?"

"It was indeed."

~ VI ~

Assembled in the most formal of Pemberley's drawing rooms for tea that afternoon were the three Darcys, Colonel Fitzwilliam, the Chandlers, the Ashtons, and Lady Catherine. (Lord Harold had politely declined but would be joining them at dinner.)

Elizabeth was about to pour when Lady Catherine lifted an imperious hand. "I insist we discuss the banns first, for time grows short." Her chilling glance rested momentarily upon Mr. Chandler. "I could have arranged for them myself, had I been informed of the groom's parish."

"Anne and James are already legally wed, making the reading of the banns unnecessary, Aunt Catherine." Darcy dared voice what the others were more than likely thinking.

"No!" Lady Catherine banged her elegant walking stick

somewhat ineffectually against the carpet. "They will follow the laws of *this* country! Not of Scotland, a land of ne'er-do-wells!"

Those seated close enough might have seen Anne take firm hold of her husband's hand, his face having grown increasingly flushed.

Lady Catherine continued, unaware. "By English law, the banns must be published on three Sundays during the three months prior to the wedding day. I have consulted the calendar, and there are yet four Sundays before the seventh of October, the date she—" her eyes rested on Elizabeth "—proposes to hold the ball. Before I agreed to come here, it was decided that such an event would only take place *after* the official wedding service."

In the chilling silence Mary ventured to say, "Perhaps I do not perfectly understand, but would it not be more prudent to attain a special license?"

"Such a measure would cause little or no speculation," added her husband helpfully. "And would make reading the banns unnecessary."

"I agree with Christopher." Colonel Fitzwilliam was seated near a window to take advantage of the breeze. "And, as the marriage is a fait accompli, the banns are no longer necessary."

Mr. Chandler gently removed his hand from Anne's and rose to his feet. "I can say with authority that neither the banns nor a special license is required. Do excuse me—I will return shortly."

After he left the room, glances were exchanged and a few eyebrows lifted. Elizabeth quietly pressed tea upon her guests, with ale or sherry as an alternative, indicating the tray of plain biscuits recommended by Lady Catherine as the ideal complement for tea in the afternoon.[12]

Anne took a glass of sherry from the footman's tray despite her mother's disapproving looks, sipped, and raised her chin ever so slightly.

With a trace of despair, Elizabeth said, "I understand your bridal dress is nearly finished."

"Mary's maid is an extremely talented designer; the dress is utterly beautiful," said Anne with a grateful smile. "The final fitting is tomorrow morning."

---

[12] Lady Catherine was known to say with great frequency, "If one must eat at such an hour, it should aid the digestion."

"She has a growing reputation in town, and offered to make our dresses for the ball," said Elizabeth quickly, to prevent a particular person from interrupting. "Each is derived from a painting of one of Fitzwilliam's ancestors."

"What did you say?" demanded Lady Catherine. "Two servant girls were allowed to enter the gallery? Not to clean, but to stare at members of my family?"

Darcy rose abruptly. "They could hardly make a design of something they had not seen." He crossed the room to join his cousin at the window.

Shoulders back, Anne faced her mother. "I understand Aunt Matlock has commissioned Mrs. Ashton's maid to make several gowns."

Lady Catherine huffed. "Then it is time Mrs. Ashton engaged another abigail, if this one is so busy making dresses." She turned to Mary. "You are in luck; Mrs. Penn-Withers wrote only last week to tell me she dismissed her lady's maid, and with good reason."

Before Mary could think of a reply, Mr. Chandler returned, approaching Elizabeth with a rolled sheet of parchment in hand.

With great care, she removed the ribbon and opened the document, reading the contents silently while the others looked on with varied levels of curiosity, and in one case ill-disguised impatience. "It is a special license issued by the Archbishop of Canterbury," she announced. "Dated the sixteenth of June this year, for the legal marriage between Miss Anne de Bourgh and Mr. James Chandler."

The resulting silence was broken only by the nervous trill of a warbler, during which Darcy went to his wife's side to read the document before addressing his aunt. "Anne and James were married by special license in England, *prior* to crossing into Scotland. It is indeed official."

Lady Catherine's chin was high as she rose from her chair. "Then we must only wait for Mr. Collins to give his counsel to the couple before we determine the day of the wedding, to be held at Pemberley Chapel." With her gaze focused on a portrait of a stern-looking Darcy ancestor, she said in an equally firm voice, "I find this warm weather trying, and will therefore take a tray in my rooms for dinner this evening." To Anne she said, "Come to my apartment a quarter hour prior to your fitting tomorrow morning.

I will accompany you."

"Yes, Mamma." Just then, Anne looked and sounded very much like her former self—the torpid heiress of Rosings—but only until Mr. Chandler gathered her in a loving hug.

Later in the day, Elizabeth nearly gasped when Lady Catherine appeared in the oval anteroom where they had arranged to gather prior to dinner. Needless to say, her presence had a dampening effect on the entire party, and the easy conversation they had been enjoying became stilted and remained so throughout the meal.

It was during the dessert course, consisting of sweetmeats, ices, and fruit grown on the estate, that Elizabeth boldly addressed Lord Harold from the opposite end of the table. "As you will be departing at dawn, I must take the time to thank you once more for thwarting the plans of that horrid man from York, and for the heroism you demonstrated in saving my two sisters from harm." Her misty glance went from Georgiana to Mary.

Lord Harold's smile was charming as always. "It was not only my duty, but my great pleasure, Mrs. Darcy."

"Our rescue was nothing short of wondrous," said Mary. "Especially given that none of us, including the horses and our dear puppy, suffered any harm."

"The bravery and quick thinking of Colonel Fitzwilliam and Major Ashton made the rescue possible," insisted Lord Harold.

"Given what ultimately happened to Darcy's carriage, the magnitude of your actions cannot be understated." The colonel lifted his glass. "We are in your debt."

Lady Catherine rose regally from her chair. "Undue praise should not be given for the simple execution of one's duty." Her sharp glance landed upon Elizabeth. "It is time for the gentlemen's port."

Her hostess nodded graciously but did not allow her husband's aunt to have the final word. "Lord Harold, I wish you a safe journey, and a timely conclusion of affairs in Vienna."

The others chimed in, apart from Lady Catherine, who looked upon the hero of the moment with narrowed eyes.

It was only when the ladies had withdrawn that the gentlemen began to speak in earnest about what they hoped might be accomplished at the conference. Darcy clearly found it an interesting discussion, but before the usual time suggested they adjourn to the music room. "I would not wish to incommode Elizabeth further; she had little sleep last night."

"I will go, but only to say goodnight." The colonel just managed to cover a yawn.

Mr. Chandler was out of his chair before the others. "It has been a trying day for us, so I think we will do the same."

When they entered the music room, Georgiana was playing an aria transcription of incredible beauty. At the end of the piece she waited until the sound died away, then deliberately pulled the fallboard over the keys.

Anne was first to speak. "Thank you, Georgiana. I never tire of hearing you play."

Lord Harold approached the pianoforte. "Nor I, Miss Darcy. It is something I will miss intensely."

Georgiana looked up at him. "When you are in Vienna, you may have the opportunity to see Herr Beethoven perform. If so, please commit all you see and hear to memory so you can describe the experience to us upon your return."

"It would be my pleasure." He made a formal bow.

Lady Catherine had observed the exchange with thin lips. "It is past time I returned to my chamber, though I doubt I will sleep. An owl has been screeching near my windows for two nights." She motioned to the colonel. "You will accompany me, Richard."

"One moment, Aunt Catherine, if you please." Colonel Fitzwilliam went to say a few words to Lord Harold before leading his aunt from the room.

The Chandlers were next to go, followed by Georgiana, Mary, and Christopher, leaving Darcy and Elizabeth alone.

"Shall we go to the nursery?" suggested Darcy, who was rewarded with a pleased smile.

Tiptoeing into the airy room, they found Gregory sleeping peacefully and acknowledged the nursemaid in silence before proceeding hand in hand to their own chamber.

They were soon in the bed, nearly asleep when he whispered, "Lizzy?"

Not altering her position, she opened her eyes, a smile playing about her lips.

"Do you think we will ever stop feeling so tired?"

At this, she patted his chest and closed her eyes again. "After the ball, dearest."

He kissed the top of her head and with a look of contentment closed his eyes.

CHAPTER TWO

Pemberley, in Derbyshire

~ I ~

In the sewing room, Molly was examining the handiwork her friend had just completed. "The pearls are nice and even."

Lucy made a face. "Thanks, Moll. I worry that my work will not be good enough."

"Just remember, Mrs. Chandler called the dress *glorious*. It wasn't until her mother started coming to see it that we got so nervous." Molly carefully stuck her needle through the sheer fabric of the overlay, continuing the invisible hem.

In the short time they had left the two worked in a silence disturbed only by the chattering of starlings, until Lucy exhaled and slid her needle into the pincushion on her wrist. "All done, unless her ladyship wants more pearls added again."

Molly glanced at the timepiece attached to her pinafore. "I have a bit more to do."

Just then Mrs. Chandler's cheerful abigail stepped into the room.[13] "My mistress sent me to ask if I can help tidy before her

[13] Called Wilson by her mistress and Dora by the servants, she had been personally chosen by Mrs. Chandler directly after her marriage.

appointment."

"Yes, please!" Lucy returned her smile, pointing to several lengths of fabric on one of the tables, then to a large armoire with a tall looking glass in the center. "It shouldn't take long to tuck it all away."

While the other two folded and stacked, Molly continued sewing and had just finished when the clock began to chime eleven. With calm, sure movements she snipped the thread, then carried the gown to the wicker-work dress form, carefully placed it over the top, and arranged the skirt into graceful lines.

From far down the corridor came Lady Catherine's unmistakable voice. "I still say you should have insisted they come to us, for you must be ever watchful of your health. If they have not completed the tasks I set for them, all this walking about will have been for naught." The soft reply was unintelligible, soon after which that lady, followed by her daughter, entered the room.

By then, the three maids were standing in a neat line.

Lady Catherine approached the dress form, lifting her lorgnette as she bent forward to examine the gown. "It seems you have done fine work, but we shall have to see how it looks on my daughter." She eyed Molly narrowly. "I trust, for your sakes, you have removed all needles."

"Yes, milady." With great care Molly lifted the gown from the form.

"It is so beautiful," breathed Mrs. Chandler.

Lady Catherine eyed her daughter's abigail, who silently followed her mistress behind the screen.

When Mrs. Chandler stepped out again, she spun round, displaying the flattering style and perfect fit. The pearl-encrusted overlay was an ideal complement to the satin slip, and Molly and Lucy shared a proud glance.

The mistress of Rosings was silent as she circled her daughter, but even she was unable to find fault with the alignment of pearls on the bodice and hem, the lace-edged gloves, or the flattering cap. Her only comment was: "It will do well enough for a small chapel wedding."

Mrs. Chandler was in no hurry to remove the gown and stood before the looking glass, twisting back and forth. "I will always treasure this."

With an audible huff, Lady Catherine moved to a sewing table at the far end of the room, upon which lay several pieces of fabric that had been cut into various shapes and sizes. "What is this?"

After a furtive glance at Molly, who nodded sharply, Lucy hurried to the table. "It is one of Mrs. Darcy's older dresses, milady, taken apart to use as a pattern so we know the proper length and fit for the new one."

The mistress of Rosings lifted one of the pieces. "Show me."

Lucy, a trifle confused, hesitated.

"I want to see how you intend to make the gown!"

"I'm so sorry, your ladyship." With slightly shaking hands, Lucy arranged the length of butter-yellow satin, then placed a pattern piece atop it. "This is one of the sleeves for Mrs. Darcy's gown."

"And what will you do with all the others?" Lady Catherine used her walking stick as a pointer.

Lucy took up a few more pieces, placing them just so upon the fabric. "We lay them along the bias—" she ran a finger down the line to demonstrate "—and once all are arranged correctly, we pin them in place, then cut them out."

She stood aside as Lady Catherine eyed the satin.

"I see no lines here. You are mistaken."

At that moment Mrs. Chandler, once more in her morning gown, stepped out from behind the screen. "Mamma," she said gently, "I believe it is time for your appointment with Mrs. Ashton."

Lady Catherine, after consulting the gem-encrusted watch hanging from a long chain about her neck, turned on her heel and approached the door.

Mrs. Chandler followed, turning back to smile encouragingly at the maids before stepping from the room.

Those three stood quite still, allowing enough time for the ladies to be out of hearing before they released a collective breath.

"Can we go below-stairs now?" asked Lucy. "You know how hungry I get when I'm nervous."

~ II ~

Before dawn that same morning, Lord Harold had departed without fanfare, taking with him a parcel containing bread, cheese, and sundries that Mrs. Reynolds had thought to request from the kitchen.

By tacit agreement, Elizabeth and Darcy did not mention Harry at the breakfast table, where only Georgiana had so far appeared. Instead, they chose to talk about the Bingleys' proposed date of return to Pemberley.

"Sadly, Mr. Hurst cannot be moved yet. Jane says he is in too much pain." Elizabeth eyed her husband. "Perhaps I should ask that the cherries be taken out of storage."

Darcy looked up, somewhat distracted. "Cherries?"

"For the treatment of gout," she explained.

He nodded. "Perhaps Chef Renault could make something with them for us as well."

Elizabeth smiled at him, fully aware of his fondness for the fruit, then turned to Georgiana. "What else could we do to ensure his comfort?"

"I think Mr. Hurst would be better off in town, where his physician can attend him." Georgiana's tone was uncharacteristically sharp, and she immediately lowered her eyes. "If you will excuse me, I have a slight headache." She waited only for their silent nods before leaving the room.

Once she was gone her brother and sister-in-law looked at one another with concern, then Darcy pushed his chair back. "This must be about Harry. I'll speak to her."

"One moment, Fitzwilliam," said Elizabeth gently. "She may need only a little time by herself, and will no doubt find solace in the music room. If you approve, I'll look for her there in a little while, and will bring Gregory with me."

Darcy gave her a grateful look. "He does enjoy music."

In the nursery, baby Gregory was wide awake and smiling. Elizabeth bent over and smiled into his eyes as he took one of her fingers in his tiny hand. Cooing, she lifted him from the cradle, kissed his cheeks and held him tight while she shared her plan with the nursemaid, who was known to say the Darcys took more care with their child than anyone else in her experience.

"Would you like me to come to the music room at some point to fetch him, madam?"

"You know my son well." Elizabeth's dimples appeared. "I may be ringing later, thank you."

The young mother then made her careful way to the music room, stopping first at a window so Gregory could view the deer running through the park, next to allow him to contemplate the beauty of a marble statue, and finally to giggle over a portrait of one of his ancestors.

Outside the music room, she was surprised to find Darcy's aunt standing near the door, both hands resting upon her cane as she listened.

"Good morning, Lady Catherine," said Elizabeth quietly. "I thought you were to oversee Anne's fitting."

"I have already accomplished that task and have approved the gown."

Elizabeth acknowledged this with a slight dip of the head before quietly entering the room, still cradling Gregory in her arms.

Georgiana had just lifted her hands from the keyboard, having come to the end of a haunting piece in a minor key. Turning round on the bench, she smiled as she saw Elizabeth approaching and held her hands out to take the baby.

Lady Catherine had moved so quietly that Elizabeth started visibly when she spoke. "It is most unfashionable, the time you spend with my nephew's heir." Darcy's aunt, since coming to Pemberley, had yet to recognize the presumptuous Miss Elizabeth Bennet as having had anything to do with the birth of said heir, thus in part carrying out her threat made nearly two years earlier.[14]

Elizabeth had so far managed to tolerate such slights. "I hoped the music might be soothing. His father observed him making an unusual face earlier this morning and fears it might signify discomfort."

The three ladies studied the baby's face for a few moments, but all he did was smile and reach up to touch Georgiana's chin.

---

[14] Reportedly, Lady Catherine's words were: *Your name will never even be mentioned by any of us.*

"Spending time with my child is a great pleasure," continued Elizabeth. "And I would happily recommend it to any lady in society as a remedy for boredom." It was the closest she had come to answering back since Lady Catherine had arrived at Pemberley, but her detractor did not appear to notice.

Lady Catherine's features might have softened as she lightly touched Gregory's cheek. "It is normal for a baby to alter its countenance. I will tell Fitzwilliam so myself."

Georgiana looked up at her aunt. "Gregory's cousin, little Eliza Bingley, will be here soon. She is but three months older than he, and is delightful."

"All this talk of children!" Lady Catherine stood straight, eyeing Elizabeth. "I have noticed, by-the-bye, that your elder sister has not come to pay her respects."

"Jane is currently at the whim of her own guests, Lady Catherine—Mr. and Mrs. Hurst and Miss Caroline Bingley—but I know she looks forward to making your acquaintance."

In response, Darcy's aunt made a dismissive gesture. "It is past time I met with Mrs. Ashton. There is an enormous amount of work to do before the book is publishable. I only came to remind my niece to play music appropriate for accompanying conversation, and that the performance of melancholy works is capricious." She turned on her heel and was soon gone, leaving two visibly relieved young women behind her.

Georgiana rose and handed her nephew back to her sister-in-law, keeping her voice low. "Lord Harold left without saying good-bye."

"I feared the suddenness of his departure might affect you, but you hid your feelings well last night." With the baby in her arms, Elizabeth absently rocked back and forth. "I wish I could say something wise, but all I can think to do is advise caution until the truth about Harry's alleged misdeeds is known to us."

"Mary suggested we ask Lord Exeter about it." Georgiana sat back down on the bench, trying to smile.

"You may have to wait to do so; he has yet to confirm his arrival."

"I thought he meant to come for the ball."

"He has written to say he may have to decline."

"Poor Caroline."

"Poor Caroline, indeed! Forgive me, but you above all people should not feel undo concern over misfortunes brought on by her own actions."

"She *has* caused me unhappiness." Georgiana frowned. "Still, I do not care to think what might have happened had she not stolen Mr. Petersham's attentions from me."

"Perish the thought!" Elizabeth wore a look of mock horror.

Idly, Georgiana played a short, melancholy phrase, then took her hand away from the keyboard. "I have tempted fate more than once with bad judgement. Just think where I would be now had I eloped with Mr. Wickham." She looked down, clasping her hands. "Somehow I feel Harry is different. He showed great kindness to Catherine Leigh when she fell ill at an assembly in town. And he took great risk in saving us on our journey from York." She looked up, her expression beseeching. "My belief in him must be justified. It *must* be." Despite those fervently whispered words, there was an element of uncertainty in her tone.

Elizabeth's eyes strayed to the music rack, which held a piece called *Flow My Tears*, and said brightly, "Is it not time to exercise Matilda?"

"It is." Georgiana squared her shoulders. "And I must go now or I'll miss the others."

When she had gone, Elizabeth gave the music a disapproving frown.

~ III ~

Earlier that same morning, at Christopher's suggestion, the Ashtons shared a simple breakfast in their apartment so they would have time for a leisurely stroll before Mary's session with Lady Catherine.

Seated at the small table, Mary spooned marmalade onto a crumpet. "Each day she wants something new changed, including plot elements. I begin to think the book might never be finished."

"I have no doubt you will prevail, my dear." Christopher chose a pear from the basket. "The little house near the chapel is undergoing changes. It would make a pleasant walk, if you care to go in that direction."

Having just taken a bite, she nodded her agreement.

Shortly afterwards they were outside, proceeding hand-in-hand to the formal garden, following the winding path through hundreds of flowering plants and shrubs, all jealously tended by the head gardener.

As they passed under a trellised rose bush filled with buds, he asked, "Have you noticed the time it takes to get from our chamber to the breakfast room?"

She tipped her parasol back. "It is a big house."

"Quite different from the little one in York."

"It is indeed," she responded with mock seriousness.

"Which makes me think about our future house in town."

"You would prefer to take fewer steps to get to breakfast?"

He grinned. "I had not thought in terms of steps, but when we start looking for a house we might want to consider it. What if I wished to speak to you suddenly, but forgot the subject during the long walk to your study?"

They stepped onto a wooden bridge, pausing to view the flowing water below. When they resumed walking, Mary said thoughtfully, "A library and music room would be nice, but they could be combined in a single space if it was large enough to accommodate a pianoforte and a few chairs." She glanced up at him. "I notice you haven't taken out your violin since our return from York."

Christopher shrugged. "The days are so full here, what with riding, fishing, bowling on the lawn—"

"And convalescing from injuries incurred during archery competitions?"

"Yes, that too. And don't forget extensive reading. I need to prepare for the next time I converse with my father-in-law." He reached up to move a low-hanging evergreen branch to the side. "When in his company, I feel like a schoolboy."

"You might do well to sharpen your skills at backgammon and chess as well, both at which my father excels." She paused. "I've noticed one of your brothers-in-law has taken a sudden interest."

"Darcy? He does challenge one to table games more frequently of late." Christopher glanced down to catch her eye. "What with all those things, and you so busy with Lady Catherine, it's a wonder we see one another at all during the day."

Mary laughed. "It is the price we pay for being guests in a

country house."

They walked in companionable silence for some time until Christopher asked, "Have you and Darcy's aunt come to an agreement about the ending?"

"For the most part, yes. An explosive element has now been added to the tale, although I argued against anything so violent. She claims it will add verisimilitude—her word—but we have yet to agree upon the who and the why elements. I don't care to have the story reflect so much of what really happened in York."[15] Mary shuddered. "Though in retrospect it seems exactly like what one expects in a novel."

"Since first meeting you, my dear, so many unbelievable things have occurred." Christopher looked at her fondly. "But I have news. The carpenter wrote—your model house is complete." He referred to the commissioned doll-sized version of the house they inhabited while in York.

Again, Mary shifted her parasol. "He will send it here, I presume."

"I have instructed him to do so."

"It is such a thoughtful gift—thank you. I will ask Jane and Elizabeth who made all those tiny rugs, bureaus, bed frames, and the darling paintings for their own model houses, and, if it arrives in time I think Mamma will love to see it."

Christopher stopped for a moment to reach inside his breast pocket. "I hope you will treasure this even more."

"You need not give me any more jewels," said Mary with slight alarm, for she was frugal by nature. "I am perfectly content."

"This is something more precious. At least I hope it will be." He held out a folded sheet. "Would you care to read it?"

Mary took the paper from him and, reading it, drew in her breath. "The house on Grape Lane is yours?"

"*Ours*, my dear. As well as most of the furnishings, though I'm sorry to say the owner refused to sell the writing table you used whilst we were in residence."

"It was a nice desk, but what fun it will be to search for one like it." She let her parasol drop to the ground to embrace him, regardless of who might see. "Have I told you how much I value

---

[15] Mary is referring to events described in *Mayhem at the Minster*.

being married to a truly gentle man, especially one who tolerates an authoress for his wife?"

"You have mentioned it once or twice."

After a few moments he retrieved the parasol from the stone path and handed it to her. "Would you care to continue on to the chapel house?"

"I would. And once under the canopy of trees, I will leave this bothersome thing behind."

It was an easy walk to the edge of the wood, and the path to the chapel house was heavily shaded by trees planted many generations earlier. So much so that Mary did leave her parasol leaning against a tree trunk.

Soon they could hear hammering, and not long after they had stepped into the clearing where the house was located, one of the workmen came to greet them.

"Jack Farley—acting foreman and one of Mr. Darcy's tenants," said the man in response to Christopher's introduction, his eyes going to the other men, who had continued to work. "We've been asked to get this house ready in a hurry." As an afterthought, he removed his cap. "Would you like to see what we've done inside? You'd only have to mind the floor. There are stray boards and nails lying about."

Mary nodded eagerly and they followed the foreman through the newly painted front door. Inside, he pointed out the fine details in the wood floor and wainscotting. "All it took was a bit of scrubbing and it came back to life."

They passed from room to room, Mr. Farley pointing out the work he had just completed on the deep windowsills and carved mantels. Stepping back into the narrow corridor on the first floor, he asked, "Would you like to see the attic?"

After a quick glance at his wife Christopher shook his head. "We won't delay your work any further. Thank you for taking so much of your time."

"My pleasure." The foreman led them back down the stairs into what he called the receiving room. "We'll finish repairs by the end of day. Once cleaned, with the furniture in place, it will look a right cozy place."

The Ashtons were retracing their steps, nearly half-way to Pemberley, when one of Darcy's phaetons came round a corner with Colonel Fitzwilliam on the driver's box.

"There's been an incident in the village. I've come to bring you both back to the house." His eyes were on Christopher. "You and I are wanted in Lambton."

~ IV ~

From the stable yard, Mary watched the colonel and her husband ride away before walking slowly to the house. Once inside, she asked a servant for the whereabouts of Mrs. Darcy and soon found her sister in the nursery, tucking a blanket under her baby's chin.

Upon hearing Mary's tale about visiting the chapel cottage and the apparent emergency leading to an unplanned ride to Lambton, Elizabeth frowned. "Did Richard say anything about the incident?"

"He did not. And, whether it was due to lack of time or out of discretion I cannot say." Mary went to the window and looked out upon the open park, in time to see Darcy and his sister approaching on horseback. "Georgiana does not seem happy."

Elizabeth joined her at the window. "I spoke to her earlier. It's this business about Lord Harold." She shook her head impatiently. "She is a fortunate young woman, free from encumbrances who will soon be of age, but sadly one who grows attached too easily."

Mary turned away from the window. "I wish we could know what made his uncle disinherit him. Perhaps Christopher and I should start attending card parties when we are back in town, so we can hear the gossip."

"You may be disappointed. There is either a very deeply hidden secret or nothing to discover." Elizabeth took a few steps and tugged on the bellpull. "Will the house do for Mr. Collins?"

"It is charming, with room enough for him, Charlotte, and their child."

"I doubt she will come, but if so, we must do all we can to keep them apart from Mamma and Papa."

"I don't envy you the task." Mary glanced at the wall clock. "It is time for me to be in the library."

The nursemaid came in response to the summons, and after a brief exchange with her, Elizabeth followed Mary out to the passage. "Whilst you work diligently to maintain peace in this house, I may take advantage of the lull and have a nap."

Mary considered her sister for a moment. "Motherhood must be very taxing."

Elizabeth laughed. "In this case it is not so much motherhood, but the entertaining of hostile parties!"

~ V ~

Riding to Lambton, an easy distance from Pemberley, Colonel Fitzwilliam told Christopher about the local constable's message.

"A courier representing the foreign secretary's office has recently been frequenting this area. Given the constable's brief description, I think the missing man could be Matthew Baker, who has worked with Harry in the past."

Christopher was thoughtful. "Was anything left behind to indicate the man's identity?"

"A well-hidden saddlebag, empty, barring a fragment of blank foolscap sewn into the lining. The Lambton constable—Dunn is his name—has a brother in high office who told him weeks ago not to pay particular attention to a certain visitor in his town; I believe he was referring to the courier." Colonel Fitzwilliam gave him a side glance. "Our good constable questions the reason for hiding a trimmed piece of blank foolscap."

"A secret message?"

"It's possible. If so, we'll want to guess correctly which medium to use to reveal the message, if there is one."

Christopher thought for a moment. "I've always preferred to begin with heat over milk or vinegar."

The colonel nodded his agreement, and by then they had reached the outskirts of Lambton.

Constable Dunn was waiting at the inn and led them directly to the first floor. "The innkeeper thinks our man fled in the dark to avoid paying for the room. Given what my brother told me, I thought it best not to disabuse him."

"When was the man reported missing?"

"I heard about it around ten o'clock this morning, Colonel, but

I can find no one who recalls seeing him yesterday. A chamber maid found the room empty and the innkeeper sent for me, hoping the man could be detained and forced to pay."

The constable unlocked a door with a painted number eight on it, and they entered the small room. It was clean and tidy, with nothing personal in sight save the saddlebag.

"Where was it found?" asked the colonel.

"The maid was cleaning the hearth when she heard a sound she thought might be a bird. She used her broom handle to scare it and down the bag fell."

Going to the single window, the colonel looked down upon the high street. "I very much doubt he left this way. It's too narrow, even for a small man." He turned to the constable. "I'd like to see all possible means of egress, and to speak with the chamber maid."

"Certainly. Follow me." The constable grabbed the saddlebag and they left the room.

After determining there was only one door by which the courier might have exited the inn without notice, the constable left the other two in a private salon and went to fetch the maid, who was soon sliding into the chair he indicated.

"This is Belle, whose duties include daily cleaning of the guest chambers." The constable turned a kindly face to the maid before taking a seat near the two officers. "Please tell these gentlemen what you saw yesterday in the first-floor passage."

"I'd just finished one of the rooms," she said clearly. "It was late in the day, and hot, and I was in a hurry to be done with my work." She glanced over at the constable as if for approval before continuing. "That was when I saw a man come out of number eight, carrying a satchel. At the time I thought nothing of it, but then this morning, in the same room, the bed wasn't at all ruffled, and there was no sign of the man staying there." She pointed to the saddlebag. "Except that. It was stuffed up the chimney."

"Could it have been there before the missing man took the room?" asked Christopher.

"No, sir. I do a quick going-over of the chimneys between each guest and would have noticed it."

"Very good. Did you happen to look inside the saddlebag?"

Belle shifted slightly in her chair. "No sir, I just went about my work."

The colonel was leaning forward. "Can you describe the man with the satchel?"

She shrugged. "He was like most that come here, and as I had no notion anybody would be asking, I didn't pay much attention." She paused, frowning. "But I did notice the satchel. It was a handsome one, with four straps."

"Thank you, Belle, you've been very helpful." The colonel stood up straight and motioned for the other men to do the same at his side. "Can you say which of us is most like him in height and build?"

Belle held a finger to her lips, then pointed shyly at Christopher. "More like you, sir, but portly, and not so well-dressed."

The colonel stepped forward, holding out a coin. "Should you remember anything else—even the slightest detail—please inform Constable Dunn without delay."

The young maid's fingers closed tightly over the silver. "Thank you, sir! I will."

After she had gone the constable opened the saddlebag to remove the trimmed foolscap, holding it so the others could see. "Judging by the edges it was torn, not cut."

He gave the piece to the colonel, who went to hold it up against the window. "Is there a lantern? If this paper holds an invisible message, a little heat might reveal it."

"I'll be right back." The constable hurried out and returned with one, the flame protected by a glass cylinder.

The colonel held the paper high above the flame. "As it warms, anything written will be visible only briefly. Don't take your eyes from it." He steadily lowered the scrap as the other two watched closely.

Gradually, as if by magic, words appeared for just a few seconds, then faded to nothing.

"Did you see?" asked the colonel.

Christopher straightened. "Four words in French: *s'échapper caporal la violette.*"

The constable, wide-eyed, nodded. "I saw it too."

"My French tutor was never very pleased with my work," said the colonel wryly, "but 'escape' is a word I do know. Also, the major and I are familiar with several code names used by Napoleon's supporters when referring to him." He wrapped the note in a clean handkerchief and carefully placed it in a pocket of his jacket. "We must report this."

On the way to the stable, the colonel asked Constable Dunn to organize a discreet search for the missing courier. "But take care—if Baker's mission was related to what was on that paper it could be a dangerous undertaking."

The constable vowed to be careful. "I'll send word of our results. Where can I find you?"

"London," answered the colonel, scribbling his address on the back of a small card. "But you must be as discreet in sharing any information as you are in obtaining it." He handed two coins to the constable. "I hope this will satisfy the innkeeper."

"Thank you, Colonel Fitzwilliam. I'm certain it is more than enough."

On the road back to Pemberley Christopher brought his horse alongside the colonel's. "I suppose it will be to town for me as well. When do you plan to leave?"

"Tomorrow morning."

"Mary will not be happy when I tell her I will soon be following you."

"I don't see why. She has Aunt Catherine to distract her, after all."

"Very funny." Christopher was quiet for a few moments before asking, "Do you suppose the courier is in danger?"

"Since we know nothing of his reasons for being in Lambton, his sudden departure could be explained in several ways. There might be a woman involved, for example, or he left suddenly to follow some suspicious character and hasn't yet returned. But it could also indicate a serious situation. Months ago you and I tried to convince our superiors how unwise it was to award *any* freedom to Napoleon, let alone an island to govern and his own small navy to command. What is more, if our information is correct, he has a considerable number of supporters still in France, and the words on the message may indicate that a plan is being made for his escape. Or worse, one is already in play." The colonel looked up at the sky. "Will we never be rid of him?"

Both were silent as they reached a good section of road and urged their horses to a gallop.

~ VI ~

The two men went to find Darcy upon their return to Pemberley and were soon closeted with him in his study. Shortly afterwards they left to compose a coded letter to their superiors, and it was only when the dressing bell rang that they parted company.

Mary had been waiting to speak with her husband, and prior to dinner took advantage of their few moments of privacy. "The incident, as Richard called it, must have been quite serious to take so much of your time."

Christopher, who had excused his valet so he could ask his wife to tie his cravat, lightly touched her cheek. "We can speak more of that later. Right now, there is something of greater importance."

Upon hearing her husband's plan to return to London alone she turned quite pale, the ends of the silk tie slipping from her fingers. "You would leave me?"

He retrieved the ends and held them up for her. "My duties in town will keep me much occupied. I can't say when I would be free, and it could be intolerably lonely for you."

Mary blinked rapidly. "It is not how I would wish it, Christopher."

He gently raised her chin. "Nor I."

Before they left their chamber, he took up a parasol placed near the door. "Look what I found on the return journey."

The weather being fine, Elizabeth arranged to have dinner served outside on the west loggia. Prior to the first course, they were given cooling ices made from late-summer fruits.

Lady Catherine, after having pronounced it far too hot to eat, complimented Darcy's French cook, Monsieur Renault, who, unbeknownst to her, had prepared the frozen beverages with wine. After her second glass she expounded upon the dangers transported by a summer breeze, then upon the multitude of diseases transmitted by insects. To outsiders, her audience might seem to have been participating in an experiment by Franz Mesmer, except for the glances passing between them.

Dinner was well into the second course when Elizabeth was finally able to take advantage of a brief lull in the soliloquy to make an announcement, her eyes on James and Anne Chandler.

"My father has written to inform us that Mr. Collins is preparing to depart from Lucas Lodge—Mrs. Collins' family home in Hertfordshire," she explained for the benefit of those few who were unfamiliar with Meryton and its environs, where she and her four sisters were raised. "He will start tomorrow, breaking his journey mid-way for one night." She glanced at her husband whose countenance remained unchanged. "Therefore, barring the unforeseen, we can expect him in two days."

Lady Catherine was the only one to look pleased. "This means we can choose a date for the wedding." She paused, ever so briefly. "Tomorrow sennight should do, so long as Mr. Collins has time enough for counseling." She turned to her nephew. "Fitzwilliam, I will speak with your housekeeper in the morning about the wedding breakfast."

The master of Pemberley looked at his wife, who quietly signaled the servants to bring the dessert course, a humble selection of fruits and nuts as recommended by her ladyship.[16]

Before his mother-in-law could pass judgement on even such simple fare, Mr. Chandler said to his wife—in a tone meant for one in particular to hear—that as he was feeling tired perhaps they could return to the lake house without delay. There was no argument from his hosts, who undoubtedly felt the emotional strain each time Lady Catherine and her son-in-law were in the same room.

Elizabeth rose suddenly, addressing her husband. "I assume you would like to discuss what took the major and the colonel away from us today." She turned to Georgiana a trifle desperately. "We can take our coffee in the music room. Would you care to play for us?"

"I would be happy to," responded her sister-in-law without

---

[16] Unbeknownst to her, Elizabeth had asked that trays of delicacies from the excellent kitchen be brought to each of her guests' rooms (save one) so they might enjoy the treats without suffering a lecture on the adverse effects upon their digestions.

hesitation. As they proceeded inside, she quietly asked Mary to play through a duet that her former companion, Mrs. Annesley, had sent as a gift. "It is a set of variations on *Robin Adair*."

"I have lapsed, as you know, but will do my best," promised Mary. "The melody is familiar enough, as it was often performed in Hertfordshire."

Once they were seated at the instrument, Georgiana said softly, "You were unusually quiet at dinner."

Observing Lady Catherine's narrow gaze on them, Mary placed her hands on the keyboard. "Later," she whispered.

Meanwhile, the three remaining men decided upon Pemberley cider in lieu of port, the colonel having suggested it was more palatable in such heat.

After they settled into comfortable chairs away from the table, Darcy asked his cousin when he planned to leave.

"At first light. I would like to make my report in person as soon as possible."

"Then may you find good horses at the posting inns." Darcy lifted his tankard by way of a toast. "You're convinced the missing man was the courier, and that he did not go willingly?"

The colonel shrugged. "Given the secrecy surrounding his presence in Lambton and the invisible message, it is a reasonable assumption. Additionally, the maid's description of the one who took the satchel is all wrong. Matthew Baker is short and trim, and has frequently passed into France disguised as a woman because of it. The constable's brother described our man as such, and the innkeeper as well."

"Any suspicion of treachery is reason enough for me to go to London as well," said Christopher.

None of them being fond of conjecture, they lit cigars and sat back to watch the light grow fainter. Finally, the colonel stretched out his arms. "Rising in the early hours grows increasingly difficult for me when I'm here. You make us too comfortable, Darcy."

"I'll remember to have the feathers in your mattress replaced with straw." His cousin rose with him. "You must promise to return as soon as possible. If Aunt Catherine has her choice of the day, it appears you will miss the wedding, but perhaps you could come back for the ball." He paused. "I believe Elizabeth invited a certain young lady on your behalf."

His cousin did not rise to the bait. "I'll do my best."

Darcy was quiet as he and Christopher approached the music room, the melody from *Robin Adair* discernible amongst trills and scalar passages. Before they entered the room he stopped to say quietly, "Is it mere coincidence that Lord Harold left us at nearly the same time the courier went missing from Lambton?"

Christopher stared. "You suspect Harry?"

"I find the timing curious."

As they stepped into the room, Lady Catherine lifted her lorgnette to peer at her nephew.

"You were too long; so much port is not healthful. And I see Richard is not with you. If he chooses to join us at cards after we have begun he will have to sit out, for nothing is more inconvenient than a change in players during a game. Come now—" she motioned to a footman "—get the table ready. It is past time we started."

The games lasted longer than Mary might have wished, and she was forced to wait until Christopher dismissed his valet before returning to the subject that had disturbed her equilibrium in the past few hours. "Must you go to London before the wedding?" Her eyes searched his.

"As I have not yet resigned my commission, it is my duty to report without delay. You do understand?"

She turned away slightly, dabbing at her eyes with a delicately embroidered handkerchief. "I do, but is it not my duty as your wife to be at your side, especially in times of trouble?" She looked up with a misty smile. "I am no stranger to solitude and might be of some comfort to you in town." Suddenly her eyes lit up. "Perhaps Georgiana would like to come with us. There would be the footmen Darcy insists upon attending her whenever she leaves Pemberley, and Molly and Lucy as well. You need not be concerned with us at all."

Christopher wrapped his arms about her, whispering, "I can deny you nothing, Mary." He drew back to give her a look of mock severity. "But if you do come with me, you must promise not to be involved in any part of this investigation. You, Georgiana, Molly, and Lucy—all of you seem to attract trouble."

"There will be no adventures," promised his wife. "Or misadventures, as you sometimes call them."

CHAPTER THREE
Pemberley, in Derbyshire

~ I ~

Breakfast the following morning was a somewhat hurried affair, with Darcy anxious to see to the readiness of the chapel cottage, Elizabeth wishing to warn Mrs. Reynolds about Lady Catherine's imminent summons regarding the wedding breakfast, and Christopher already dressed for his ride to Lambton, where he would speak with Constable Dunn about the courier and perhaps do a bit of discreet investigating himself, if the man was still missing.

When the others had gone and they were left alone at the table, Mary asked Georgiana if she would like to go to London with them. "I'm not certain when, but we may need to leave before the wedding."

Georgiana finished her tea. "I would welcome the distraction and believe Anne would understand, but first I must speak with Elizabeth and Fitzwilliam." She rose and went to the door, turning back to say, "I'll look for you later in the library."

Alone in the room, Mary went to the sideboard to pour a cup of coffee. She took it with her to the open window, standing there quietly until the clock chimed the hour. With a sigh she placed her cup on a tray and turned her steps towards the library.

Once there, Mary and her somewhat impatient collaborator went directly to work and within a single chapter two new scenes were added, each involving the actions of a miscreant servant.

"They can never be relied upon, save to do the wrong thing." Lady Catherine also claimed to have had a dream the night before that left her with a strong conviction. "The poisoner in the tale must be a man, not a woman. Poison is a vile weapon; I cannot sanction a woman taking part in it."

Having based her original plot on actual events during the previous summer, Mary might have had a reasonable objection. Instead, she sighed inwardly before crossing out several lines of manuscript and inserting the new material exactly as the great lady dictated.

Hours later, when Molly came to inform her that Major Ashton had returned, she set her pen down with finality. "Lady Catherine, my husband is called back to London, and I am to go with him. Therefore, we must put aside the novel until my return."

Lady Catherine blinked. "You are going away?"

Mary straightened her shoulders. "Yes, and our departure is imminent."

"Can you not continue to write whilst in town?"

"Certainly, but—"

"There are no buts about it, Mrs. Ashton. If you are to get this book published in a timely manner you must be diligent. Leave the remaining chapters with me. Georgiana can transcribe the changes as I dictate them, and have the corrections sent to you each day by special messenger." She tapped one elegantly clad foot against the parquetry. "You are stubbornly silent."

Mary's shoulders sagged. "I will look forward to receiving your corrections."

~ II ~

Earlier, when Mary was on her way to the library, Georgiana found her brother and sister-in-law in his study, where they often escaped of late. Elizabeth smiled upon hearing the plans for London, then looked closely at her husband, who was frowning. "Surely you do not object? Christopher and Richard will be there, and you can send as many footmen as you deem necessary to ensure Georgiana's safety."

"Given all that has happened to Georgiana and Mary, an entire regiment might not give adequate protection on their journey back to town," grumbled Darcy.

Georgiana was radiant. "Thank you, Fitzwilliam!"

He gave her a stern look. "You must promise to have no adventures."

"I promise!"

"Very well. Will you be riding this morning?"

"It will take but a few minutes to change." With a burst of energy, his sister left them to look upon each other in silence.

Elizabeth was first to speak. "Georgiana seems to have forgotten Harry, at least for the moment. It is good to see her smile again, but when she and Mary are gone we will be in dire need of diversion for your aunt...shall I ask Jane and Charles to come sooner than planned?"

Darcy nodded sharply. "Today if at all possible." He glanced at the ormolu clock on his desk. "They could easily arrive by mid-afternoon."

"Then I will write to say how very much they are wanted."

Justifiably confident that her sister would agree to come, no matter the inconvenience, Elizabeth sent her note with a messenger and went to speak with Mrs. Reynolds.

As it turned out, Darcy correctly anticipated when the Bingley carriage would arrive at Pemberley. Having been alerted by the gatekeeper's son, he and Elizabeth were already outside, waiting for their visitors.

"Jane!" Elizabeth embraced her elder sister. "It is so good of you to come today."

"Had it not been for our kind servants, I doubt we would have been here before dark." Jane smiled, motioning for the nursemaid to bring the baby over to them and Elizabeth immediately held out her arms to take the child.

Watching them, Bingley leaned towards Darcy. "We took our fastest horses."

Darcy, drawing nearer to his wife, lightly touched his niece's plump cheek, smiling when the baby girl grabbed his finger. "We're a fast-diminishing party, I'm afraid. Richard left early this morning, and Harry before him. Lastly, Christopher, Mary, and Georgiana will be returning to London soon."

"I thought they were all to be here for the wedding." Bingley frowned. "And the ball."

"There were...developments."

"Developments, eh? Let me think. Richard and Harry gone, and Christopher nowhere in sight. What could this possibly mean?" Bingley looked closely at Darcy's countenance. "I see you are stubbornly reticent but perhaps you will tell me more when we are more comfortable. My older butler packed several bottles of prosecco with a block of ice; by now it should be the perfect temperature."[17]

"How thoughtful of you. It will be a welcome panacea," said Darcy as he led the way up the wide stone steps to the portico.

Elizabeth, upon entering the cool hall, turned back to glance through the open doors. "Jane, should we expect the Hursts and Caroline?"

"They were not yet ready to go when we left, but I imagine they are not too far behind." She cast a wry glance at her sister. "Charles has begun to talk of visiting Kitty and Edward in York, so he can see a new invention...something called a steam engine."

"That would of course mean leaving Caroline as mistress of Beechwood."

Jane lifted her brows but said nothing.

After the nursemaid took charge of the baby, Elizabeth looked up and down the corridor. "Fitzwilliam and Charles seem to have disappeared. Would you like to change now?"

"Please. The roads were a bit dusty, due to so little rain recently."

The sisters soon came upon Lady Catherine in company with

---

[17] Charles Bingley had retained Mr. Walker, his kindly octogenarian butler from Netherfield, when he and Jane moved to Beechwood Manor. All duties assigned to Mr. Walker in the new house were light and pleasant, designed to retain the status below-stairs he deserved. The younger 'butler-in-training' was chosen primarily because he showed proper respect by automatically deferring to the elder man. (Thus, Mr. Bennet was correct in his prediction that Jane and Charles, once married, would be 'easy' on their servants.)

Georgiana and Mary, the latter two apparently relieved to see them.

Elizabeth introduced Darcy's aunt to Jane, who dipped her head in the proper manner. "It is a great pleasure to meet you, Lady Catherine."

That lady dipped her head regally in return before addressing Elizabeth. "My maid said it was to be a large party. Where are the others?"

"The second carriage from Beechwood is expected soon." Elizabeth's amused glance was on Mary's stained cuffs. "I see you have been hard at work."

Mary peered at the tell-tale ink, then unceremoniously tugged at her left cuff, surprising the others by pulling off what appeared to be a long sleeve attached to the dress. "This is Molly's design," she said proudly. "I haven't ruined a dress in ages." She frowned then, possibly recalling the recent stain on the skirt of one.

"How clever," remarked Jane.

"Too often I have seen you rest your elbows upon the ink before blotting the page." Lady Catherine took the false sleeve from Mary to examine it more closely. "You must tell your maid to share the design with Dawson."[18] She handed the sleeve back and eyed Jane. "I understand you have a child, Mrs. Bingley, though unfortunately it is a girl."

"Yes," responded Jane with no sign of offense. "We named her Eliza, after my sister."

"I believe *Queen Elizabeth* ruled long before your sister was born—" began Lady Catherine, but further oration was mercifully curtailed by Simms, the butler, who announced the arrival of a second carriage.

In response to being introduced to Bingley's sisters, Louisa and Caroline, Lady Catherine lifted her nose. "I understand your father's fortune comes from trade." To Mr. Hurst she offered a slightly warmer reception, as there was no known stain of trade in his family. "I understand there are plans for an afternoon excursion, about which Dawson could tell me very little." With accusing eyes on Elizabeth, she added, "Have you informed my daughter?"

---

[18] Dawson is Lady Catherine's abigail, a thin, worn-looking woman.

Elizabeth nodded and said to the newcomers, "Mr. and Mrs. Chandler are staying at the lake house and will join us shortly."

"They reside there together?" asked Miss Bingley with a hint of censure. "I would have thought separate quarters more appropriate." Perhaps she hoped to gain the approval of the mother, but a sudden, cold silence in the hall resulted instead. "For appearances sake only—" she faltered "—until after the wed...*second—*"

Thankfully Mr. Hurst interrupted. "I must have a chair! And where is Charles?"

Quickly, Elizabeth motioned to the waiting footmen. "Please take Mr. Hurst where he would like to go."

The footmen stood on either side of Bingley's brother-in-law, lifting him in concert as if he were a chair, and carried him down the corridor.

Before Lady Catherine could reproach Miss Bingley, which she clearly intended to do, Elizabeth addressed them all. "I imagine you would like to change into something cooler for the outing."

Lady Catherine banged her stick on the shining marble floor. "I am in no need of a change of clothing and will therefore wait in the portrait hall for my daughter. I can see her approaching the house from there." She motioned to Georgiana. "Attend me."

Mary was smiling as they watched the lady and her niece walk away. "Your efforts are already being rewarded, Elizabeth. Lady Catherine referred to Anne as her daughter."

"She does seem to be relenting in some little way. My greatest wish now is for her to rescind the disinheritance." Elizabeth made a face. "For her to recognize James as her son-in-law may be too much to hope for."

~ III ~

Molly's sister Harriet had lost her way below-stairs again and was standing in the middle of a long corridor, contemplating the dizzying number of doors when a Pemberley maid came round the corner.

"I'm glad to see you, Dora!" exclaimed Harriet, the two maids having become friendly in the course of the Bingleys' frequent visits to Pemberley. "I was looking for the stairs to the sewing room, but got all turned around."

"It's easy to do in this house." Dora tipped her head to the side. "Is that a new dress? It's very pretty."

"Molly made it." Harriet unconsciously plucked at the skirt. "I'm to help her with the ball dresses today."

"I'll take you there." Dora walked a few steps and opened the nearest baize-covered door. "Maybe I can peek at the marriage dress. They say it looks as if fairies made it."

Harriet had no chance to respond, for Dora was accustomed to moving swiftly, as well as silently, throughout the house.

When the two maids entered the sewing room, Molly was alone, cutting the final piece from a length of silvery-blue satin. She greeted them with a welcoming smile. "You've come none too soon!" Her teasing eyes went to Dora. "I didn't know you could sew."

Dora laughed. "Not a stitch! I only came along to make sure Harriet didn't get lost." A few quick steps brought her to a series of long tables with a neat array of pattern pieces laid out upon them. She shook her head in wonder, then caught sight of Mrs. Chandler's dress on the wicker form and gave a low whistle. "You are clearly magicians." She stood staring at the dress for a few moments, then gave a pert wave and was soon out the door.

Molly set her work aside to give Harriet a hug. "How was your visit?"

"Mum was busy making a fancy dinner so I helped in the kitchen, and at teatime I read your letter to her." Harriet grinned. "She wants to hear more about York."

"I did leave out a few things." Molly motioned to the nearest table. "The yellow sarsenet is for Mrs. Darcy, and the silver for Mrs. Bingley. We need to stitch those pieces together."

Harriet nodded, her eyes on the dress form with Mrs. Chandler's gown. "The overlay looks like spun gold, it's so fine."

"We kept the underdress simple so it won't affect the fall of the lace," said Molly, who regularly read descriptions of fashion in *La Belle Assemblée* and other ladies' magazines.

"I wouldn't know where to begin."

"With a good pattern." Molly pointed to the yellow pieces she had numbered with the precious porte-crayon given to her by Mrs. Ashton. "Why don't you start with these and I'll do the silver, but take care with your needle."

"Don't worry, Moll. I'll be careful."

In a few minutes the sisters were so intent upon their work that they started visibly when Lucy greeted them.

Molly held a hand to her heart. "You gave me a fright!"

"I'm sorry," said Lucy, her bright smile belying her words. "I've just finished with Miss Darcy's trunks. What would you like me to do?"

"Would you help Harriet with Mrs. Bingley's gown?" asked Molly as she continued to sew. "Between the three of us we should manage to have that and Mrs. Darcy's ready for Miss Finks to do the hemming and fancy work.[19] We'll take the pieces for Miss Darcy and Mrs. Ashton's gowns with us to London." She came to the end of a seam and made a loop, pulling the thread through to create a knot.

"Since there are to be no more adventures," said Lucy, catching Molly's eye, "we should have plenty of time."

The three grew quiet as they worked and for a while the only sound in the room was birdsong drifting through the open windows.

Having finished her part on the yellow gown, Molly went to see how her sister was progressing, and nodded her approval. "It shouldn't take much longer, if Mrs. Bingley can spare you."

Harriet kept her eyes on her work. "She said to stay as long as you need me."

"We're lucky, you know." Lucy looked up briefly from her stitching. "There are mistresses who keep a maid so busy she doesn't have a minute to spare all day, and long into the night."

Harriet reached the end of a seam and snipped the thread. "Our mum says our mistresses are akin to angels because they taught us to read."

"And to write," Molly reminded her.

"Mrs. Bingley says I'm almost ready to write letters all on my own," said her sister.

"Then you can write to us while we're in London."

"I'll try, Moll, but it takes a long time." Harriet caught her breath. "I haven't said what else happened—after I read your

---

[19] Molly is referring to the Pemberley seamstress.

letter twice through, she asked me to read a story to her while she went back to cooking."

Lucy frowned and pulled out two stitches. "What did you choose?"

"It's a story called 'Little Snow White' from the book you lent me, but why it says they're written for children I can't understand. What I've read so far gave me the frights, and I'm almost fully grown!"[20]

"We haven't read that one yet," said Molly, collecting the pieces for Miss Darcy's gown.

Harriet tied a knot in her thread and reached for the scissors. "It's about a sweet girl who was the only child of a rich king. Her mother died when she was very young, and one day the king married again. Snow White's new step-mum was always staring into the looking glass to ask, 'Who in this land is the fairest of all?' and it always answered, 'Thou, oh queen, art the fairest of all.' That is, until one day when it said Snow White was the fairest." Harriet looked up to see if the other two were still listening. Satisfied, she resumed her stitches. "The queen was so jealous that she ordered the huntsman to take Snow White into the forest and to return only with her heart. But the huntsman couldn't kill such a sweet little girl, and he let her run away." She was silent for a bit, cutting the thread and tying the two ends together, just as Molly taught her, before pulling out a fresh length from the spool.

"What happened next?" demanded her sister.

"Oh, sorry. The huntsman let Snow White go free, and he killed a wild boar instead. Then he brought the heart to the cook at the castle, who added salt and baked it for the stepmother's dinner. That evil woman really thought it was Snow White's heart, and said it was delicious."

"How horrible!" Lucy shuddered. "What then?"

"That's as much as I had time to read," admitted Harriet. "But I want to know what happens, so maybe I can read more tonight."

"You can read it to us before we go to bed, if you like," said Molly. "When Mrs. Ashton was first teaching me, I read a little to her almost every day. I can't tell you how proud I was to be able

---

20 The book is a collection of folk tales by Jacob and Wilhelm Grimm: *Kinder- und Hausmärchen, or Children's and Household Tales,* first published December 1812.

to read her first novel, and to ask the meaning of only a few words. But you have to keep practicing, Harriet. Lucy and I still read stories to each other."

Harriet nodded eagerly. "I promise to work hard. Can you remember one of those stories?"

"Let me think." Molly carefully placed the pieces for the two gowns yet to be sewn into a travelling box. "Which story do you like best, Lucy?"

"*Cinderella*, except for some parts."

"Me too." Molly went to arrange Mrs. Bingley's gown on another of the dress forms, all the while telling the story of the unfortunate girl whose stepmother and stepsisters treated her so poorly.

~ IV ~

Mr. Greene, Darcy's steward, was at his desk when the foreman in charge of the improvements to the chapel cottage knocked on the frame of the open door.

"Jack! It's good of you to come so soon." Mr. Greene closed the accounts book and indicated the chair opposite his desk.

"It was no trouble." Mr. Farley removed his cap and sat down.

The steward slid a packet across the smooth surface. "Mr. Darcy asked me to include a bonus and to say he couldn't be more pleased with the timeliness and outcome of your work."

"Thank you. He's a generous man to be sure." Mr. Farley glanced at the packet but did not take it. "There's something I think I should tell you. Normally I wouldn't bother with what may be a trifle, but the missus insisted."

Mr. Greene, though unmarried, looked understanding.

"My youngest daughter, Belle, is a chambermaid at the Lambton Inn. She was talking with the cook after being questioned by the constable and two officers about a guest who left without notice, when suddenly she remembered finding two cigar ends in the grate of the chamber next door to the man who scarpered."

"Cigars in the grate aren't unusual, surely?" asked Mr. Green with a tolerant smile.

"No, but Belle says that particular room wasn't in use and only went in to see that it was ready for a new lodger. She'd cleaned it the day before, you see, and all was as it should be. But on the same day she found the cigars, the bed looked as if someone might have sat or even laid upon it, and there were those spent ends. It may be nothing at all, and I wouldn't have said anything about it, but for the missus. Some days there's no arguing with her."

"She's a wise woman." Mr. Greene leaned forward. "What did your daughter do with the cigar ends?"

"She put them in the ash bucket."

Mr. Greene stood. "Colonel Fitzwilliam has returned to London, but Major Ashton is still in residence. I'll speak with him; in the meantime it might be wise not to say any more about it."

With a look of understanding, Mr. Farley nodded, took the packet, and lifted it by way of farewell. Only when he was a few steps from the office did he replace his cap, whistling lightly as he walked away.

As soon as he was gone, Mr. Greene went in search of the major, only to be told by Simms that he had gone to Lambton.

"I'd like to speak with him as soon as he returns."

"I will see to it, of course, though I feel it is my duty to inform you that Mrs. Darcy has an outing planned and is expecting Major Ashton to be one of the party."

"Duly noted," said the steward.

An hour or so later, Christopher was passing through the great hall when he came across Darcy's butler. "I saw Mr. Bingley's carriage at the stable, but no one seems to be about."

"The ladies are dressing for the outdoor excursion, sir, and the gentlemen are taking refreshment on the west loggia," said Simms. "Will you be joining them?"

Christopher indicated his riding clothes. "As soon as I can be made presentable."

"The reason I ask, sir, is Mr. Greene wished to speak with you rather urgently."

The other man's surprise at the unusual request was clear. "Then I shall go to him first. Will you please inform Mr. Darcy?"

"Certainly, sir." Simms dipped his head and Christopher went directly to the steward's office, where Mr. Greene lost no time in sharing what he had been told.

"Spent cigar ends in an unoccupied room may mean nothing, Major Ashton, but I thought it best to inform you immediately."

"There may be no connection to the missing man, but the timing could be significant, and I thank you and Mr. Farley for your prompt action." Christopher paused. "I don't want to exaggerate the possible implications of this man's disappearance from Lambton, but neither should I understate them. Should Farley's daughter recall anything else, please send word by special messenger. The colonel will be in London soon, and I plan to leave for town tomorrow."

Christopher then went to change, his valet informing him that Mrs. Ashton had already gone down to meet the others. "I have prepared the shower-bath for you, sir." He referred to one of four such apparatuses Darcy had purchased for Pemberley in recent months.

Before the shower, however, Christopher sat down to compose a brief note to Constable Dunn and a coded message to the colonel.

~ V ~

Mary, meanwhile, was in Georgiana's dressing room where the latter's trunks were ready to be taken down and loaded on the fourgon.

"Mrs. Reynolds sent two maids to help with the packing," said Georgiana, leading the way to an alcove where the French windows were open to catch the breeze. She motioned to a pair of overstuffed armchairs and they sat down. "I went to see Elizabeth and Jane's gowns earlier. Lucy and Molly will finish ours in London, but given current relations between Aunt Catherine and Mr. Chandler there may be no wedding at all, and no ball either."

"Elizabeth may decide to hold a ball even if she must wait until your aunt returns to Rosings." Mary paused. "A letter came from Aunt Gardiner this morning. They are remaining at the seaside."

"And who can blame them?" Georgiana sighed. "I would love to visit Sanditon."

A light knock preceded a housemaid with news of the major's return and Mary rose. "I had hoped to speak with him before the outing."

Georgiana followed her to the door. "Despite the possibility of missing the ball, I am very much looking forward to our journey tomorrow."

"I am as well, even though Lady Catherine promises to send corrections daily." Mary made a face, waved gaily, and proceeded down the corridor.

Christopher, about to leave their apartment when she arrived, smiled and took her hand. "I'm sorry to be later than planned, but I had an unexpected meeting with Darcy's steward." He glanced round the room. "I see all the luggage has been removed."

"We are fully prepared for an early morning departure." She looked up at him. "Though, if necessary, I could have dispensed with trunks and taken only a satchel."

"But where would you put your books?" He smiled mischievously, lifting her hand to his lips.

When they reached the gallery leading to the main staircase he asked, "What do you know of this excursion?"

"Very little. Elizabeth has been remarkably secretive."

"If everyone is to attend, we will be a large group—eleven in all."

Mary stopped in the middle of the stairs. "I believe you miscounted."

"Miscount? Me? My math was always quite good in school."

"I count thirteen. Elizabeth, Jane, Anne, Louisa, and I are each married, which makes ten. That leaves Lady Catherine, Caroline, and Georgiana." She looked up at him. "Thirteen."

He shook his head. "That is too many for three carriages. Perhaps you and I could take a phaeton...I don't believe we've ever ridden in one together."

"I still have some memory loss, so cannot say if I have ever been in one.[21] Is it safe?"

Christopher nodded. "Perfectly."

---

[21] Mary's memory loss is due to an event described in *Mary, Mary, How Extraordinary*.

Outside in the courtyard, Darcy greeted the Ashtons with evident relief and led them to where the others were standing in line near three open carriages. “My aunt has begun to assign seats.”

“So I see,” said Christopher quietly as they joined the group.

Lady Catherine was using her parasol as a pointer. When she attempted to separate Mr. Chandler from his wife, however, he firmly but politely refused to comply.

His mother-in-law’s eyes narrowed dangerously, and for a breathless moment it seemed that Elizabeth’s strategically planned outing might fail before it had begun.

Happily, Darcy intervened, calmly suggesting the Chandlers take their seats with Jane and Charles in the Bingleys’ landau. “It can be covered at a moment’s notice, should Anne feel there is too much sun.” He turned to his aunt. “I assume you would prefer to ride in your own barouche. Perhaps Georgiana will accompany you.” He glanced at his sister, who gave a sharp nod.

Lady Catherine, her lips forming a thin line, accepted her nephew’s assistance into her luxurious equipage. She sat in the forward-facing seat, patting the open place beside her. “Georgiana, you will sit here.”

Mary, standing next to Elizabeth, opened her parasol and under its cover asked, “Where is Mr. Hurst?”

“Sadly, the gout keeps him from joining us.”

“There goes the phaeton,” whispered Christopher.

With the hint of a smile Darcy said to him, “You and Mary can take my landau, along with Caroline and Louisa. Lizzy and I will ride with my aunt and Georgiana.”

The coachmen were instructed to drive past the primary water features, then down a shady lane where the Darcys’ guests might glimpse wildlife through clearings in the managed woodland. Next was to be a stop at the orchard, which boasted a fine view. Light refreshments would be served, and baskets would be available to any who cared to pick apples. The chapel was to be the final stop, as Elizabeth hoped it would lead to preliminary discussion about the wedding service.

Throughout the first part of the drive, Mr. Bingley’s sisters waved elaborate fans in one delicately gloved hand while holding parasols with the other, their faces hidden by the fringe. Mary and Christopher attempted conversation at the onset but soon surrendered to silent admiration of nature.

The middle carriage, with the Bingleys and the Chandlers, was the liveliest of the three, and the two couples inside it were in the midst of animated discussion when they reached the orchard.

In a small clearing a series of benches made from felled trees formed a circle. The area was shaded by a canvas tarpaulin, and at Darcy's invitation they partook of a light repast. This included Chef Renault's delicious ice, which pleased Lady Catherine.

In due course, Christopher confessed a desire to stretch his legs and suggested a walk through the brimming trees. "I believe a freshly picked apple is one of the greatest pleasures in life."

Mary, who had heard this statement before, turned to him with a smile. "A food and drink in one."

Anne was suddenly on her feet. "I have never picked apples," she admitted, surprising no one.

Mr. Chandler took her hand in his. "You will enjoy it, I promise." He led her outside the covered area, away from his mother-in-law whose countenance left no doubt of her displeasure at the thought of her daughter engaged in anything so rural.

The others followed his example, and once outside Georgiana happily accepted a basket from Elizabeth. "What a charming idea!"

Elizabeth could not have looked more pleased. "My sisters and I used to pick them at Longbourn when the weather was fine."

Mary, in a tone reminiscent of her past persona, corrected her. "As I recall, Kitty and Lydia might have accompanied us, but they *never* deigned to pick."

Elizabeth laughed. "You are absolutely right."

Miss Bingley joined them, looking extremely pretty in dotted muslin as she waved her fan back and forth lazily.

"You are coming to pick apples with us?" Her brother could not completely hide his surprise.

"Thank you, no," said Miss Bingley coolly.

"It is far too warm for exertion," agreed Louisa at her side, her fan refusing to open at the first flick of her wrist.

"September was always an intemperate month in my younger days," said Lady Catherine, raising her parasol to block the sun as she stepped out. "We simply grew accustomed to it. Young people are not as resilient as we were then."

Darcy took one of the baskets. "Will you join us, Aunt Catherine?"

"Certainly not!" The great lady sniffed and stepped back under the tarpaulin.

Bingley eyed his long-time friend. "Care to engage in a friendly competition?"

"A fine idea, Charles, but we are an odd number for teams," said Darcy.

"I suggest we gentlemen do the picking, in company with our wives. You and I against Christopher and James. Georgiana can go with the team that wins a halfpenny toss."

There was a slight delay until one of the footmen discovered a coin of that value in his pocket. The toss was then performed and Georgiana was assigned to the Ashton-Chandler group.

The competitors went their separate ways, leaving three ladies bent upon remaining silent under the comparative coolness of the shaded area.

The Ashton group as a whole rejected the first several trees, until Anne stopped under the low branches of one she thought promising. "What about these? They are as perfect an apple as I have seen."

The tree passed a brief inspection by the two gentlemen and after much pointing by the ladies, who often rejected an apple in place of another even higher up, their baskets were filled.

"We can watch the other team from here," observed Christopher with satisfaction as he picked a few prize specimens and handed one to each of them. "Why not enjoy the fruit here, in this beautiful place? We have time, for I see there is still room in Darcy's basket." It was pleasant in the shade, with a soft breeze, and after throwing his apple core into a nearby copse, he lay back on the soft grass, arms folded across his chest, as if intending to sleep.

Anne and Georgiana were discussing dresses, so Mr. Chandler turned to Mary. "When I was last in London, I found your novels at my preferred bookseller—the Temple of the Muses. Anne and I are reading *The Wine Cellar* to one another now and would consider it a great privilege if you would inscribe our copy."

Mary's cheeks grew rosy, knowing Mr. Chandler to be a writer of far more serious bent than she.[22] "I would be happy to."

"I understand Anne's mother contributed to the book." He glanced at his wife, the picture of health as she chatted with her younger cousin.

"Yes, she did." Mary did not admit that there were in fact few such contributions remaining in the final work.

"Which has led to your current collaboration?"

Mary kept her voice low. "It is as good a term as any, I suppose, though I cannot say I always agree with the changes she wishes to make."

"Your efforts have not gone unnoticed, or unappreciated." Mr. Chandler too spoke quietly. "Any distraction must be considered a benefit to us all."

"You are kind to say so." Mary plucked a long piece of grass from the ground. "How do you like the lake house? Christopher and I stayed there after our wedding in June." A smile played about her lips. "Should you chance to enter the kitchen, you may see burn marks on the worktable. A testament to my attempts at cookery."

"Cookery? I have never heard of a lady attempting it."

"And you will probably never hear of it again, for I have given it up. I now devote my free time to more conventional activities, such as music, so I can prevent taxing Georgiana's patience when she suggests a duet."

"I hear nothing amiss when you play together. When I was but a young boy, my family often visited Devonham, as you probably know. I recall a few times when Richard allowed Georgiana to join us in our games, and even at so young an age she demonstrated not only patience, but tenacity, and a profound sense of fair play." Mr. Chandler looked fondly upon his subject. "It is with pride I now call her cousin."

"I value her friendship a great deal," said Mary, running the grass along her husband's hand, whose fingers moved but his eyes did not open. "Do you plan to return to Scotland after the ball, or will you remain at Pemberley, as my sister hopes?"

---

[22] Also, she might have blushed had he known that when first introduced to him at the ball at Devonham—when she learned he was a childhood playmate of Miss Darcy's—she had considered him an ideal candidate for Georgiana's affections.

"It will be Anne's choice, though I admit to an ever-increasing desire to be away...even the largest of Darcy's drawing rooms can feel confining at times. But my greatest wish is for my wife to be happy, and she very much wishes to be back in the good graces of her mother." He caught Anne's eye and she smiled. No one watching could doubt their mutual affection.

Mary applied the grass to Christopher's hand a second time and one of his eyes opened. "Have I missed anything interesting?"

"You have." Mary rose to her feet, brushed off her skirt, then offered her hand to help him up. "And it appears the other team is returning."

"Then we must hurry!" He was up in an instant.

Despite their increased pace, Darcy's team returned first, their four brimming baskets prominently displayed on the ground. Elizabeth declared the Darcy/Bingley team the winner and the four gentlemen shook hands.

In the next moment they heard, but could not see, Lady Catherine. Her voice came from behind a nearby hedge, her tone sharp enough to quell even the most tenacious disputant. "I am not accustomed to hearing the opinions of *unmarried* females of *advancing* age, especially when offered without invitation, and without benefit of foundation!"

Anne stood quite still, holding tightly to her husband's hand, her eyes on the ground. Louisa Hurst remained quietly seated, Mary and Georgiana exchanged a wide-eyed, speaking glance, Charles, Jane, and Elizabeth were suddenly interested in a handsome yellow bird some distance away, and Darcy took Christopher with him to speak with the coachmen.

During this burst of activity Miss Bingley stepped out of a break in the hedge, her words well pronounced. "My information comes from a confidential, reliable source. There can be no argument. The king's illness is the real reason behind the extraordinary changes to the queen's drawing rooms!"

When Lady Catherine appeared from around the greenery, a sharp cry came from Anne, who had bent low to examine her ankle.

"Help her!" Lady Catherine marched forward. "She should never have been forced to walk so far." This second remark was directed at Mr. Chandler who had but a moment before been holding the hand of his perfectly healthy, perfectly contented wife. Confused as he probably was, he lifted her into his arms and carried her to the landau where he placed her on the seat with great care. What she whispered to him as he did so no one else could determine.

He faced the others, who had followed them to the carriage. "She is quite all right—it is but a broken strap on her slipper."

As testament to this assertion, Anne nodded vehemently and pointed to the offending shoe, partially hidden by the flounce at the hemline of her walking dress.

Although Lady Catherine reluctantly agreed that there was no immediate need to send for a physician, she insisted, "A damaged slipper can be dangerous. As a precaution, Anne must be carried indoors upon our return."

Mr. Chandler, now seated next to his wife in the carriage, addressed Elizabeth. "Had you planned to go anywhere else this afternoon?"

"I hoped we might stop by the chapel cottage, which has recently undergone improvements," responded their hostess.

Lady Catherine's eyes narrowed. "That house was never in need of change when my dear sister was mistress of Pemberley."

"If possible," said Anne in a clear voice, "I should like to see the chapel as well as the house."

"Then you shall, and if necessary I will carry you inside," said Mr. Chandler loudly enough for his mother-in-law to hear.

Once more underway, the Ashtons rode with the Bingley sisters, who were again in the forward-facing seat. Only a few minutes had passed when Caroline stilled her fan and rested her fingertips against her forehead.

"Are you feeling poorly?" asked Mary with the appearance of genuine concern.

"It is a headache, no doubt from too much heat and sun." Miss Bingley smiled thinly. "Please order the driver to stop at the house. I fear I must forgo the pleasure of viewing the chapel today."

Christopher turned round to do as she asked, helping her down as soon as the carriage came to a stop.

"I hope you will recover enough to join us for dinner this evening," said Mary politely.

"We shall see." Miss Bingley focused a look of impatience upon her sister. "Come Louisa, you must attend to Mr. Hurst."

When the carriage was moving again, the Ashtons now on the forward-facing bench, Mary took Christopher's hand in hers. "Tension can be quite taxing."

"I have noticed." He smiled at her. "Do you think they would notice if we were a bit late in reaching the chapel?"

Also smiling, Mary shook her head.

The chapel, which Lady Catherine insisted upon viewing first, was a plain, small building, reflecting the more sober of Darcy's ancestors.

"The position of the benches and the pulpit make it impossible for a proper service. They must be moved." She continued in earnest, making plans for her daughter's wedding service, which was more than Elizabeth had hoped.

Darcy, Georgiana, and the Chandlers were attending to Lady Catherine, presumably committing to memory what needed to be done, enabling Elizabeth, Jane, and Bingley to slip out unnoticed. They entered the cottage moments later, passing idly from room to room.

"Mr. Collins will be very comfortable here, Lizzy," said Jane.

"Is he bringing Charlotte, I wonder, and their son?" Bingley lifted the top of a davenport desk, then closed it, circling round. "How can one be comfortable in a house so small?"

Laughing, Jane rested a hand on her husband's arm. "One could learn to be, if necessary."

Elizabeth's hands were on her hips. "I can imagine no better place for our cousin. Should Charlotte come, she will no doubt spend most of her time at the main house...one more child in thc nursery will not be a difficulty."

As they were leaving, Jane stopped to admire the inlaid pattern of the polished wood floor. "Lizzy, you and I might have lived out our days in a house such as this."

"*Might* have," emphasized Elizabeth, lifting her brows. "Come, they must be finished at the chapel by now. Gregory and Eliza will be awake, and I wish to speak with Mrs. Reynolds about adding a few things to make Mr. Collins so comfortable he will not think about being moved elsewhere."

"He is extremely partial to madeira, though he never admits to caring much for spirits," commented Bingley as he held the door open.

"What has you all smiling?" asked Darcy, who had come looking for them.

"We were considering what would make Mr. Collins more comfortable here," responded his wife.

"Madeira," he said without pause, and Bingley smiled broadly.

~ VI ~

Upon reaching Pemberley, Elizabeth spoke with Mrs. Reynolds about sending a few more items to the cottage, including several bottles of madeira, a cask of the estate cider, and beeswax candles. At Darcy's suggestion, she included a selection of tomes, sermons, and similar items recently removed from his study to accommodate his more recent acquisitions.

"Very good, madam." There was a discernible twinkle in the housekeeper's eyes as she made note of the requests. "I *had* thought it might be convenient to send a selection of breakfast items along with the reverend's tea each morning...allowing him more time for study and reflection."

"Mrs. Reynolds, you are a treasure!" Elizabeth's glance was filled with admiration. "But I hope you are not overtaxed? You must promise to engage additional servants if ever you feel the need."

"Thank you, madam. I will do as you ask, but those we engaged shortly before Lady Catherine arrived have learned quickly and are most helpful." Mrs. Reynolds hesitated. "If you don't mind me saying so, your kindness to us below-stairs, and to Mr. Darcy's tenants, has not gone unnoticed. The house has not been the same since Lady Anne passed, but now you are here, and Mr. Darcy is so very happy—" she retrieved the handkerchief tucked beneath one of her sleeves to dot her eyes.

Mr. Darcy's wife, blinking rapidly, surprised the other woman with an impulsive hug.

Following that meeting, Elizabeth was on her way to see Gregory when she came across Georgiana, who said, "I was hoping to see you before dinner. Might I speak with you privately for a few minutes?"

"It would be my pleasure. Why not come with me to the nursery?"

Georgiana readily agreed and matched her sister-in-law's pace. "I will be sorry to miss the wedding, which now seems likely to take place." She smiled gently. "I wanted to thank you for all you've done to reunite my aunt and cousin."

"Any reconciliation will not be through my devices alone, but I thank you for crediting me." Elizabeth glanced to the side. "Do I sense a second reason for seeking me out?"

Georgiana blushed charmingly. "Sadly, I find myself once more in a confused state regarding a certain gentleman, and before his return I must somehow know if it is truly love I feel."

"You refer to Lord Harold?"

"It *is* Harry, but I have begun to question the exact nature of my feelings. If I am so desperately in love, should I not have felt ill and weak since his departure? Should I not be starving myself, unable to stop thinking about him even when out riding or playing music?" She shook her head as if disappointed with herself. "I was irritable for a time directly after he left, for which I must apologize, but now my thoughts have turned to London and I feel only happy anticipation. In which case, how will I ever be certain that what I feel for him—or any man—is a true, lasting, affection?"

Elizabeth stopped at the foot of the stairs, one hand resting on the newel post. "I cannot claim special knowledge or experience, you know. I was blind to my own feelings until I learned what extraordinary measures Fitzwilliam had taken on behalf of my family when Lydia acted so foolishly." Her expression softened. "Only after admitting the truth was I able to recognize the signs that I had been falling in love with him since our first...nay, second meeting."

"Everything he did was for your sake. He loved you dearly then, and does even more so now." Georgiana sighed. "I want what you, Jane, and Mary have achieved in marriage, nothing less. It is something of a marvel, really, to witness such partnerships day after day. Your mother must think it fairly wonderful to have three daughters so happily wed."

"I doubt she would be so pleased had we married men of little means, no matter how well matched we were." Elizabeth gave her a mischievous glance. "I notice you do not include Kitty or Lydia."

Georgiana looked down at her hands. "I know nothing of the Wickhams, but, since observing Mr. Darnell and Kitty in York, I believe she has not been so fortunate in love." Her chin went up. "If she could try to understand him better, and not think only of how *she* feels, I believe they could be happier."

"You astound me, Georgiana. What makes you think you are unable to judge true, lasting affection? You are far wiser than you know."

"I wonder. Despite my near-disastrous experiences with Mr. Wickham and Mr. Petersham, I still have good reason to question my judgement."

"In each case, you realized you were in danger before it was too late," Elizabeth reminded her. "You are still young...younger than I was when I first met Fitzwilliam. But tell me, how do you feel when you think of Lord Harold? This very minute."

"I do not *feel* anything just now—other than a little hungry—though I admit to being curious about his travels." A wistful smile appeared. "He will soon be in Vienna, where he will hold court with the wealthiest, most charming ladies on the Continent. They will tempt him with sparkling manners, shocking gowns, and brilliant conversation...and I do not think he will be able to resist them."

Elizabeth somehow managed to hide her shock at the bold words. "Truly?"

"Yes. And I feel disappointed in him, despite having no personal knowledge of any wrongdoing."

"If so, perhaps it might be best simply to say it is friendship you feel, not love."

"But the question is, will I allow myself to admit it?"

Elizabeth laughed openly. "If you are able to talk about yourself in such a way, I doubt you are in much danger."

"I do hope you are right." Georgiana squared her shoulders. "I will leave off thinking about Lord Harold for the time being, and should a gentleman with fine manners, spotless reputation, and a good understanding of music come into the picture, it might make it easier to do so."

~ VII ~

Half an hour before dinner, the Bingleys and Darcys met by design in the oval anteroom. Setting his glass aside, Mr. Bingley cleared his throat. "A friend from my school days means to visit us soon—you may recall I spoke of Hartleton some months ago, when he was desperately in need of a new valet." He paused briefly, but his hosts did not appear to recall the name.

"In any case, he was recently turned out of Albany on account of his dog—they're rather strict about noise—and is at loose ends until he can find new lodgings or purchases a house." Bingley stopped to sip his wine, then barreled on. "Hartleton is a scholarly type, somewhat absent-minded, who often forgets plans with his mates, and when he is out with them scarcely pays attention to what is said."

Elizabeth was smiling. "It seems to me, that as you and Jane are here with us rather than at Beechwood, he must be invited to Pemberley as *our* guest."

"I was rather hoping you would welcome him," said Bingley with a grateful look.

"Of course we will, Charles," said Darcy. "Why not tell us a little more about your scholarly friend?"

Bingley glanced at Jane, who gave him an encouraging nod. "Hartleton is the best of men—always willing to stand up with one's sisters at a dance, for example, and likes to invite chaps to his club for dinner. He's very fond of music, and goes to concerts and so forth. I recall one particularly cold December day when he invited a few of us to sit in his box to hear a work for orchestra and chorus. We all accepted, thinking it would be something of a lark." Bingley went silent then, seeming to be smiling inwardly.

"And did you enjoy the music?" prodded Elizabeth with a side glance at Jane.

"Enjoy?" Bingley thought for a moment. "As I recall, the composer is an Englishman—or was. A famous one, but the name escapes me. He wrote grand pieces for the king and such. Anyway, there wasn't an empty seat in the place. The music was fine at first, some parts very jolly, but Hartleton did not like us to move about during the show, and after two hours one does need to stretch one's legs, or seek refreshment."

"Your friend Mr. Hartleton and Georgiana have something in

common," said Elizabeth. "She too does not like to see people leave their seats during a concert or lecture."

At that moment Lady Catherine entered without warning, sat down in great estate, and refused refreshment with an autocratic wave of the hand. "I heard you talking about music. Of all things, it is a topic close to my heart." She began to describe a seemingly endless series of musical evenings attended before her marriage, not breaking off when the other guests came in and sat down, each eagerly taking a glass from the footman's tray.

Caroline and Louisa were last to join them (Mr. Hurst had again ordered a tray in his rooms), and suddenly Lady Catherine changed her subject. "As we saw earlier today, Pemberley Chapel is far too small to accommodate even as many as are gathered here—" her eyes rested momentarily upon Caroline and Louisa "—and therefore, according to English custom, only members of the family will be present at my daughter's wedding."

Anne and Mr. Chandler seemed about to object but they were forestalled by Simms, who announced dinner.

The topic was not revisited, as once they sat down Lady Catherine was intent upon another. "What is behind this sudden need for everyone to be in London? It is most vexing! First, Richard left without warning or explanation! And now Major Ashton must go and my work with Mrs. Ashton will suffer. What could possibly be so important?"

Waiting until after the soup was served, Darcy replied calmly, "Richard and Christopher are understandably obliged to return to their regimental duties during Lord Castlereagh's absence."

Lady Catherine pointed a long finger at Mary. "But *she* need not go, nor Georgiana. This will not do! There will be no one to visit in town, and they will be far more comfortable in the country."

Bingley bravely took advantage of the ensuing moment of silence. "I must say, Elizabeth, this afternoon's outing was decidedly pleasant. Nothing was wanting. The wine was perfectly chilled, the weather fine, and the Kentish Pippins the best I ever tasted. I've a mind to speak with one of your gardeners about starting a few for our orchard at Beechwood."

Darcy sent him a grateful look. "It may be prudent to take a few from the Pemberley orchard that have already borne fruit. If done with care, you will see apples sooner."

Lady Catherine set her glass down hard upon the table. "I was not finished! I must know the reason behind this order to return to town. Why are my wishes being thwarted?"

Darcy turned to her, a model of patience. "It is a matter of business for the crown, Aunt Catherine. I daresay the major is not able to speak of it."

Happily, Lady Catherine was distracted by the appearance of delicate boat-shaped china containing artichokes and truffles, one of the few dishes she could not resist.

With his mother-in-law's attention thus averted, Mr. Chandler managed to say, "The chapel cottage appears to have undergone a good deal of change since Anne and I saw it a few days ago when we were out walking."

"It was done with Mr. Collins' comfort in mind." Elizabeth's twinkling eyes met those of her husband.

"I would not care to be tucked away amongst the trees." Miss Bingley sniffed. "It would be most inconvenient to walk, or to wait for conveyance to the main house." She turned wide eyes on Elizabeth. "But perhaps that is by design, given the nature of your visitor." She lifted her glass, almost hiding a sly smile.

"*You* may not care for it, Caroline," said Bingley, his somewhat sharp tone leading to more than one raised brow. "But there are some who enjoy the benefits of a brisk walk in fresh morning air."

Lady Catherine's narrowed eyes went to Miss Bingley. "A daily walk keeps the mind—as well as the body—active and strong. Some ladies, especially those past their prime, would do well to adopt the habit."

This led to a sharp intake of breath, but Lady Catherine immediately launched into her next subject: her idea of a proper ball. "A simple harvest celebration will not do. This must be the social event of the decade."

Unaware of her nephew's deepening frown, she exhausted the topic before advising the Ashtons on choosing the correct style of house in London for entertaining, and how to go about engaging the best servants. "One must insist upon excellent references, Mrs. Ashton. I will write to my dear friend, Lady Metcalfe. She will guide you."

The main dessert was an English Charlotte filled with

Pemberley apples, during which Lady Catherine moved on to the subject of improvements she deemed necessary to the chapel prior to the wedding.

Darcy was unconsciously rubbing his temples, and Elizabeth could be seen doing the very same.

Mary waited until Lady Catherine was forced to take a breath before saying in a clear voice, "When we first laid eyes on our spaniel puppy, I named her after my dear friend Georgiana. The choice has since proved short-sighted, for it is most confusing to have both a Georgiana and a Georgy in the house. Therefore—" she eyed her husband across the table "—we have decided to change the name, and welcome your suggestions."

"Is it not unwise to change her name after so long?" asked Elizabeth.

"Apparently Georgy is still young enough," said Christopher. "We need only be patient while she adapts." He glanced at Darcy. "The kennel master advised us to choose a name ending with a 'y' sound."

"I've always liked the name Squire," said Bingley, then made a face. "But Squirey is no good. What about Harriet? You don't know anybody by the name Harry, do you?"

Miss Bingley gave her brother an exasperated look. "Lord Harold?"

"What about Lady?" suggested Georgiana quickly.

"I like it," said Anne. "Or Morgan. You could call her Morgie." She turned to her husband, who smiled at her.

"Bonnie comes to mind."

When no one voiced an objection, Mary asked, "What do you think of Bonnie Morgan?"

Christopher nodded his approval. "We can reserve the second name for when she doesn't mind us, just as my nursemaid did when I was a youngster."

When it came time to separate from the gentlemen, Miss Bingley and her sister claimed headaches, wished the others a good evening, and retired to their rooms.

After Bingley's sisters left, Lady Catherine was first to proceed to the sitting room, but Jane held Elizabeth back to ask, "Who is to be excluded from the wedding, do you suppose?"

Elizabeth rolled her eyes. "The chapel can sit twenty at least."

"If Caroline is excluded, she will leave in high dudgeon, and in a fit of temper refuse to return for the ball." Jane shook her head in vexation. "She will not be here to re-unite with Lord Exeter, will not be married, and will therefore continue as our guest for an undetermined period." It was the most Jane had ever said about the matter.

Mary, who had stopped to say a few words to Christopher, followed them and happened to hear some of the brief exchange. As a result, upon reaching the sitting room she joined Georgiana and Anne, who were doing their best to appear interested in Lady Catherine's opinion on impermeable types of shoe leather.

As soon as the topic was exhausted Mary turned to Georgiana to ask loudly enough to be overheard, "Will Lord Exeter be escorting Miss Bingley to the ball?"

"Lord Exeter?" Georgiana appeared to be surprised at the question.

"As he is engaged to Miss Bingley, I assumed he would be here." Mary turned innocent eyes on Lady Catherine. "Are you familiar with his lordship?"

Lady Catherine lifted her chin. "One cannot know *every* member of society, but he may be known to some of my acquaintance."

"Aunt Matlock invited him to a ball at Devonham, which is where we were first introduced." Georgiana had apparently caught on to Mary's scheme, and, being aware of a moderate level of competition between Lady Catherine and her sister, Lady Matlock, she added, "Lord Exeter is much sought-after amongst the ton."

"Is he indeed?" Lady Catherine's eyes narrowed. "Tell me more about this engagement."

Between them, Georgiana and Mary contrived to satisfy her.

Meanwhile, Darcy, Bingley, Christopher, and Mr. Chandler were in the dining room, the respite enhanced by an ideally-aged port.

Darcy eyed Christopher across the table. "Have you learned anything more about the missing courier?"

"Constable Dunn did hear about an unusual couple seen on the road to London—a tall, somewhat portly man with a sickly wife who is without a maidservant. According to one innkeeper, she cannot walk without aid, and a heavy veil hides her features." At their confused looks, Christopher explained, "They are of interest because the courier has successfully passed for a woman before, so as we are travelling the same road on the way to town I will make a few inquiries." He caught Darcy's eye. "Discreetly."

Bingley was surprised by a note brought to him on a salver. "I have just learned that Caroline and Louisa will be allowed to attend the wedding."

"How did this come about?" asked Darcy.

"Apparently, it was Georgiana and Mary's doing. Something about Lord Exeter."

CHAPTER FOUR
Pemberley, in Derbyshire

~ I ~

The next morning, having seen Georgiana, Mary, and Christopher safely away, Elizabeth and Jane found refuge in the nursery, where the two infants were sleeping in their cradles.

From her rocking chair facing the south windows, Elizabeth waved the letter she was reading to catch Jane's attention. "Papa sent news! According to Lady Lucas, Charlotte departed from Hertfordshire alone, the day *after* Mr. Collins left for Pemberley. Papa cannot say if she plans to come to us or to return to Hunsford. Could she and Mr. Collins have quarreled, I wonder?"

"If they had, would she not simply have remained at Lucas Lodge?" asked Jane reasonably, her attention on the pinafore dress she was making for her daughter.

"Perhaps her mother encouraged her to go." Elizabeth frowned severely. "I dread the long days with Mr. Collins constantly underfoot, his every word and action the object of Caroline and Louisa's ridicule!"

"Then it is a very good thing the cottage is ready for him." As usual, Jane remained placid in the face of her sister's vehemence. "Perhaps Charlotte was simply delayed. You and I know well enough how easily a sickly child can upset plans. She might simply have chosen to wait a day or so to make certain their son was healthy enough to travel, and with Fitzwilliam sending a carriage for Mr. Collins, would it be so surprising that he would leave his wife behind rather than discommode his patroness?" Her smile was slightly mischievous. "You may be relieved to have Charlotte here, Lizzy, for she is sometimes able to restrain our cousin's...shall I say exuberance?"

"As usual, your thoughts are far kindlier than mine." Elizabeth went to stand at the open window. "I will *not* have him bothering Fitzwilliam, and he is *not* to remain late in the evenings, forcing us to entertain when we would rather be in bed, thereby discomposing the servants!" She began to pace, the rapidity reflecting her perturbation. "And, poor Anne and James. Forced to suffer his vainglorious lecturing in silence. Do you recall the day he rushed to Longbourn on the heels of Lydia's infamy? He pretended sympathy for our plight, to condole with us during our troubled time—but you know as well as I that he was barely able to contain his triumph at our misfortune, and at the scandal it would cause. Mamma always thought we had Charlotte to thank for that." She stopped in front of Jane. "Your sisters-in-law will justifiably find him a constant source of entertainment! How are we to bear it?"

"You need not be so fearful," said Jane calmly. "Mr. Collins will be wholly occupied with his duties, and when in the company of Lady Catherine he must surely curb certain tendencies."

Elizabeth made a face. "He was forever groveling at Rosings." Seeing her sister's expression, she smiled wanly. "You are far too patient with me."

"Not at all." Jane set her sewing aside just as the nursemaids appeared. "Shall we go now to inform Mrs. Reynolds about Charlotte?"

Later, almost as soon as Darcy and Bingley returned from their morning ride, Simms informed them that Miss Bingley wished to speak with her brother *most particularly*.

Mr. Bingley went directly to her rooms, where she was overseeing the packing of her trunks. "Caroline? What is this?"

"Louisa and I must bring Mr. Hurst back to Beechwood, Charles. His gout is far worse and a quieter setting is essential."

Bemused, especially given the recent concession from Lady Catherine about them attending the wedding, Bingley did his best to dissuade her. He even went so far as to mention the strong possibility that Lord Exeter would attend the ball, but his sister stood firm and he gave up trying.

Finding Jane in their private sitting room, which had been furnished to accommodate their child, he told her about recent events.

"Caroline's concern about Mr. Hurst's health seems a bit unusual," said his wife in a calm voice as she held little Eliza against her shoulder, rocking back and forth while lightly patting her on the back. "When do they plan to go?"

"This very afternoon."

"So soon?" Jane did not ask if the Hursts would be returning to their perfectly comfortable home in London at some point. Neither did she say that Mr. Hurst had seemed more than content at Pemberley, making frequent use of Mr. Darcy's cellar, and ordering the servants about as if they were his own. What she did say was, "We won't have time to send word to Beechwood, which will upset Mrs. Graham." She referred to their current housekeeper, the first having given notice during Miss Bingley's preceding visit.

"Personally, I think this sudden change in plans has nothing to do with gout, but rather with Darcy's aunt." Bingley leaned against a chest of drawers and crossed his arms. "Another argument today, perhaps? Caroline should never have disagreed with her about the queen."

"What about Lord Exeter and the ball?" Jane's expression might have given some clue to her thoughts. "It may be her last chance at a reconciliation between them."

"Knowing Caroline, she might presume her absence will rekindle his passion."

"Such a stratagem is much overused in novels." Jane gently placed their sleeping child in the cradle. "If you would ring for the nursemaid, we can go together to speak with Lizzy and Fitzwilliam."

Happily, their search for Mr. and Mrs. Darcy was not long-lived, for one of the housemaids could tell them where the master and mistress were currently located.

The couples had a brief consultation and were on their way to speak with Bingley's sisters, when, at the foot of the main staircase they saw, or rather heard, Mr. Hurst severely scolding the footmen carrying him down. (They allegedly allowed his bandaged foot to come in contact with a banister.)

Caroline, dressed for travel, wore a look of almost convincing regret when refusing Mr. Darcy's offer to send for a physician. "Thank you for your kindness, but we must go, and without further delay. Mr. Hurst will be more comfortable in the relative quiet of Beechwood." She tilted her nose up and stood waiting until her brother realized what she wanted.

With a muttered apology, Bingley stepped forward to escort his sisters outside.

"Some of our servants are sure to give notice," said Jane as she and Elizabeth followed, waving their handkerchiefs at the fast-disappearing carriage.

Elizabeth squinted against the sun, having had no time to collect a parasol. "How many is it now since they first came to Beechwood?"

Jane did not immediately respond. "Perhaps it would be better not to dwell upon it."

~ II ~

At four o'clock precisely, the Darcy carriage bearing Mr. Collins arrived at Pemberley. He stepped onto the stone courtyard with a look of complacency, but there was no one to greet him. (The gatekeeper's son had twisted an ankle when running to forewarn the household and had not yet managed to limp all the way to the house.)

At the time, Elizabeth and Jane were outdoors, freed from entertaining Caroline, the Hursts, or Lady Catherine, who was busy writing changes to Mary's book.

Lounging upon a woven blanket laid on the grass, they tried not to laugh as they watched young Eliza, tummy on the ground, raise her arms to the side as she lifted her chin and legs.

Darcy and Bingley observed this when passing by a line of

windows and came out to join them, the master of Pemberley tossing his jacket aside before sitting next to Elizabeth, his eyes going from his niece to his son. "Has Gregory made as if to fly as well?"

Elizabeth smiled softly as she rubbed their baby's back. "He is too young, I'm afraid."

Bingley flopped down next to Jane. "Caroline says Eliza should be walking by now."

"Aunt Caroline's expectations are a bit high." Jane leaned forward to adjust their daughter's pretty muslin dress. "Our little girl will walk, have no fear, but first she must crawl. Mamma says what she is doing now is the first step." The other three smiled as they watched the baby trying to keep her chubby little legs aloft.

"Well done, Eliza!" Bingley leaned back on his elbows. "Darcy, after the ball, what do you say about going on a visit to York? The weather is sure to be fine for travelling. We can use Ashton's house, and walk everywhere. Most importantly, we can see that new steam-powered locomotive in action." He had for some time been considering an investment in the recent invention, the so-called *Puffing Billy*, designed to transport coal more efficiently to the waterways.

"You would leave your houseguests behind?" Mr. Darcy reached over to replace the little cap his son had managed to remove.

"Caroline and Louisa?" Bingley huffed. "They'll be perfectly happy at Beechwood without us, I assure you."

Darcy eyed Elizabeth. "My guess is we must wait to decide until after the ball."

Nodding, Elizabeth shifted her parasol to shade the baby. "There is something more to consider. Your aunt has not indicated when, or if, she will return to Rosings."

Darcy shrugged, resigned. "You see how it is, Charles."

His brother-in-law groaned and plucked a long piece of grass, examining it with care. "You know, one of my governesses taught me how to make sound come from a blade such as this. It has been many years, but—" he aligned the blade between his hands, held it to his mouth, and blew, producing a fowl-like honk.

Darcy found a similar piece of grass and the two men were engaged in competition until there came a distinct, masculine cough. "Please excuse me, sir, but the Reverend Mister Collins has arrived." The effect of his words was a clear termination of frivolity.

"Thank you, Simms." Darcy rose and retrieved his jacket. "Please see that he is taken to the chapel cottage and settled there."

"Thank you, sir." Simms hesitated. "Will he be taking dinner at the main house?"

"Yes. Have a gig sent to fetch him shortly before the hour."

"Very good, sir." The butler turned on his heel and without any appearance of haste was soon out of sight.

Elizabeth sighed and signaled to the nursemaids, who came to collect the children.

Jane accepted her husband's assistance to stand, then brushed at her skirt. "Now he is finally here, Lizzy, you have no further cause for concern."

As they walked back to the house as a group, Darcy was shaking his head. "Given the disparate nature of our guests, I'm not sure I can agree."

~ III ~

Lady Catherine's abigail was late in informing her mistress about the departure of Caroline Bingley and the Hursts, having been ordered to sharpen quills and refill ink bottles in addition to her other duties.

Much to Dawson's relief, Lady Catherine was pleased at the news. "It is just as well they are gone, for Mr. Collins will arrive soon."

Her abigail swallowed hard. "Mr. Simms has gone to inform the master about his arrival, my lady."

"Whose arrival?" demanded Lady Catherine.

"Mr. Collins, my lady."

"Why was I not alerted? And where is Mr. Collins now?"

"I am sorry, my lady, but I do not have an answer to either question."

"Have him sent to me." Lady Catherine dismissed her with a sharp wave of a hand.

"Yes, my lady." Dawson bowed out.

The next person to knock at the door of Lady Catherine's sitting room was not Mr. Collins, however, but Mrs. Reynolds, who patiently explained to Mr. Darcy's aunt that Mr. Darcy himself had arranged for Mr. Collins to be taken to the chapel cottage directly upon his arrival.

"When is Mr. Collins expected back here?" Lady Catherine did not sound pleased.

"He is to be at dinner, my lady."

This clearly did not suit the mistress of Rosings and, unbeknownst to the master of Pemberley, Mr. Collins was summoned back to the main house without delay.

He was not led to any of the fine drawing rooms as he might have expected, however, but taken instead to the private sitting room of his patroness, where he received detailed instruction.

From the first day his aunt had taken up residence at Pemberley, Darcy had deemed it not only desirable, but necessary, for his guests to convene for a pre-dinner glass of claret or sherry in the drawing room adjacent to the large dining room.

It was during this comparatively pleasant interlude when Mr. Collins was first seen by the other inhabitants (now down to seven). His manner was overfamiliar to Jane, Elizabeth, and Mr. Bingley, whilst towards Mr. Darcy and Lady Catherine he was cloying and obsequious.

He went to stand before the Chandlers. "It is not for me to judge the misdeeds of young people," he intoned, though he was not much older than Anne. "In a case such as this, it is best not to speak of that which has so unfortunately transpired, but of what is to come." With a look of irritation he waved away the servant bringing a tray of drinks. "Despite the scandalous, heretical, and sacrilegious nature of your actions, I am bound to comply with the wishes of my patroness, and to act as a minister of the Church of England to officiate at a nuptial ceremony officially binding you in wedlock." He lifted a hand to his breast. "This ceremony, in the company of select witnesses, will follow the rule of the Church of England. Only when the service is complete and a new license signed will your marriage be recognized by your family and friends." His voice continued to gain strength. "This does not mean, however, that my patroness can, or ever will, forget or forgive your transgressions. She has asked me, as her humble messenger, and your counsellor, to inform you that she has no plans to alter her will, which was revised after your scandalous actions, and which permanently—irrevocably—disinherits her daughter."

Mr. Collins clasped his hands and attempted the appearance of humility as he gazed upon the former Miss de Bourgh of Rosings Park. "Such is the consequence of a daughter's defiance and arrant disregard of her mother's wishes."

During this oration Anne had gone frightfully pale, and in the next moment Mr. Chandler was holding his insensible wife in his arms. "She fainted! Sal-volatile, or sherry, please!"

Mr. Darcy acted quickly, his repugnance towards the clergyman evident as he brushed past him to bring a restorative to his cousin.

Mr. Chandler gently held the glass to his wife's lips and within seconds Anne's eyes opened. To Darcy he said, "I believe it would be best if we returned to the lake house."

Anne grasped her husband's arm. "There is no cause for concern; a bit of fresh air is all I require." Her grip tightened when he might have objected. "I am well, James. Truly."

From her chair, positioned throne-like at the opposite side of the room, Lady Catherine could not clearly see them and addressed Jane, sitting nearest to her. "What ails Anne?"

"I believe something has upset her," suggested Jane gently. "The words of Mr. Collins, perhaps."

Lady Catherine harrumphed. "What do they not deserve to hear?" Her narrowed eyes were upon the couple as she thumped her elegant stick on the carpet. "What has happened? No one is to leave until I am satisfied!"

Darcy strode across the room. "Anne has taken ill. She and Mr. Chandler will not be joining us for dinner this evening."

Mr. Collins had followed him, bowing deeply to his patroness. "I have done as you requested, my lady, and believe the attack stems from guilt and disappointed expectations." He turned back to watch the Chandlers leave the room. "Such a reaction is not unexpected, for despite the affectation of post-factum submission, they have failed to gain your forgiveness."

Lady Catherine waved him away. "Mrs. Darcy!"

Elizabeth visibly started.

"Ring the bell! I will speak with the housekeeper."

Darcy lifted a hand to belay the order. "What is it you wish to say to Mrs. Reynolds, Aunt Catherine?"

"I wish to have a physician sent to Anne, and I would have the housekeeper prepare all provisions necessary to maintain my daughter's health. I will not have her fall ill again!"

Much surprised at this sudden appearance of maternal solicitude, Darcy rang for Mrs. Reynolds himself and when she appeared it was he who gave the orders.

"You must send clear broth," insisted Lady Catherine. "It is best for the digestion, and what my daughter is most accustomed to taking when experiencing these attacks."

Having witnessed everything in silence, Mr. Bingley turned to Jane with an expression of wonder. "How would Mary have described such a scene?"

~ IV ~

The next morning a disturbing note came from the lake house. Mr. Chandler thanked Mr. and Mrs. Darcy for all they had done to encourage a reconciliation between Anne and her mother, but wished to inform their hosts they were returning to Scotland forthwith.

> *Lady Catherine's manner towards me, along with her determination to dominate Anne, is something I can no longer tolerate with equanimity. More to the point, the words of Mr. Collins, at the dictate of his patroness, make it impossible for us to remain.*

This note was carried on a salver to Mr. and Mrs. Darcy in the breakfast room, at the time its only occupants.

"Everything is ruined!" moaned Elizabeth. "And it is all because of Mr. Collins!"

Darcy slid his chair back from the table. "I will go to them now. It may yet be possible to change their minds."

Jane entered the room shortly after he left. "Charles' valet was not satisfied with something or other," she explained his absence a trifle breathlessly. "And Eliza is so unsettled, I have little time for breakfast."

"Perhaps she senses a change in atmosphere," said Elizabeth drily. "But I am very happy you came down, for we have just received vexing news."

Jane read the note, then looked up. "Might you implore Lady Catherine to apologize for Mr. Collins' interference?"

"I had not thought of that." With renewed energy, Elizabeth rang the bell and requested paper, pen, and ink. When the items were brought to her, she asked the footman to wait while she wrote a message. "Take this to the lake house, John. You must make haste—it is of vital importance."

"Yes, madam." The footman bowed and left with the scribbled note in hand.

Jane, sipping her tea, gave her sister a questioning look.

"I asked Fitzwilliam to delay the Chandlers by whatever means possible while we attempt to remedy the situation," said Elizabeth softly. "We may be able to refocus a certain someone's displeasure."

At this, Jane's eyes lit up.

Bingley entered the room then, looking a bit confused. "Darcy not down yet?"

"He has gone to speak with the Chandlers," answered Jane, summarizing events while he filled his plate at the sideboard.

In the meantime, Elizabeth composed a second note, crossing out several words before sliding it across the table. "Is it enough, do you think?"

Mr. Bingley and Jane read it together:

> *A short while ago we received word of Anne and Mr. Chandler's imminent departure. Fitzwilliam hopes to convince them to remain but fears it is unlikely as Mr. Chandler blames Mr. Collins for Anne's attack last evening and insists he will not risk her health by any further contact.*

"Is it wise to place *all* the blame on our cousin?" asked Jane, and Elizabeth's brows went straight up.

Bingley tapped his knife against the top of a soft-boiled egg. "I believe you have your answer, my dear."

The revised note was soon in the hands of Lady Catherine. Moments after reading it she rang for Dawson and penned a message of her own, ordering it to be taken to the chapel cottage forthwith.

Seated at his small dining table, the unsuspecting clergyman eyed the tray before him with great anticipation. He had just taken a bite of omelette when Lady Catherine's note arrived. As he read, his expression changed from one of pleased expectation to great discomfiture, and it was due only to a strong digestion that he was able to partake of his entire breakfast in the quarter-hour allowed him.

When his lady patroness entered the chapel Mr. Collins was, as ordered, standing at the winged pulpit, with the *Book of Common Prayer* opened to The Form of Solemnization of Matrimony.

His attitude of dutiful benevolence went unnoticed, however, for she immediately struck her walking stick against the stone floor.

As he scuttled down the aisle to greet her, she raised a regal hand. "Do not bother with platitudes, Mr. Collins. I have come to give you instructions. And I warn you: any deviation will result in the loss of my patronage." It was no empty threat for she enjoyed a close friendship with the bishop, the only one who held the power to depose a clergyman.

"Yes, my lady." He bowed, listened to her instructions, and with subdued obeisance agreed to do exactly as she said. He then followed her from the chapel, stood by while a servant helped her into the barouche, and watched until it was out of sight.

Directly upon her return to Pemberley, Lady Catherine demanded to see her nephew. When Simms informed her that the master was not in the house, she took a seat in the blue drawing room and summoned Mrs. Darcy.

Surprised, yet hopeful, Elizabeth entered a few minutes later and Lady Catherine began without preamble. "I have sent a servant to find my nephew, but as time is short I have no other choice than to tell *you* what I have decided. Sit down here, for I do not like to shout." She pointed, waiting to speak until Elizabeth complied.

"I have personally instructed Mr. Collins to perform the wedding ceremony this very morning, which must take place before noon." She consulted the elegant gold watch dangling from a long chain round her neck. "Anne's marriage dress must be taken to the lake house without delay—she and Mr. Chandler must be at the chapel within the hour if it is to be done." Her eyes rested momentarily upon her nephew's wife. "You will inform them that if they agree to be wed this morning, I will reinstate my daughter's inheritance." She paused ever so briefly. "And I will never again refer to their insupportable actions."

With admirable equanimity, Elizabeth went to the ornate desk in the room and quite soon another footman was running to the lake house with a message.

Mrs. Bingley's abigail (Molly's sister, Harriet) was not far behind in a carriage, with the precious gown carefully placed on the back-facing seat.

Inside the lake house, Darcy was at the breakfast table with the Chandlers since his own repast had been interrupted. When a servant came in with the note from Elizabeth, he and Mr. Chandler were talking pleasantly about an upcoming horse auction at a nearby stable.

"What is it, Fitzwilliam?" asked Anne. "You look perplexed, if I may speak plainly."

"You may." He slid the paper across the table.

The Chandlers read it together, though with differing expressions. Then, Anne looked at her husband, her beseeching eyes effectively softening his mutinous features.

"Is this what you wish, Anne?"

"I do not want us to be forever estranged from my mother." She paused. "This is a great concession on her part."

Mr. Chandler pushed his chair back. "Then we had better change out of our travelling clothes, for we have a wedding to attend."

Darcy went to the window in time to see Harriet on the walkway, approaching the house. "Anne, your dress is here."

"Truly?" She rushed to his side. "Wait until you see it, James!"

While they were changing, Darcy penned a note to his own wife.

> *I look forward to hearing how you worked this miracle. But for now, let us all meet at the chapel as soon as may be, in whatever state of dress it is possible to achieve in so little time. I will ride in the carriage with Anne and James—we require nothing more.*

Meanwhile, there was a great flurry at Pemberley.

The housekeeper met with Monsieur Renault and Mr. Simms to make plans for the wedding breakfast and the subsequent entertainment. Jane and Elizabeth had so little time, they chose only to enhance their morning gowns with lightweight spencers and lace bonnets. Lady Catherine always dressed in a formal manner, and the three ladies were waiting near the main entry when Mr. Bingley appeared in his riding clothes. Moments later, the four were stepping into the carriage.

Inside the chapel they found a dour Mr. Collins repeatedly wiping his forehead. He paced back and forth, and in the little time it took them to be seated, he opened his pocket watch six times.

The bride, groom, and Mr. Darcy arrived precisely at eleven-thirty, giving Mr. Collins time only to perform the solemnization ceremony, without his customary embellishments. Had the witnesses dared, they might have exchanged confused glances, for the majority of what he read was nearly unintelligible, it was done so rapidly.

Mr. Collins slowed ominously when it came to the question of any impediment to the marriage, but Lady Catherine impatiently waved him on. When he paused over the rings, it was Mr. Chandler who hissed, "Do keep going!" The scripture passage, chosen by Lady Catherine, was three lines. At last, he gave the final blessing, and it seemed the building itself released a sigh.

Darcy discreetly showed the time to Elizabeth, who bit her lip. Following the newly re-wed couple outdoors, she whispered, "I began to feel quite breathless at the end."

Bingley came to Darcy's side, holding out a sovereign. "Had we met prior to this ceremony, I would have bet that it was impossible to complete the service in the time allowed, given the, er...talkativeness of the officiant." He grinned. "Thus, I give you what you would have won."

An elegant table was set with the finest china, crystal, and silver in Pemberley's most formal dining room. The delicacies were taken from what was to have been served at dinner, leaving Chef Renault in a quandary about what to serve for the evening meal.

Mr. Collins joined them at the table, but was uncommonly silent, and later, when they left the dining room, Lady Catherine pulled him aside to speak privately.

When she entered the airy ballroom alone, Darcy remarked on his absence but she would only say, "It is time Mr. Collins administered to his own parish." This led to raised brows and shared glances, but no further questions were asked.

Until the trio of local musicians engaged that very morning arrived, Elizabeth suggested each guest contribute to the amusement.

Mr. Bingley and Jane were first to volunteer, performing three à cappella duets they often sang at Beecham Manor for their own amusement. Elizabeth was next, playing two pieces at the pianoforte but absolutely refusing to sing. Mr. Chandler surprised most of them when he produced a collection of Scottish airs and asked Elizabeth to accompany him as he sang.

Following the last performance, Lady Catherine crossed the room to speak with Anne. Although no one could hear exactly what was said, they rightly assumed a reconciliation was taking place when they saw the mother gently take her daughter's hands in her own.

Mr. and Mrs. Darcy observed this from their place near the open French windows. "We may yet see them at Rosings Park." Elizabeth's misty eyes went to Jane and Mr. Bingley, who were smiling at one another. "It is a wonderful thing to have two couples very happily wed."

"Three couples, for we must include ourselves." He lifted her hand to his lips. "Thank you, my dear. I would not have thought such joy was in store for Anne."

The twice-wed couple came to thank their hosts for all they had done. "And for holding a ball on our behalf," added Anne shyly. Her glance went to her mother, who was instructing Mr. Bingley on the management of orchards. "She will allow the ball to be as you originally planned—to celebrate the harvest as well as the wedding."

By then the musicians were ready to play. The dancing was not so formal as some would have expected, but was highly satisfactory to the participants.

One truly surprising occurrence was when Darcy asked the musicians to slow the tempo, then invited his aunt to be his partner for a courante.

She accepted.

That evening, after the Chandlers had returned to the lake house and Lady Catherine retired, the Bingleys and Darcys stepped outside to view the waning crescent moon.

Jane was standing next to her sister. "Did you find it odd that Mr. Collins did not remain with the party?"

Elizabeth kept her eyes on the moon. "His manner at the wedding breakfast was *most* peculiar."

"Do you suppose he will leave before Charlotte arrives?"

Elizabeth's eyes widened. "Oh my—I completely forgot about her!"

Jane patted her hand. "Never mind for now, Lizzy."

Not much later, when Mr. Darcy stepped out of his dressing room, Elizabeth went to him without pause, resting her head against his chest. "What a time this has been!"

He held her for a moment, then pulled back with an affectionate smile. "Would you not be more comfortable in the bed?"

Elizabeth nodded. "I am very tired, and if Charlotte comes she will have her son with her, and I've been looking forward to a few peaceful days—" she left the sentence dangling and glanced up at him. "I don't care to admit it, but his resemblance to Mr. Collins is a bit unnerving."

Darcy gently tucked a lock of hair behind her ear, then frowned. "Charlotte Collins is to be one of our guests?"

"It is not a certainty, but I have a feeling Mr. Collins will leave us soon, and if she arrives after he has gone what are we to do?"

"Perhaps if we get some sleep, things will seem less daunting in the morning," he suggested softly.

She looked up at him. "What did I ever do to deserve you, Mr. Darcy?"

"I do not know, my dear."

— THE SECOND PART —

CHAPTER FIVE

London

12 September 1814

~ I ~

Two days after the wedding was held at Pemberley, the Ashton carriage stopped before a handsome brick house on Hertford-street in London. It was a family home, frequently used by the major's Aunt Hermione who was en route to Vienna.

Inside the hall the three weary travelers were greeted by the servants, who had quickly assembled upon their arrival. Once they were introduced and had dispersed, the housekeeper suggested baths for the young ladies, who were most appreciative.

"You are a treasure, Mrs. Chadwick," said Christopher with evident affection, then turned to Mary. "This good lady has been with our family ever since I can remember. She'll take good care of you both whilst I attend to some business."

He had already told Mary and Georgiana his plans to personally inform Colonel Fitzwilliam that the courier's satchel had been found in a thicket near one of the coaching inns along the way, and that the innkeeper there gave the same description of the two travelers as had Constable Dunn.

"I can't say how long I will be—we'll need to stop at Bow-street to enlist the aid of the runners and their informants to search for our man." Christopher turned to Mrs. Chadwick. "I imagine Colonel Fitzwilliam will join us for dinner."

A few hours later they were enjoying a meal prepared by Aunt Hermione's excellent cook, when Christopher asked Mary and Georgiana if they found the house accommodating.

"We did not see much," admitted his wife, who had stepped over its threshold for the first time that afternoon. "Mrs. Chadwick kindly led us around the ground floor, but I'm afraid the tour ended once Georgiana and I entered the informal room leading out to the back garden."

"The enclosed outdoor space is charming," said Georgiana brightly. "Mary and I spent the remainder of the afternoon there, and with the French windows open we went in and out as we pleased."

"I was shamelessly idle," admitted Mary. "And might have fallen asleep."

Georgiana nodded. "With Bonnie on your lap." She turned to her cousin. "Mary and I have dubbed it the garden room. I started looking at a catalog that listed what was shown at this year's art exhibition at the Royal Academy, and came across something I think would interest you, Richard—a description of the portrait of a man and wife, aged ninety-six and eighty-eight respectively, who lived in the wood upwards of fifty years, carrying their hut from place to place as his work required, along with their eight children." She frowned in thought. "He was called a charcoal burner, something you mentioned recently."

"Your memory serves you well," said the colonel. "It is a respectable occupation that requires considerable skill. Some time ago I considered an investment in the product and learned something about the process. The charcoal is made when wood is stacked with a flue in the center, then covered with dirt or clay. The fire is carefully controlled by so-called colliers, and the product burns cleaner than wood, and hotter."

"You learned quite a bit," said Christopher. "Did you make the investment?"

"No." The colonel took a sip of wine. "But I am interested in the new steam engine Charles mentioned."

The remainder of the meal passed pleasantly, and soon after the gooseberry fool he thanked his hosts. "I have an early start in the morning but must say I will accept an invitation to your table at a moment's notice, for you have an incomparable cook."

~ II ~

On their third day in town, upon returning from a morning walk with Georgiana, two ladies' maids, two footmen, and a puppy, Mary was given a parcel sent by special messenger.

Inside were several pages from her novel with revisions written in two hands—one she did not recognize—along with a note from Lady Catherine.

Dear Mrs. Ashton,

I was truly vexed, having been forced to ask my nephew for the location of your residence in Town so as to send you my latest corrections in the most expedient manner. You can expect to receive more pages soon, for I have someone to assist me now. You may be surprised to hear it is Mrs. Collins, who, in a shocking state of dishevelment, arrived at Pemberley in a farm cart quite late on the day after Anne's wedding. It was a good thing she did not arrive the day before because it would have disrupted the celebration considerably.

Mrs. Collins had her sickly son with her, but no nursemaid, thus making it imperative for him to be placed in the care of one of my nephew's tenants and for the mother to be housed in a chamber farthest away from the family wing. We cannot risk Darcy's heir being exposed in any way to putrid infection.

Currently, Mrs. Collins claims to be too exhausted to explain her actions, or to follow her husband to Hunsford (he was on his way back to Kent directly after the wedding breakfast). However, she has made herself useful by reading pages from your book aloud to me, then writing the changes as I dictate, which I then review (you will see I have made notes in the margins as well as she; the difference in our penmanship is surely remarkable, for my tutor in the art was forever complimenting my hand).

I understand the house in which you currently reside is the property of your husband's family. No matter who was mistress in the past, you must be firm with the servants from the very first.

Yours sincerely,
Lady Catherine de Bourgh

n.b. I have taken up the quill with ever-increasing frequency and Dawson has not been able to make writing sleeves to my satisfaction. Do have your maid make a pattern, carefully write the instructions as she tells you, and send all to me in the next post. Even as I write this, it occurs to me that she can make the sleeves there and you can send them along with the pattern, for I require several sets.

Mary rose with a sigh and went to find Georgiana in the music room, which was spacious and high-ceilinged, with painted wainscoting, and room enough for a handsome Broadwood grand pianoforte with mahogany veneer, much like the one at Pemberley. She was playing a sonata by Herr Beethoven but ceased when Mary came to her side.

"You have news?"

"Yes, from your Aunt Catherine." Mary gave her the letter.

Georgiana remained seated at the keyboard while reading, giving Mary a pointed look when reaching the end. "Did I not wake you to say I thought I saw Charlotte Collins huddled amongst the passengers inside a mail coach on the second day of our journey? We dismissed it as ridiculous, but apparently I *did* see her, *and* she was making for Pemberley." She pointed at the third paragraph. "Evidently Charlotte is not well enough to follow Mr. Collins to Hunsford, but why did he not wait for his wife and child before returning to their home? And, how could Anne's wedding have taken place so soon? I thought it was weeks away."

"It seems much has happened in a very short time. Perhaps Elizabeth has been too distracted to write."

"She left many questions unanswered," mused Georgiana. "Shall we write to her now?"

"Yes," said Mary. "So long as you wield the pen."

The two went directly to the morning room, where Mary did a fine imitation of Lady Catherine as she paced back and forth in front of her friend, who was writing furiously.

Once the letter was resting on the hall tray, Mary said she had better see Molly about the stain-preventing sleeves. "Then I suppose I should make the suggested changes to the novel. If I put it off the task will become akin to The Twelve Labours of Hercules."

Georgiana laughed. "Very well, if you must allow my aunt to browbeat you from afar, but I had hoped we might go to Hatchards this afternoon. It is a pleasant walk from here to Piccadilly-street, or so Lucy was told below-stairs."

"I will stop at the end of an hour," promised Mary, who returned to the little study off her dressing room where a writing desk was placed against the window. A few minutes later she was motioning for her abigail to sit in the chair beside it.

"Molly, Lady Catherine would like you to create a pattern for writing sleeves so her maid can make them, but in the meantime she asks if you would please make a few pair for her immediate use. Is this possible?"

Molly nodded. "I can have them finished in an hour or so, madam, and making the pattern would be simple."

"Thank you." Mary indicated the pages spread across the desktop. "Before you go, Lady Catherine is again advising me on a novel, and, as you are aware, I do not always agree with her suggestions." She paused, considering her efficient, kind, and intelligent maid. "Her perception of those below-stairs is far different than my own, you understand."

Again Molly nodded, this time more vigorously. "You are an unusual mistress, if you'll forgive me for saying so, madam. When I first told my mum about the lessons you gave me, and how you lent me your own set of *The Mysteries of Udolpho* to read, she had to sit down."

"I take that as a compliment." Mary was smiling as she placed a finger near a lengthy revision in Charlotte Collins' scrawl. "Lady Catherine thinks the maidservants in this story should act in a certain way, but my models for this tale are you and Lucy, as you are thoughtful and independent-minded." At Molly's look of confusion, she said, "Listen to this and tell me what you think real maids would do."

Jenny, the housemaid, saw the visitor in the servants' quarters with the missing kitchen maid's travelling case in hand, and hurried to inform her mistress.

Mary looked up. "Now, do you think Jenny, a close friend of the missing maid, would have allowed the intruder to leave the house with the travelling case whilst she reported the theft to her mistress? In York, you and Lucy bravely followed Miss You-know-who from the house—at your own peril, mind—and ultimately solved a mystery." She pointed to notes written in the margin. "Lady Catherine claims no one will believe a maid would dare risk her position for a friend, and that it is inappropriate to write a scene in which a maid demonstrates independent thought, or goes against the orders of her mistress in any way, for it may give those of inferior birth radical ideas."

Molly hesitated. "Excuse me for saying so, madam, but great ladies don't usually take time to think about their servants. Maybe Lady Catherine believes those who read your books would expect it to be that way."

"It is a valid point," said Mary wryly. "But perhaps if the servants in my stories act as if they have brains it might lead to these great ladies—if such read my books—having a bit more consideration for those who serve them. But there was something else." She leafed through several pages. "It is when the kitchen maid discovers the cat in the back garden. This is how Lady Catherine wants it to read:

Carelessly, Myrna dropped the dish of milk, screaming at the top of her lungs as she ran back to the house.

"What's all this fuss?" demanded the cook, a large wooden spoon in hand.

"Oh, Mrs. Withers! The cat has taken ill! I think it may be beyond help!

"Earlier in the story, Myrna is clearly afraid of the cook. I mentioned this to Lady Catherine when we were discussing this section, but she insists that the first thing a young maid would do is seek the advice of a superior. In this case, the cook. What do *you* think?"

Molly bit her lip. "What really happened was different than this, of course, but the maid in the story might have run inside once she saw the poor cat and blurted it out to the first person she met."

Mary marked the page. "I suppose it is best not to go against her wishes too often." She glanced at the open letter on her desk. "I hope this request for the pattern, instructions, and sleeves is not too much extra work."

"It is no bother, madam. If Lucy can help, we'll have everything ready long before the afternoon post." She stood up. "May I add a letter for my mother? She asked if I would write as soon as we were in London."

"Of course. Write as often as you wish. And do tell her the starching she suggested was much appreciated."[23]

"I will, madam. She says it makes a difference in how well a person sleeps in a strange bed."

"She is quite right." Mary smiled and dipped her quill in the inkpot.

Having written three novels, she could be efficient and with fifteen minutes to spare was blotting the pages, easily enough time to change into the walking dress Molly had prepared for her.

Their steps were light, parasols held at a jaunty angle as the two young ladies strolled along Piccadilly-street past The Green Park (followed discreetly by their maids and the footmen). Despite so many of the inhabitants already gone to Vienna—or perhaps because of it—there was a lively energy about the city.

Before they stepped inside the bookshop, Georgiana motioned down the street. "Richard's rooms are only a few buildings away."

~ III ~

At breakfast the next morning, Mary and Christopher were perusing different newspapers for a response to the coded

[23] Molly had starched and ironed the bed linens at each of the coaching inns on the way to London, making them seem freshly laundered.

message he and the colonel had submitted as part of their efforts to locate the courier.

"There is nothing but scandal in these pages." Mary lowered *The Morning Post* just below her eyes. "Should I assume the same of yours? That is your third sigh."

"I didn't realize I was so vocal. Forgive me." Christopher folded his copy of *The Times*. "With each passing moment I fear for Baker's fate and begin to think it might be wise to approach that Westmacott fellow."

"Westmacott?" She set her newspaper aside.

"A scoundrel in the guise of a writer. Richard thinks he may be able to help us, for he is said to possess the secrets of rich and powerful people—a master blackmailer in fact. He is also suspected to have secret dealings with the French, though his loyalty is to himself only. In order to approach him, we would need an introduction in a social way, not so he could make a connection to anything relating to the government." Christopher drummed his fingers on the table. "We may have to take Exeter into our confidence, for he is acquainted with the man."

"I can send an invitation to him. Lord Exeter, I mean." Mary had already thought of doing so, but her motive was to glean information about Lord Harold's past. "Would dinner this evening be too soon?"

"Since we are practically in-laws—assuming he goes through with the marriage to Caroline—I see no reason to stand on ceremony. I'll ask Richard to join us." Christopher set his coffee down. "On a happier note, I received word from Mr. Nolan, the house agent. He will contact you directly when he finds an appropriate house to tour. Do you and Georgiana have plans for the day?"

"We have a commission to perform on Anne's behalf. But first there is Bonnie's walk. She tends to mind the servants best, so Molly thinks a bit of training with me is in order."

"I wish I were free to escort you myself. When this business is finished we'll go along South Carriage Drive in an open landau. I think you and Georgiana would enjoy it."

"Any ride in an open carriage on a warm day sounds delightful."

Despite the possibility of being seen, he came to her side, bent down, and kissed her. "You are my idea of a wife."

In the park, Mary followed suggestions from Molly and one of the footmen, William, whose father was the kennel master at Pemberley. At first, Bonnie was distracted by a squirrel, then a bird, then a bee, but with patience and coaching the puppy stopped pulling on the lead.

When they reached the edge of the Serpentine William threw a stick into the water for her as a reward. During this activity Georgiana and Mary sat on a nearby bench to read a letter from Elizabeth, delivered just before they left the house.

My Dear Sisters,

There is so much to tell, I hardly know where to begin. However, Jane thinks this will read more like a novel if I start with a wedding, and so I shall.

As fate would have it, on the day after you left, Anne and James' marriage service was held, and the documents signed before noon. There was little warning and we all went as we were dressed. This sudden change in plans stemmed from something Mr. Collins said (at the instruction of his patroness), which appeared to upset Anne terribly. Mr. Chandler took great umbrage and sent a note the next morning to say they were leaving that very day. Once informed of this, Lady Catherine ordered Mr. Collins to perform the wedding service at once.

After the breakfast we managed a bit of dancing, despite so few people (Caroline and the Hursts returned to Beechwood prior to the day, though the reason is still unclear to us). Dare I say it was a relief to all that Mr. Collins did not take part in this part of the celebration?

Incredibly, there is yet more to tell: on the following day, another surprise arrived in the form of Charlotte Collins! It was then Lady Catherine informed us that Mr. Collins had already departed! She would only say, 'It is time he returned to his duties at Hunsford.'

Jane is beside me as I write and has reminded me of something else. Anne is once more the heiress of Rosings!

But there is more to tell about Charlotte. She was bedraggled and overheated from travelling in a crowded mail-coach, and upon hearing that her husband was on the road to Hunsford she burst into tears and fainted!

Lady Catherine was convinced that Charlotte's son was sickening from something, and insisted he be taken away (his disposition was even worse than I recall so he might actually be ill). Mrs. Reynolds wisely recommended a kindly couple to care for him, the wife being a nursemaid. The good news is that Charlotte has not fainted since then and has become useful to Lady Catherine. Still, she is dispirited, and I have begun to wonder if she is ill herself.

Jane was convinced we should all retire to Beechwood to avoid contagion, but the physician assures us the boy and his mother require only rest. Nonetheless, I have alerted Mrs. Reynolds to the possibility of a hasty departure.

You may think this is enough for one letter, but do not set it aside just yet. Will it surprise you, I wonder, to hear that Anne and Mr. Chandler have gone away? On the day after their wedding he asked if we might postpone setting a date for the ball, as he wished to take Anne on a wedding-trip. She was positively radiant as the carriage pulled away.

We will choose the date for the harvest/wedding ball upon their return, which may be for the best, because by then the weather should be cooler. In any case, I can now forewarn our guests.

Lady Catherine has just given me a note for Mary, which I enclose, and the nursemaid has come with Gregory. Do write soon, both of you, with full details of your adventures.

Affectionately,
Elizabeth and Jane

n.b. Jane also suggests I warn you that Caroline and Louisa may be returning to town.

As they walked back to the house, Mary broke the silence. "Are you more surprised by the suddenness of the wedding, or by the actions of Mr. Collins and Charlotte?"

"I am sorry for them, of course, but am exceedingly surprised and pleased to hear about my cousin," said Georgiana, who then whispered fiercely, "I do *not* want Caroline to come to London!"

That afternoon they took the carriage to Pall Mall, with Molly and Lucy inside with them. The two footmen rode on the back because Mary preferred it to their running alongside the vehicle.

Their first stop was Harding Howell and Company, where Mary and Georgiana pretended to look at fabric for their own use, asking Molly and Lucy's opinion for each bolt they considered.

Finally, Georgiana asked them to tell the assistant how many yards they desired of those they liked best.

Neither maid understood her meaning, and Mary took immense pleasure in revealing the secret. "Mrs. Chandler wishes you to have any fabrics you choose, to thank you for making her marriage dress."

"But, madam, how can we accept such a gift?" Molly's eyes were on several bolts of muslin.

"Gracefully," said Georgiana with a smile. "Now, if you please, give your instructions to the assistant for we have another commission."

Their second stop was at a haberdashery, where the two maids looked with wonder upon the array of ribbons and other trimmings on offer.

It was mid-afternoon when they returned to the house, where Lord Exeter's acceptance for dinner that evening was waiting on a salver.

"Happily, I remembered to alert Mrs. Chadwick," said Mary as they ascended the stairs.

"I assumed he would have a prior engagement," said Georgiana. "Is it possible he is eager to hear news of Caroline?"

Mary shrugged. "I suspect he never goes anywhere without motive."

Later, seated at the table, Mary was given good reason to wonder why she had hitherto found Lord Exeter so irritating.

He employed exceptionally good manners, displaying no airs as he entertained them with tales of the past season, most notably the incident in Saint James's Park during a celebration of the Hanoverian centenary and Lord Nelson's Battle of the Nile. During the festivities, a seven-story pagoda built for the occasion was aflame. While it burned, the crowd applauded wildly, having inaccurately assumed it was an intended part of the gala.[24]

"The incident was not without a few casualties," remarked Colonel Fitzwilliam. "It's dangerous to mix gaslight, fireworks, and timber."

Lord Exeter nodded. "Sometimes I wonder how the follies of our age will be reported in the history books." His seriousness led to quizzical looks and he immediately lightened his tone, touching upon another subject of constant interest to society: the latest whispered exploits of Lord Byron. "There are hints of a serious liaison, and, unsurprisingly, the identity of that individual is a point of limitless conjecture."

Christopher, lifting his brows, turned the subject to society's exodus to Vienna. "That city will soon be bursting, with nowhere to stay."

"Proving yet again how little individual thought exists amongst certain factions of the upper class," grumbled the colonel.

Lord Exeter smiled in response. "It is my understanding the congress was to be comprised of but a few representatives from each country affected by Napoleon's wars."

"The lifting of two decades of travel restrictions allows the elite to witness this historical event whilst enjoying the benefits of European society," said Christopher before taking a sip of Madeira wine. "Some of their number may hope to gain influence, for it is within the drawing rooms of society where most political decisions are made and secrets shared, is it not?"

"True, though I'm surprised to hear you admit it," said Lord Exeter with a half-smile. "In fact, my inclination is to witness this historic event myself."

---

[24] The pagoda was destroyed by fire 1 August 1814. The wooden bridge it was built upon survived but was taken down in 1825.

Mary asked, with no sign of mischief, "Has your charming friend Mrs. Beasley gone to Vienna as well? Georgiana and I had hoped to call on her."[25]

"I am certain she would take great pleasure in such a meeting when she returns to town; she is currently visiting a friend in Sussex."

"Is she?" Mary did not ask how he knew her movements so well. "I will write to her in any case. Is Mr. Beasely at home, perchance?"

Lord Exeter's countenance remained unchanged. "Mrs. Beasley is a widow of several years."

There was a slight interruption when the fish course was served, after which Georgiana returned to her subject. "I am sorry to say that the guests at the Pemberley ball to celebrate my cousin's wedding will not include Caroline Bingley. Mr. Hurst's ill health prevents it." She assumed the air of an ingénue. "There is another who cannot attend, because of the congress. I believe you have met Lord Harold?"

"We have met. I was not aware he was called away."

"Such a commission from Lord Castlereagh must surely be a reflection of his loyal service."

"Assuredly, Miss Darcy." Lord Exeter eyed her curiously. "Lord Harold is fortunate to have loyal friends."

At this point, the colonel sighed somewhat impatiently. "The foreign minister holds Harry in high regard." He leaned forward slightly. "What are your thoughts on this conference, Exeter? Do you think it possible for the heads of state to agree to a fair distribution of land, and to fund the reconstruction of war-torn areas?"

To his credit, Lord Exeter exhibited no shock at the discussion of political issues when ladies were present, and he responded freely. "It is not for me to say, but I feel certain Lord Castlereagh will protect our interests."

"What of France?" asked Christopher. "Do you think our greatest enemy will be allowed concessions?"

"*Former* greatest enemy," corrected Lord Exeter cheerfully.

---

[25] A few weeks earlier, Lord Exeter escorted Mrs. Beasely to an assembly in York (as described in *Mayhem at the Minster*), where he had introduced her to Mary and Georgiana.

"It is my understanding France will be well represented, and will no doubt present a convincing argument. But I would not care to wager whether they will be awarded anything."

Later, during the mushroom fricassee he admitted to having read Mary's three books.[26] "I have enjoyed them enormously. You write so convincingly, the adventures might in actuality have occurred."

Christopher laughed. "I can never guess where Mary is going to take her characters."

Talk of recently published books lasted throughout the dessert, after which Mary's husband signaled with a prearranged movement of his hand. She turned to Georgiana, who, without blinking, rose gracefully from her seat and followed her out.

As they walked the length of the corridor, Mary said gently, "Such strong opinions regarding Lord Harold might become the subject of speculation. Assuredly so if our guest lives up to his reputation."

Georgiana grinned. "My hopes exactly."

Mary shook her head in amazement, slowing her steps as they approached the formal sitting room. "I would far rather be outdoors, where we might at least feel the whisper of a breeze."

The two pivoted on their heels and turned their steps to the garden room.

Back in the dining room, Colonel Fitzwilliam turned to Lord Exeter in a confidential manner. "It has fallen upon us to investigate an incident that may have serious political implications." He glanced at Christopher. "And we're hoping you can assist us."

Lord Exeter showed no surprise. "How may I be of use?"

The colonel was not one to prevaricate. "We would like to be introduced to Charles Westmacott."

For a few moments Lord Exeter focused his attention on the candlelight playing against his glass of port. Finally, he looked up. "A casual introduction at a social gathering would be best. I

---

[26] Mary's novels were all published anonymously—written by 'A Lady'—but a small number knew her secret, including Miss Caroline Bingley, who would have enjoyed informing Lord Exeter.

happen to know he will be at an upcoming musical soirée hosted by Mrs. Penrose. It would be a simple matter to arrange invitations for your party." He leaned forward, voice low, looking from one man to the other. "This fellow is not one I would approach unless I were desperate, mind." He paused. "I assume you can give me no details?"

The other two shook their heads, which he accepted with good grace. "Westmacott generally slips in after all the guests have assembled and departs before the encore—perhaps because he fears someone might call him out." His smile was barely discernible. "Thus, I will do my best to introduce you prior to the start of the music."

The three soon decided to join the ladies, perplexed at finding an empty sitting room, but happily re-directed by a footman.

When all were seated comfortably in the back garden, Christopher mentioned the likelihood of receiving an invitation to a musical evening.

Mary's smiling glance rested on Lord Exeter. "I assume we will have you to thank for this?"

He dipped his head. "Mrs. Penrose is quite fond of music, but she also takes pride in her literary salons." He paused. "May I tell her you are an authoress?"

Surprised, Mary did not take time to think before acquiescing.

For a short while they discussed what music they should expect to hear, and when the subject was exhausted Lord Exeter thanked his hosts and departed.

Once he had gone, Christopher turned to Mary. "Is 'literary salon' an alias for the bluestocking club?"

"It may be. If so, would you be willing to escort us?" asked Mary, her eyes teasing.

"You may find it interesting," said Georgiana, addressing the two gentlemen. "According to Caroline Bingley, the great writers are sometimes guests at these salons. Even Miss Fanny Burney, who once visited Mary at Darcy House on an errand for the queen."[27] She thought for a moment. "Miss Burney has been married for many years, but I can't recall her husband's name."

"Alexandre d'Arblay," said Mary.

---

[27] This event is chronicled in *Mary, Mary, How Extraordinary*.

"A Frenchman?" The colonel sat straighter in his chair. "Ashton, I think it would be a very good idea for Mary to attend this literary club."

"The thought of meeting critics and serious writers makes me nervous," she admitted, catching her husband's eye. "Do you think my being associated with bluestockings could reflect poorly on you?"

"Not at all." His smile was easy. "I would be happy to attend. And Richard would as well."

It was Georgiana's turn to laugh.

~ IV ~

Prior to going down to breakfast the next morning, Mary was recounting the events described in Elizabeth's letter to her husband.

"Was I unclear about something, Christopher? You look...perplexed."

"Well, many things happened at once, but apart from Mrs. Collins' singular situation, most of it is perfectly reasonable. To my mind Mr. Collins' sudden departure was precipitated by Lady Catherine, and in defense of her daughter."

"I had no idea you were a student of maternal instincts."

He stepped closer. "It is one of my many talents. Would you mind?"

Mary sighed. "One wonders why you keep a valet."

"There are times when a man would rather have his wife adjust his cravat."

She took the ends of the long strip of white silk, arranged it as Molly had taught her to do, then stood back to look. "You are not in uniform."

"I was wondering if you would notice. Richard and I go incognito today." He turned to the looking glass as if to preen, and she brushed an imaginary speck from his sleeve.

"You may excuse your valet whenever you wish. I will always be happy to tie your cravat."

"I knew I was wise to marry you." He took her hand. "Shall we?"

Breakfast was not a lingering affair, with Christopher expected at the Bow-street station, and Georgiana taking a tray in her room.

After seeing her husband to the door, Mary went directly to her study to begin the work assigned by Lady Catherine. It was not long before she set the quill down, however, chin resting on her hands as she looked out the window.

Molly's knock at the door brought her back from a pleasant reverie. "A note has come for you, madam, from a Mr. Nolan. The messenger is waiting for your reply."

As Mary read, a smile appeared. "We can view a house today." She scribbled a response and handed it to her maid. "You may tell Lucy we will be going out this afternoon!"

Mary was making her way to the music room when she came across the butler, Mr. Fletcher, who informed her of a visitor. "Shall I say you are in, madam?" He held the salver for her to take the calling card.

It was from Mr. Bingley's good friend, Mr. Hartleton. "I will certainly see him. If you would escort him to the—I don't know what to call it, exactly—the room with the blue walls and cream wainscoting?"

"The withdrawing room, madam?"

"Yes, that's the one. I will collect Miss Darcy; please tell our guest we will be with him shortly." She began to walk away, then turned round. "I may ring for tea."

"Very good, madam."

Mary, her mind no doubt still on the house agent's message, almost skipped to the music room, where she found her dear friend kneeling on the floor, surrounded by stacks of manuscripts.

"Georgiana! What are you doing?"

That young lady placed a piece of music on the pile to her left and rose, readjusting the skirt of her morning dress. "Organizing Aunt Hermione's collection. There is a great deal of music, some of it quite old." She pointed to an ornately carved cabinet, its doors ajar. "No order at all, just tossed inside."

"I think you might prefer to do something else." Mary told her about the note from Mr. Nolan. "But first we must see our visitor. Mr. Hartleton has come to call."

Georgiana tipped her head to the side, frowning slightly. "Mr. Hartleton?"

"The scholarly, absent-minded friend Charles has mentioned a few times."

"Oh, yes." Georgiana smoothed her hair. "But I must change first."

"There is no need," insisted Mary. "Being a scholar, I doubt he would notice anything was amiss." She motioned to the door and Georgiana somewhat reluctantly followed her down the corridor.

"Mr. Hartleton, how kind of you to call on us," said Mary as they entered the withdrawing room, where Bonnie was sitting at their guest's feet, tail wagging as he bent down to pet her. "My husband will be sorry to have missed you." She introduced Georgiana and their guest made a handsome bow.

"It is a great pleasure to meet you both. Charles wrote to say you were in town and I thought only to leave my card, not wishing to disturb you."

"As a dear friend of my sister's husband, you need not stand on ceremony." Mary smiled and looked down at their puppy. "This is Bonnie, whose training is ongoing."

Mr. Hartleton's eyes were on the little spaniel. "She is adorable. I too have a dog, but she is quite large. Some of my fellow residents complained so now I am in search of a house."

Mary nodded in understanding, for Charles Bingley had mentioned the dog as the reason his friend was forced to leave the Albany. A sudden thought brightened her eyes. "Mr. Hartleton, the major and I are looking for a house as well, and just before you arrived I received a note from the house agent saying we can tour one this afternoon. It will be the first Miss Darcy and I have seen." She glanced at her friend, whose look of comprehension was almost imperceptible. "Perhaps you would care to join us? We are to meet him at two o'clock."

"I would, yes." Mr. Hartleton took out his pocket watch. "There is time enough for me to arrange a carriage so I might escort you properly—I hailed a hackney on my way here."

"You are kind to offer, but with the servants there will be six of us. Why do we not meet at the house?" Mary gave him the street name and house number.

"I shall see you there." With a gentle smile Mr. Hartleton bowed once more and took his leave.

Once he was gone Mary and Georgiana went to their rooms,

where their maids were waiting, and it was almost exactly on the stroke of two when they stepped down from the carriage onto the stone pavement, their heads tilted back to view the white-brick, three-story building.

Mr. Hartleton had arrived before them and was standing outside on the pavement. "Mrs. Ashton, Miss Darcy." His eyes went to the footmen. "You come well attended, I see."

"We do indeed," answered Georgiana with a shy smile. "Due to past incidents, my brother insists upon it whenever we leave the house."[28]

He asked no questions and followed the two ladies up the steps to the shining black door, which swung open as if by magic.

Behind it was Mr. Nolan, a soft-spoken man of advanced years. He introduced himself to each of them, mistaking Mr. Hartleton for Major Ashton.

Mary gently corrected him and he pushed his spectacles up. "Oh, please do forgive me. I have never met the major in person." He motioned to one of the rooms off the entrance hall. "Shall we begin?"

Before starting the tour, however, Mary asked if the servants might go below-stairs on their own. "I would like to know their impressions."

Mr. Nolan did not appear at all surprised at the request and agreed without demur. "Perhaps they might like to view the garret as well? I find it uncomfortably warm today." He dabbed his brow with a handkerchief before stepping over to the footmen to tell them where to find the doors leading to the servants' areas.

Mary spoke briefly with Molly. "Do mind the heat. If it is uncomfortably warm in the garret, I should like to know."

"Yes, madam." Her cheeks pink with anticipation, Molly followed the others through the baize door indicated by Mr. Nolan.

The house agent commenced the tour of the ground floor, leading them from one spacious, beautifully furnished room to the next, some connecting, and some with access only from the main corridor. He then led them out to the back garden,

---

[28] Mr. Darcy's precaution stems from incidents in *Mary, Mary, Not So Ordinary*; *Mary, Mary, Oh So Contrary*; *Mary, Mary, How Extraordinary;* and *Mayhem at the Minster.*

surrounded on all sides by a high stone wall, with espaliered fruit trees against it. There were shade trees just off the spacious patio and a serpentine path through flowering plants and shrubbery. The centerpiece was an active water feature with spouting metal fish, which Mr. Hartleton compared to one he had seen in Hampshire.

Mr. Nolan ran his fingers through the water and dried them with his handkerchief. “It can be a practical feature as well as ornamental.”

Mary silently agreed with him as she stood looking at the fountain, head tilted to the side. When Georgiana and Mr. Hartleton walked off to see more of the garden, she remained behind to dip her own handkerchief in the water and dab at her wrists. Upon their return she said, “If we are ever to stay in town during the summer months, I think we must have a fountain.”

Upon hearing this Mr. Nolan took out his leather-bound notebook, along with a graphite pencil, and began to write.

Georgiana simply smiled and took her friend by the arm as they followed the house agent back indoors, where it was considerably cooler.

The grand staircase led to a galleried landing, off which was a ballroom. “This is something I did not expect to see,” said Mary.

“Nor I,” admitted Georgiana. “But it is lovely.”

The tour continued through the billiards room, the smoking room, and another with several elegant game tables. By the time they ascended to the second floor, Mary was feeling overwhelmed. “It seems the people who live here do nothing but entertain.”

“Oh, the house is vacant, Mrs. Ashton, and the owner is offering most of the furnishings.” He motioned to the side. “If you would care to see the bed chambers.”

After viewing several, each with a dressing room, all sizeable and beautifully furnished, they returned to the ground floor.

“Do you like the house?” asked Mr. Nolan once they reached the hall.

“It is lovely, but difficult for me to see as a home,” admitted Mary.

He nodded and opened his notebook, running his fingers down a list. “I think I have a better option for you.”

After hearing his description of the second house Mary eagerly set an appointment time for the next afternoon, and Mr. Hartleton gladly accepted her invitation to join them.

Back in the carriage, she and Georgiana tried to recall the arrangement of rooms, but ended up laughing because they could not agree on several.

"It might help to start with the first we saw and go from there." Georgiana began to do so, but when she used the term 'library' (just as Mr. Nolan had done) to describe the smallest of the sitting rooms on the ground floor, Mary was dismissive.

"Library indeed! There were but a few shelves placed against a single wall. The library I wish for will have them on all sides, all the way to the ceiling, with sliding ladders and perhaps a set of circular stairs leading to a gallery. It should be a refuge, with shining wood floors, and tall windows with comfortable seats, where one could read for hours on end."

"The ballroom seems large enough to be converted," mused Georgiana as she flicked open her fan and began to wave it. "But there are other concerns. The nursery, for example, was quite small."

"Ours at Longbourn was larger," mused Mary. "Hopefully the house we see tomorrow will have a real library, a decent-sized nursery, *and* an impressive water feature." She leaned back with a sigh. "Mr. Hartleton seemed to like the house very well."

"I don't think he is absent-minded," remarked Georgiana, quite casually. "In fact, he was nothing like what one would expect, given Charles' description."

Just as casually, Mary said, "I would go further and say the description does not do him justice. He is well-spoken, well-mannered, and particularly good with dogs."

"Perhaps we should introduce him to the Miss Leighs?" Georgiana looked pointedly at her friend, who laughed.

"Now you are teasing me, which is well-deserved. I am no matchmaker."

Georgiana lifted a single brow in perfect imitation of Elizabeth. "He might do for Deidre Burnaby."

That evening, Mary and Georgiana had only Christopher to tell about Mr. Hartleton's visit, the house they had seen in his company, and another one on the morrow.

"Exeter has offered to escort you to one he knows of on Lower Grosvenor-street, and I've sent a note of inquiry to Mr. Nolan." His glance went from one to the other. "Also, we have an invitation to the musical evening."

Mary eyed Georgiana. "Lord Exeter is being extremely helpful."

"Perhaps he hopes to regain Miss Bingley's affection and desires our approbation in that respect." Her tone was such that had Lord Exeter entertained aspirations towards Miss Darcy, he would have been sorely disappointed.

"Speaking of Caroline," said Mary, "why does he not postpone his travel until after the ball? I had thought the elbow incident was forgotten, and forgiven."

"Affairs of the heart are too complex for a simple-minded man," said her husband. "I prefer to expend my energy on other topics, such as what we're having for dessert."

"Peach ice, there being a surplus of the fruit in town," said Mary. "Or so I have been informed."

"No doubt, with fewer people to consume them." He pulled at his cravat. "We should be grateful ice is procurable in this heat."

Later, Georgiana suggested they might be entertained by a novel she purchased on their recent visit to Hatchards, and as soon as they were comfortable in the back garden she opened the first volume. "I will begin with the preface, written by the authoress."

> *My skill in the composition of various sorts of puddings has never been questioned: my epistolary talents have been commended by my few correspondents, and not denied by myself: but that I possessed the inherent qualities necessary to write a book, was not suspected by me, until lately.*
>
> *I had been reading a celebrated novel, written by a celebrated Lady, which appeared to me of that kind called prose run mad. Beauty, sentiment, and description rose to such a pitch, that their effect was reversed. What should have excited admiration, became burlesque; and I found myself obliged to laugh, where it was intended I should have wept. "Surely," said I, as I laid down the book,*

"Surely I *could write as well as this!"*[29]

"What is the title?" inquired a bemused Mary.

"*The Miser Married*, by Miss Catherine Hutton. The bookseller did say it is a first novel, as her words attest."

"Thankfully, 'celebrated novel' and 'celebrated Lady' do not apply to me." Mary grimaced.

"I wonder if we have read the book she refers to." Georgiana flipped back the pages as if in hopes of finding the title.

"There are too many matching that description for us ever to know," said Christopher. "I'd like to hear more, if you're willing, so we can decide for ourselves whether this lady succeeded where she claims others have failed."

Mary agreed, her eyes on Bonnie as she patted the cushion of the settee. The puppy jumped up, then crawled over her lap to snuggle between her and Christopher.

"She grows bigger each day," commented Georgiana.

Mary rested a hand on their tired pup. "She wants to be as big as Samson."

"Bigger, I'd say," said Christopher. "And she may soon achieve her goal, at least in girth."

"You think her overfed?" Mary was frowning.

"We might ask the servants not to treat her so often...just think of Mrs. White and her pug."[30]

Mary and Georgiana volubly objected to this condemnation of that little dog, and he held his hands up in mute surrender.

With an amused shake of her head, Georgiana turned to the first chapter and began to read.

Letter one. To Mister William Mendall, Winterdale, February fifteenth, eighteen-twelve.

I hope you get on with business. Tell the rascals I will not abate them a farthing. Because their fathers and grandfathers had the lands for nothing, I suppose they will think it an infringement on their rights to be made to pay for them....

---

[29] See "Selected Resources."

[30] Christopher refers to a lady they met frequently in the course of their time in York, who was tremendously fond of her dog (as described in *Mayhem at the Minster*).

All was going well until she began the second letter, supposed to have been written by a servant. "I am sorry," she said after stumbling a third time, "but so many words are spelled strangely—I believe Miss Hutton is imitating how she thinks a servant would write." She took a breath and began again, but more slowly.

Howsomever, I thot to myself, as they all knod I was the squrs—

"Pardon me...I believe the word is *squire's*." She began again.

...squrs howskiper, Ide furbitch myself up a bit, among sich fine fokes;—"

At this point Mary and Christopher were laughing openly.

Georgiana closed the book with a snap and placed it on the low table between them. "It is difficult not to take offense on Lucy's behalf."

"And on Molly's, but not all servants' mistresses are willing to teach them as you two have done." Christopher leaned forward to take the book, the crease on his forehead growing deeper with each page he turned. Finally, he closed the volume with a condemning shake of the head and placed it back on the table. "There are several more letters written in that manner and though it is tempting to disregard them one must assume they include information vital to the tale."

"The man at Hatchards was so full of praise." Georgiana sighed. "I will continue reading it on my own and tell you what happens." She looked up, a teasing glint in her eyes. "Which means either we are reduced to reading the serials in Aunt Hermione's magazines in the evening, or we must return to the booksellers."

"Then to the bookshop we go, for Molly frequently regales me with those stories." Mary looked up through the trees to see patches of blue sky. "It is still light. What do you say we take Bonnie for a stroll before retiring?"

It was nearing dusk as they stepped out onto the pavement, their chosen path bringing them behind a lamplighter, handsomely dressed in the signature hat and coat of the trade.

Christopher held tight to the curious puppy's lead as they

watched the man set his ladder against a lamppost, take a metal pitcher from the boy he had with him, climb up, add the oil, light the wick and climb down again. Before moving on to the next, he tipped his hat to the Ashton party, whistling as he tucked the ladder under his arm and motioned for the boy to follow him.

Georgiana was fascinated. "I had no idea it was done this way. How many lamps are there in London, I wonder, and how many men are required to light them?"

"Hundreds, I would think," said Christopher as they resumed walking. "It is a community of trustworthy men who frequently act as night watchmen as well. A proud vocation, which is passed from father to son. One evening, we might take a drive along Pall Mall, and on to Westminster Bridge. Both are lit by the new gaslights, and the result is described by many as dazzling. I witnessed a demonstration by a man named Winsor a few years ago, who claimed the whole of London will be lit by gas one day."

The evening walk was so pleasant that the three made plans to do the same each night they were at home. "Somehow I feel safer out walking at this time than I ever did in the country," observed Mary as they entered the house.

"Probably because it is never this light there," responded Christopher with a grin. "Except during a full moon."

The walk had succeeded in making them think about their comfortable beds, and once tucked under the covers Mary began to describe as much as she could recall about the house they had seen that day. "The ballroom must be half the width and length of the building. The ceiling is high, though perhaps not as high as in the library at Pemberley." She turned her head to see his face, half hidden by the feather pillow. "Do we need a ballroom?"

Her husband, eyes closed, mumbled something in the affirmative and took her hand in his, holding it close to his chest.

~ V ~

The next day, prior to dressing for the house tours with Lord Exeter and Mr. Hartleton acting as escorts, Mary and Georgiana were together in the morning room. One could be heard sighing occasionally as she read Miss Hutton's novel, and the same for the other as she rewrote sections of her own book.

Mr. Fletcher interrupted the scene with a discreet cough, bringing with him a letter for Miss Darcy.

With something like a look of dread, Georgiana broke the elaborate seal. "Caroline has written."

Mary set her quill pen aside and applied the ink blotter. "What news has she to share?"

"Miss Bingley is kindly offering advice on finding the best house on the best street." Georgiana looked up with a wry smile. "Thankfully, her benevolence will come from afar since she claims intolerance to this heat, especially when so many of her friends are going to Vienna. Also, she wonders if we have had any visitors, and would like me to see her modiste personally to ensure her order is not delayed."

"Regarding visitors, does she name anyone in particular?"

"No, but I imagine she would like to know the whereabouts of Lord Exeter. Shall I admit we have seen him once already, and that we are doing so again today?"

Mary considered for a moment. "It is possible that any little thing could cause the chance of reconciliation between them to go awry."

"Then I shall only mention Mr. Hartleton." At that point the hall clock chimed once and Georgiana opened the cover of her gold watch, attached to a long, filigreed chain. "If we go up now, we will not risk being late."

In Mary's dressing room there was a slight modification to the usual schedule when Molly suggested a different hair style. "I think it will suit your new hat very well, madam."

Mary agreed, for she had not yet worn the elegant article, and the work was done in little time. "You continue to work wonders, Molly. Where do you get your ideas?"

"This one I saw in an older magazine." Molly fussed with the location of a pin. "When I asked Mrs. Chadwick if there were any in the house, she suggested we look in the attic. There were quite a few, so Lucy and I will have more stories to read." The hat was placed satisfactorily and she stood aside. "My mother tells me I can never thank you enough for teaching me to read and write."

"You may tell your mother it was my pleasure." Mary glanced at the mantel clock and rose with alacrity.

Molly and Lucy were given the task of collecting shoes at a shop on Montague-street during the time their mistresses would be viewing the first house. They were to go in the carriage with the footmen as escorts and upon completion of their assignment were to proceed to the house on Lower Grosvenor-street and make their way below-stairs, view all available rooms, and report to Mrs. Ashton and Miss Darcy later.

Molly and Lucy's first errand was at a cordwainer's shop, where the assistant brightened considerably upon learning the identities connected to their errand. "Oh, yes. Two pair of dancing-slippers." He opened the order book and ran a finger down the page. "Do excuse me. I'll be back in a moment."

During his absence Molly and Lucy went from table to table to view the footwear on display and had seen almost the entire stock by the time he returned with two bandboxes tied with handsome ribbon.

He left them on the counter and joined the maids at one of the tables. "Here you will always see the latest styles, although inventory is low at the moment because a great number of customers were suddenly in immediate need of this and that, and no time for the usual process." With a disappointed shake of the head, he took up a handsome pair of half-boots and held them for the maids to see. "They were interested only in the daintiest models rather than practical walking shoes such as these."

The two maids showed genuine admiration for the cordwainer's art and in a few short minutes had chosen those they knew would suit their mistresses very well. Shortly afterwards, the footmen were placing several parcels inside the carriage.

Their next stop was on behalf of Mrs. Chadwick, only a short walk up the street. A bell above the door announced their presence and the cobbler looked up from helping another customer. He suggested they take a seat in the narrow vestibule, where they found an errand boy already waiting.

He was a cheerful lad, who removed his cap and rose from his seat, sitting down after them, and volunteering the information that he was waiting for a pair of boots for his master. "Mr. Brown won't like it if I don't come back with them today."

"Mr. Brown?" Molly, like the errand boy, had no qualms about speaking to a stranger.

"He's the butler, miss, at one of the finest houses on Lower Grosvenor-street. I'm the boots."

"How interesting. Our mistresses are viewing one on that very street this afternoon."

"It's a grand area, for sure," he said. "Where are you staying now?"

"Near Piccadilly-street," answered Molly, less openly.

"I know that area too. There'll be plenty of fine places to let now, because so many folks are leaving town to go to a fancy conference where men from different countries are going to decide what to do now the war is over." He leaned forward to say quietly, "Jones, one of the footmen, is politically minded, you see. When the master is away—he's always visiting at one great house or another—he, Jones, I mean, reads to us from the newspapers." He turned his attention to Lucy. "And what about you, miss?"

Lucy was less frank in the company of strangers and said only that she was in London because their mistresses were dear friends.

Undaunted, he smiled at her and returned to his topic. "There's an empty house on our street where a titled young gentleman used to live. Always giving parties and the like for society, he was. Jones says the prince was a guest there more than once, and when my master and mistress were invited they didn't come home until after breakfast the next day. Then, a few months ago, the gentleman suddenly left. Slipped out in the night, so they say." He grinned sheepishly. "I know nearly all the servants on our street."

Just then the cobbler appeared with a pair of highly polished tall boots in hand. The boy dug the correct coinage from a pocket, gave it to the man, then lifted his cap to the maids. "I hope to see you again someday." He hurried out.

The cobbler motioned for the two maids to step forward, and when Molly explained what they wanted he disappeared behind a curtain without a word. In a few minutes he returned with the shoes. "Two pair with new soles and new heels. Five shillings."

Earlier, out on the York-street pavement, Georgiana and Mary, along with the two gentlemen, were looking up at the facade of the house they were to view.

"I wonder if one can get a feeling for a place, even before entering," said Mary, with a little shiver despite the warm day.

"An adverse reaction to a property is something you shouldn't ignore," said Mr. Hartleton. "I've stayed in many historic places when assessing the contents of libraries, and have on more than one occasion felt extremely uncomfortable for no discernible reason."

"Shall we see what it feels like inside?" Cheerfully, Lord Exeter took the few steps up to the shining door and lifted the lion-head knocker.

As on the previous day it was opened by Mr. Nolan, who ushered them into the cool entrance hall. Following a proper introduction to the new member of their party, Lord Exeter, the house agent pointed out the beautifully painted ceiling high above them, and the fine craftmanship of the staircase leading to the galleried landing.

"It is lovely," said Mary, but something in her tone caused the house agent to commence the tour without further comment on fine details.

After viewing the rooms on the ground floor they went outside to see the back garden. The fountain was an attractive feature but, as Georgiana noted, there was no place to sit and run one's fingers through the cool water.

Back inside, Mr. Nolan led them to the first floor where they passed from one richly furnished room after another, but when he asked Mary if she cared to see the garret or to go below-stairs she declined.

"Then shall we continue on to Lower Grosvenor-street?" suggested the house agent, and led the way out.

As pre-arranged the party of four rode together in Lord Exeter's carriage, and as they passed through the residential streets the topic of conversation naturally turned to the house they had just seen.

"Mrs. Ashton, did your feelings change once you were inside?"

asked Lord Exeter.

"It may simply have been the heat, but I felt oppressed throughout," she admitted.

"Perhaps some or all the inhabitants are, or were, terribly unhappy," said Georgiana. "And, as in Mrs. Radcliffe's novels, such feelings might affect the atmosphere in the house, to which some are sensitive."

"It is interesting you should say that, Miss Darcy." Mr. Hartleton was eyeing her curiously. "I have read a few things written by Dr. Franz Mesmer. He believes there is a universal magnetic substance of some kind connecting all living things, and to some extent inanimate objects, although his theories have not been widely accepted."

Lord Exeter was nodding. "The man is thought to be a charlatan by some and a genius by others, but no doubt he would say you were wise to recognize and respect your feelings about that house, Mrs. Ashton."

"Mary and I have attended interesting lectures at the Royal Academy," said Georgiana. "Has Dr. Mesmer ever presented there?"

Mr. Hartleton shook his head with a look of regret. "I believe he asked the committee to consider him, but was refused."

"It would be most interesting if his theories were validated," said Lord Exeter before tapping the roof of the carriage with his cane, for they had arrived at the next house.

They were there ahead of Mr. Nolan so again stood as a group on the pavement, looking upon the exterior of the house.

"It is impressive without being ostentatious," said Georgiana, tipping her parasol back to see the top story. "And the garret seems a reasonable height."

At that point, Mr. Nolan's hackney carriage pulled up. Full of apologies, he soon had them inside the grand entrance hall.

Three sets of eyes rested on Mary, who said good-naturedly, "I feel nothing, save a desire to see more of this house."

As the tour progressed, Lord Exeter relayed several anecdotes. In the red drawing room he said, "I recall a disastrous game of five-card loo in here; I lost several pounds to Lady Jersey." In the next he said, "Despite the ballroom on the first floor, there was often dancing here because it is open to the back garden. After dark, with the lanterns alight, it could be utterly enchanting."

Much to Mary's delight there was a proper library on the first floor, with ceiling-height shelves, cleverly disguised doors, and cozy alcoves built round each of the front-facing windows. Her attention was caught by a cylinder writing desk of French design, so much so she did not hear Lord Exeter's latest anecdote.

Georgiana, having come across an entire section devoted to French novels, had come to stand by her friend, her cheeks stained with pink. "It is a very handsome piece."

"I have never seen the like." Mary looked up. "Mr. Nolan, does the owner wish to sell any of the furnishings?"

"I'm glad you asked, Mrs. Ashton. The representative tells me he would entertain offers, as part of the sale."

"I like this very much." Briefly, she rested her hand upon the desk before taking a final look round the room.

Next, they viewed the family bedchambers, as well as two rooms modified for bathing, one boasting a showering apparatus such as those Darcy and Bingley had lately installed in their homes.

They viewed the guest bedchambers and finally the garret, where the corridors were not too narrow, the rooms modest but comfortably furnished, and the ceilings high enough for the gentlemen to stand erect.

Mr. Nolan was obviously pleased with their reaction to this detail. "The architect was most particular about the design, being of the opinion that those content with their living situation would carry that contentment into their work."

"Any house we consider must offer the same or better accommodation for the servants," said Mary, with a hint of Lady Catherine's manner.

Mr. Nolan took out his notebook to write a few lines before they returned to the first floor, where Mary wished to view one of the larger chambers a second time.

She had just stepped into the dressing room and was looking at a large built-in armoire when there was a slight scratching sound behind it and the entire front swung to the side, barely missing her foot as she backed away.

A face appeared through the opening.

"Molly!"

"Madam!"

"Mary!" Georgiana had rushed into the room just as Lucy sheepishly appeared.

"I'm so sorry to disturb you," said Molly. "We thought we heard someone coughing behind the wall in the corridor outside the kitchen, and when we started talking about it we heard what sounded like someone running up the stairs." She motioned towards the aperture. "We found the door to these steps by accident. Down there it looked like a cupboard built into the wall."

"Might it have been William or John you heard?" asked Mary.

Molly shook her head. "They were with us when we heard the cough, and said they'd wait at the bottom until we came down again."

"I thought Mr. Nolan said the house is unoccupied," mused Georgiana as she looked inside the passage. "These steps were likely designed to be used only by the most trusted of servants, such as a lady's maid or valet I imagine." She was backing away when something caught her eye and she bent down to pick up a gold locket attached to a long delicate chain. She showed it to the maids, who said it was not theirs.

"If you'll excuse my saying so, Miss Darcy," said Molly, "it looks very fine and must have come at a dear price."

Georgiana glanced at Mary. "Should we leave it with Mr. Nolan?"

Mary nodded, then said to Molly in a tone that brooked no argument. "Go back down and stay with the footmen in the servants' hall until we fetch you." Her eyes softened. "No more adventures, remember?"

"Yes, madam." There was a slight twinkle in Molly's eyes as she stepped back through the opening. Lucy went next, taking hold of a handle on the inside of the false wardrobe and pulling it back in place.

"Do you sometimes think we have a bad influence on them?" asked Mary as they left the room.

Georgiana smiled. "Perhaps."

They met the gentlemen in the library, where Georgiana gave the locket to Mr. Nolan, saying only that she had found it on the floor of the dressing room.

After a brief examination of the intricate piece he wrapped it carefully in a handkerchief, then tucked it into an inner jacket pocket. "I'll see if the rightful owner can be found, Miss Darcy."

To Mary he said, "Would you care to see below-stairs, or the garden?"

"I think we should see both."

With a pleased look, he led them down the main stairs and to the nearest baize-covered door.

In the kitchen he pointed out the abundance of natural light due to a special window built into the ceiling at the edge of the exterior wall. "You can see how this part of the room extends beyond the front of the house."

Mary was last to view the upper window, then looked straight out at the plain stone steps leading to the pavement above. At that moment she caught sight of the hem of a green dress and the tips of brown boots at the top of those very steps. Without looking away she said, "Mr. Nolan, does anyone have keys to this house? A cleaning maid or caretaker, perhaps?" As she watched, the woman turned on her heel and hurried away.

"As far as I know, the owner has had no one here since the last tenant departed," he said, unconcerned, then led them down the length of the servants' hall, pointing to various rooms without going inside them. At the end of the corridor he said, "The back garden has a large fountain. Shall we go there?"

On their way, Mary stopped in the servants' hall to ask Molly and Lucy to wait inside near the main entrance. "We will find you there shortly." To John and William, she said, "I would like you to wait outside, a bit away from the house, but close enough to see if anyone not of our party enters or leaves it."

"Yes, madam," said John, the elder of the two.

Lord Exeter had not exaggerated the charm of the back garden, with its multiple paths winding between rows of exotic evergreens of varying height. The focal point was a grand water feature with three stone nymphs clad in Grecian dress gracing the center.

Georgiana watched the water falling from the hands of the nymphs. "This is beautiful."

"A student of Capability Brown designed everything you see," said Mr. Nolan. "Would you care to visit the conservatory? It is well-situated, at the far end of the stone path."

"Thank you, but I think I will leave that to Major Ashton, should he care to see the house," said Mary as she flipped open her fan, just as Georgiana had done moments earlier.

When they were once more out on the pavement, near the waiting carriages, Mr. Hartleton noted how remarkably quiet it was. "I notice several doorknockers have been removed."

"The residents may well be on their way to Vienna," said Lord Exeter, facing Mary. "Did you like the house, Mrs. Ashton?"

"Very much. It is grand enough to host even the most auspicious of our acquaintance." Her teasing glance went to Georgiana. "Your aunt, for example."

"It is doubtful Aunt Catherine will come to London any time soon, unless it is to consult with you on your latest novel," responded Georgiana in kind. "If so, she can stay at Darcy House."

Before Lord Exeter could come to an erroneous conclusion, Mary explained, "Miss Darcy's aunt was kind enough to advise me on certain societal aspects in my last novel and has agreed to do so again with my current work. However, she does not care to have this widely known."

"Of course not." Lord Exeter dipped his head.

The two ladies thanked the gentlemen for their escort and accepted Lord Exeter's hand to help them into their carriage, where the two maids were already seated.

"It has been a great pleasure." Mr. Hartleton spoke to them through the open window. "One which I hope we will repeat soon."

As the carriage drew away, Georgiana asked, "Did you really find the house to your taste? It was difficult to tell by your expression."

"I did, although I prefer Aunt Hermione's, which is a comfortable size without being overwhelming."

"The last one had a good library."

"Yes, it did." Mary sighed.

Upon returning to Aunt Hermione's house, Mary asked the footmen to follow her and Georgiana into the nearby sitting room, at which point she asked if they had heard or seen anything unusual in the house after the two maids went up the hidden stairs.

"No, ma'am," said William. "But later, there was something outside. I'm not sure how unusual it was, but as you wanted us to watch for anyone coming near the house, well, there was a man and a woman just passing by when we stepped out. She was all bundled up even though it was so hot, and too weak to walk, for he was almost carrying her."

The two ladies sat straighter, and Georgiana asked, "Can you describe them?"

"The man was tall and a bit heavy-set, but his head was turned so we couldn't see his face," responded William. "Or hers, either, for she wore a dark veil."

John was nodding. "She seemed sickly and weak. I thought she must be a widow, with her black dress and veil. Maybe in service because her clothes looked second-hand. Didn't you think so, William?"

"Now you mention it, her skirt was worn at the bottom."

"You are very observant," said Mary. "Did you see where they went?"

"They turned at one of the houses on the same side of the street." William paused, then glanced at John. "Which one, do you think?"

"The third or fourth one down—it might have had a green door."

Mary rose and thanked them. "Major Ashton and Colonel Fitzwilliam may want to speak with you later."

Once the footmen had gone, Georgiana said quietly, "You think it could have been the courier and his abductor?"

Mary shrugged. "The description is too similar to ignore, do you not agree?"

"But why be anywhere near that street, where they were likelier to be seen, especially since the carriages were out there? Why not remain hidden until they were certain we were gone?"

"Those are likely the same questions Christopher and Richard will ask." Mary turned to her friend with a glimmer of excitement.

"But, if it is those they are seeking, it is far more likely we will be attending the ball!"

Just then the hall clock chimed the half-hour, and Georgiana's eyes went to the smaller timepiece on the mantel. "I was hoping for a cool bath before dressing."

CHAPTER SIX
London

~ I ~

Mary was right about Colonel Fitzwilliam and Major Ashton's interest in what was seen and heard by the maids and footmen at the house on Lower Grosvenor-street. It was the first information to give them some hope of finding the courier.

They began their investigation by speaking with Mr. Nolan. He claimed to be unaware of any secret doors or hidden passageways in the house, and gladly handed over the keys. He also gave them the necklace. "You have far better resources than I to find the rightful owner."

Inside the house, their steps echoing in the main hall, Colonel Fitzwilliam remarked on the heat and removed his jacket. "I've been to many card parties here; the play was always high."

Christopher also removed his jacket, taking a moment to assess the richly appointed hall.

"Do you know this was Harry's house?" asked Colonel Fitzwilliam. "That was before his uncle disinherited him, of course."

"Truly? Lord Exeter didn't mention it. Do you think he knows?"

Colonel Fitzwilliam shrugged. “Harry didn’t always attend his own parties. After the use of the house was rescinded, full ownership returned to his uncle, who let the house to a wealthy admiral with a wife especially fond of counting titled people amongst her guests.” He paused. “You know, I used to think of Harry as a jackanape.”

“And now?”

“I don’t know what to think. He has proved himself many times to be a reliable agent, and he recently risked his own life to save my cousin and your wife, so for now I must describe him as a brave and loyal comrade.”

“Then I will keep my good opinion of him.” Christopher looked up at the galleried landing. “Since you’re familiar with this house, where would you like to begin?”

“In the garret, where it’s sure to be hottest. We’ll want to pay particular attention to dimensions.”

“You anticipate more hidden passages?”

“Absolutely. Some of those parties were rather...lacking in restraint, shall I say?”

In the garret they discovered nothing out of the ordinary. The side attics held disappointingly few furnishings, and a hot, dusty search of old trunks yielded only outdated clothing and moth-eaten linens.

It was in one of the larger bedchambers on the floor below that they discovered a latch hidden behind a loose brick near the hearth. When lifted by means of a thin piece of metal (in this case Christopher’s pocketknife), a catch was released and a section of the wall broke free, revealing a well-disguised door. They passed into the adjoining chamber, where the opposite side of the door was cleverly disguised as part of a painted scene on the wall.

“We shouldn’t be surprised to find discreet access between bedchambers in a house like this,” said Christopher.

“No, but it might be useful to ascertain the political affiliation or ideology of those who stayed here.” The colonel led the way to the chamber with the false wardrobe discovered by Molly and Lucy. After locating the mechanism to release the catch, he stepped inside and pulled the false door closed behind him. “Can you hear me?” he asked in a normal voice.

“Perfectly. Keep talking as you go down.”

The sound quickly diminished and in a short while the false wardrobe was sliding open again. "It's a handy thing for sure," said the colonel, brushing dust from his shirtsleeves.

In the library was a full-length portrait depicting a man dressed in the pre-revolution style of France. When Christopher experimentally pressed a slight indentation on the frame the entire thing shifted slightly away from the wall, allowing it to be moved aside with little effort. This revealed a recess with a raised platform upon which a grown man could stand and presumably observe a section of the room.

In response to an encouraging nod from the colonel, Christopher lowered his head, stepped into the cavity, and slid the portrait back into place.

"I assume you can see me," said the colonel.

"Quite well, in fact. Would you take a few steps to the left and then say something?"

The colonel did so, moving farther away until Christopher had to raise his own voice considerably. "It's too dark to find the latch." Moments later the portrait slid to the side and he stumbled out, taking a newspaper from an occasional table and waving it back and forth to cool his face.

"May I see that?" The colonel grabbed the daily broadsheet, a deep line forming on his brow as he skimmed the main article. "I recognize this account of a recent battle with our tenacious cousins across the Atlantic." He pointed. "Note the date."

"It is four days old."

"And how long has this house been vacant?"

"Longer than four days, which means Mary and Georgiana's visit might have precipitated a hasty departure of someone who had access to this house, as well as familiarity with it. Perhaps without the owner's knowledge." Christopher looked up. "I'm beginning to think it really could have been the courier the footmen saw on the pavement yesterday. But, if so, where was he taken?"

The colonel slid the portrait back into place. "They may have returned here later." He thought for a second. "We need more men to help with the search of this entire area, but I'd like to have a quick look at the conservatory before we go."

Set at the far end of the garden, the building was comprised of a brick base on three sides with glass panes above, and a solid brick wall at the back. It was in no way dilapidated, but weeds had begun to climb the exterior.

Despite the appearance of neglect, the key from Mr. Nolan turned easily in the lock and the door opened without resistance. Inside, they followed the stone path between a line of a once-impressive collection of citrus trees and deep frames containing the remnants of melons, squashes, and small fruits. Near the opposite end Christopher lifted the long spiny leaves of a plant to expose rotten fruit. "Nothing has been tended to recently."

"Yet the floor has been brushed clean." The colonel scraped his boot against the stone and motioned to a solid door in the rear brick wall. "Shall we?"

Finding the key on the lintel they entered a tidy space with windows on each side. Garden tools hung in neat rows against one wall, and a long potting station stood in the middle.

Approaching a door in the far wall of that room, they found no key, but the colonel was able to open it with the use of a special tool.

The interior was dark, the air fetid, and the two men held handkerchiefs to their faces as they moved forward. In the light coming from the doorway they could see a pile of makeshift bedding on the floor. Nearby were scraps of dried food and a dish of turbid water.

On the floor the colonel found a pair of trousers and a shirt. "Only a small man or a boy could wear these."

"The courier?"

The colonel's jaw clenched. "I'm beginning to think we may be on the right path." He made a small bundle of the clothing. "But it is also possible that some unfortunate person made his home here for a short while."

"Or, he was kept prisoner," said Christopher darkly as he held up a length of frayed rope.

In the next few hours a thorough search of the house, grounds, and conservatory ensued, with several Bow-street runners working alongside members of the regiment. Some searched the adjacent houses, back gardens and outbuildings, questioning the servants and masters alike, but to no avail.

At the end of the day Major Ashton went to inform Mr. Nolan personally that no one was to enter the house on Lower Grosvenor-street until further notice. "Before I go, there is a desk in the library that caught my wife's eye—"

"I know the very one," said Mr. Nolan with a smile, and the two soon came to an agreement.

~ II ~

After a long day of trying to keep busy while waiting to hear any news, Mary and Georgiana finally ascended the stairs to begin dressing for the musical evening.

It was Mary's idea for them to sit together when Molly and Lucy arranged their hair, and she had requested a tray with an assortment of small sandwiches—just enough to stave off hunger, as there was to be a late supper at Mrs. Penrose's soirée.

The two were seated at the specially arranged dressing tables, waiting patiently as Molly consulted a plate depicting an elegant coiffure in a recent issue of *La Belle Assemblée.*

"Perhaps we could do this before the ball at Pemberley," said Georgiana, sipping her tea.

"Elizabeth and Jane would love it." Mary smiled. "It makes me feel positively festive."

"Madam, if you wouldn't mind holding your head this way—" Molly tipped her own as an example "—I'm ready to begin the pinning." She glanced at Lucy. "Just copy what I do for now. We don't want the styles to be the same in the end, so I'd like to finish Miss Darcy's hair using the plate on the next page as an example."

"Okay, Moll." The younger of the two, Lucy was a student of Molly's in so many arts. She twisted a section of Miss Darcy's hair. "Is this right?"

"It's perfect. Now, do the next section in the same way."

For a few minutes the two worked silently, but Mary preferred it when Molly told stories from the magazines, so she asked if they had read anything interesting lately.

"We found an exciting tale, madam," said Molly. "It's about a handsome colonel who falls in love with a beautiful girl named Elvira. He wasn't a colonel when they first fell in love, so they had to wait. It took *years* for him to get a higher rank, then, almost as soon as they were married, he was ordered to a faraway land. Elvira couldn't bear to be apart from him, so she went on the ship too." Molly paused as she inserted a hairpin. "But then terrible trouble came." She frowned, removed the pin, and re-twirled the hair.

"They were captured by pirates," said Lucy, her eyes bright. "The worst in the whole ocean, from a place called Tunisia. Have you ever heard of it?" Her questioning glance encompassed the two ladies.

"There may be an atlas in the house," said Georgiana without moving her head.

"And if there is none," said Mary, eyeing Molly through the looking glass, "you may choose one at the bookshop next time we visit."

"Thank you, madam," said Molly before continuing the tale. "Wherever Tunisia is, it's very far from England, and there was no chance of rescue for Elvira and the colonel. The pirates always sell their prisoners at an open market, and Elvira, being so beautiful, was bought by a very wealthy prince, to serve his daughter, and to live in a—" she reached into her apron pocket to retrieve a scrap of paper, holding it so both ladies could see "—I don't know how to pronounce it."

Mary looked at the carefully formed letters. "I have heard the major use the word *Seraglio* when speaking about a particular opera, and believe it refers to the wing of a palace where only women are allowed." She paused, frowning slightly. "It was not considered proper for young ladies in Hertfordshire to sing arias from that work."

"Seraglio." Molly imitated Mary's pronunciation. "We had a feeling it wasn't a nice place." She searched the table beside her for a particular jeweled comb, then went on. "So, poor Elvira said she would rather die than live there, but the colonel, who hasn't been sold yet and is still in the marketplace, begs her to stay alive so they can be together again one day." She inserted the comb on the left side of the coiffure. "What do you think, madam?"

"Of the story?"

Molly grinned. "Of your hair."

"It is lovely." Mary slowly turned her head back and forth to view it through the mirror. "A perfect copy of the image."

Satisfied, Molly turned the magazine page and instructed Lucy on how to complete the arrangement of Miss Darcy's hair.

As Lucy worked, Georgiana asked, "What happened to Elvira at the end of the story?"

"I'm sorry, Miss Darcy, but we haven't read that far," answered Lucy as she took a hairpin from Molly.

Mary rose and crossed the room to take a chocolate from the assorted confections. "Georgiana, don't you think that reading to the end should be the most important of Molly and Lucy's activities tonight?"

"Indeed, I do." Georgiana's eyes were teasing.

"There is one thing we haven't described, madam," said Molly. "The last thing we read was the brave colonel's farewell to Elvira." She rested her hands against her chest and recited: 'Begin from this moment to dare fortune to do its worst, and rest assured that nothing but despair can prevent our reunion.'"[31]

When Christopher returned to Hertford-street he did not stop to speak with Mary, for his valet insisted there was time only to bathe and dress.[32]

Later, he found her standing at the window in their bedchamber. "May I say you look particularly lovely this evening?"

"Thank you." Mary, married three months, still could not prevent the blush rising in her cheeks. "As do you." She offered her hand, which he lifted to his lips.

He took her gloves from a table and handed them to her. "When I came in, it seemed you were lost in thought."

"I was thinking about the house on Lower Grosvenor-street. The library is nearly perfect, and even Lady Catherine would approve the location, yet I am uncertain about living there."

"There will be others," he assured her. "You are not too

---

[31] Molly and Lucy were reading "Zara; Or the Adventures of an English Wife" in *La Belle Assemblée*, Vol. 5, J. Bell, London. January 1 - June 30, 1812, pp.14-16.

[32] The valet had served as batman to a captain in the Royal Navy, and the major knew better than to argue.

disappointed?"

"Not at all. Your aunt's kindness allows us more than enough time to view as many as we care to, and to think well before choosing."

"Was that not Lady Catherine's advice?" he teased.

She only smiled in return.

~ III ~

The three members of the Ashton party left in high spirits, but once they reached the Penrose house Christopher could not repress a groan upon observing the line of fashionably dressed people. "I had not thought so many were still in London."

When they finally reached the top of the wide, curving staircase they could see Lord Exeter standing with their hosts. Mr. Penrose, a nondescript man who seemed reconciled to—if not interested in—his wife's entertainments, was polite enough, but his wife was graciousness itself.

"I understand you are an authoress, Mrs. Ashton. You must come to my next literary gathering. I have had the honour of hosting our greatest writers. Perhaps his lordship—" she tapped Lord Exeter playfully with her fan "—has told you that the great poet, Scott, has sat at my dinner table." She paused dramatically. "I shall be hosting a small group within the next fortnight—you will join us, of course. London is frightfully thin this time of year, but as Mr. Penrose is not fond of the country I must be satisfied with the dregs."

There was little Mary could say in reply, so she dipped her head politely with a murmured thank you and took hold of her husband's arm. Lord Exeter offered to escort Miss Darcy, and bestowed his most charming smile upon his hostess before leading the Ashton party into the large salon, choosing a place to stand that was well-suited to the observation of guests entering as well as those already circulating.

Near them was a group discussing the singer's repertoire and they overheard one woman say, "I am certain Mrs. Penrose will have a good deal to say prior to the recital."

Lord Exeter's eyes held a hint of amusement as he began to take glasses from a footman's tray and pass them to the others.

When they each had one in hand, he asked the Ashtons if they were interested in the house on Lower Grosvenor-street.

"I believe it has a fine library," answered Christopher, his expression giving nothing away. "But my wife's ideal is at Pemberley, and it will not be a simple matter to find its equal."

Mrs. Penrose had left her post at the top of the stairs by then and had worked her way through the crowded room. Over Mary's head she waved to attract the attention of a passing footman. "It is so good of you to share your friends with us, Lord Exeter. What a joy it is to finally meet a member of the Darcy family." She flipped open a gilt-edged fan. "And you know what pleasure I take in introducing new authors to the world."

Another footman appeared with a tray, and only after observing that each of them had a glass did she take one for herself. As she did so, she whispered, "Ask Mr. Wilkins to assign more men to wave the fans. It grows too close in here."

From where they stood, several liveried servants could be seen standing along the bank of open windows, looking quite warm themselves as they waved large palm-leaf fans.

Mrs. Penrose turned her attention to Mary. "Madame d'Arblay has attended my soirees, though I daresay she is better known to you as Fanny Burney, the famous authoress." The fan waved. "The poor thing is in mourning for her dear father, the great music scholar, gone from us these...let me think, April, May—" she counted on her fingers "—yes, five months. What a dreadful loss to society."

Mary might have been considering how to respond when Georgiana spoke. "Mrs. Ashton is acquainted with Madame d'Arblay."

"Is she?" Mrs. Penrose leaned forward slightly.

Georgiana nodded. "Madame d'Arblay, once keeper of the robes, as I'm sure you know, visited her in person to present a request from the queen."

Mrs. Penrose's attention was once more on Mary. "Then I suppose you are familiar with the painful events in Madame d'Arblay's life, including that horrid surgery?[33] Sadly, she must

---

[33] Mrs. Penrose refers to a surgical procedure performed on Madame d'Arblay in 1811, experienced without benefit of anaesthetics, and described in detail in a letter to her sister.

return to her husband in France, and who can say when we might see her again?"

Before Mary could take a breath, Lord Exeter interjected. "My dear Mrs. Penrose, I had hoped to introduce Major Ashton to one of your guests this evening. Will Mr. Westmacott be making an appearance?"

"He should be with us any time now." Again, their hostess playfully tapped her fan against his shoulder. "You know it is his habit to come last of all my guests." She added confidentially, "He is of a retiring nature and prefers to enter unannounced."

"Well, then—" Lord Exeter straightened his shoulders "—we must be vigilant."

It was growing close to the time of the concert, and their hostess excused herself. "I must see to any late-comers, including the gentleman you wish to speak to."

Directly after she left, Colonel Fitzwilliam joined them.

"Your timing is impeccable," said Christopher drily.

"It is an artful strategy."

Before they could say more, the ringing of a bell indicated it was time to take their seats.

"Will you join us, Richard?" asked Georgiana.

"Thank you, no. I will take my place just outside—there, on the balcony." His eyes focused on the area. "Not only can I observe the guests at my ease but, more importantly, it is a place from which I can better endure the caterwauling."

Georgiana shook her head in mock admonition of her cousin before graciously accepting his lordship's invitation to escort her to their seats.

The accompanist was seated at the harpsichord in the center of a raised platform, and as soon as her guests were settled Mrs. Penrose appeared from behind a screen.

"I am proud to present one of my latest discoveries, whom I had the pleasure of hearing last March at a concert of ancient music in the New Rooms at Hanover Square. Tonight's artist is a devotee of the actress and singer, Miss Kitty Stephens, and will be performing arias from the operas of Herr Handel." She extended an arm towards the screen. "And now, without further ado...Miss Elena Spire."

The audience applauded and the vocalist, adorned in a

shepherdess costume, walked out from behind the screen, first making a deep bow to her patroness, and then to the audience. "I will begin with 'As when the dove,' from *Acis and Galatea."* She smiled at the accompanist, who placed his hands on the keyboard and after the briefest pause began to play the introductory measures.

Throughout the performance, the audience was captivated by the beauty of the soprano's voice. Had anyone taken their eyes from her they would have seen more than one discreetly lifted handkerchief.

Miss Spire sang several arias from the renowned composer's operas and oratorios, all perfectly suited to her voice. She obliged her appreciative audience with two encores, but when they begged for a third Mrs. Penrose appeared once more from behind the screen. "I am so pleased you have enjoyed this wonderful music, but we must allow our artiste to rest. If you would proceed to the adjoining salon for supper, I hope Miss Spire might soon join us."

The colonel approached the Ashton party then, and Christopher asked discreetly, "Did you see him?"

"No." The colonel's eyes were on the guests slowly making their way to the salon.

Georgiana had turned round at the sound of his voice. "How did you like the music, Richard?"

"Very well." He sounded pleasantly surprised. "Our hostess demonstrates unexpectedly good judgement."

"Her performance of the aria 'Sweet Bird' was so lovely," said Georgiana dreamily. "I wish it were possible to hear it again and again, whenever I chose."

Mary waved her fan, for the palm leaves had moved into the supper room. "According to Georgiana's Italian tutor, a Spanish king suffered from terrible headaches and ordered Maestro Scarlatti to play for him at all times of the day or night."

Georgiana smiled. "Speaking of the harpsichord, I thought the accompanist showed both taste and sensibility."

"His playing allowed for superb artistry on the part of the singer, something I have rarely witnessed," said Lord Exeter, to their surprise.

"The music surpassed my expectations," said Christopher, his eyes on his lordship. "Thank you for arranging our invitation."

"It was my pleasure," he responded, then made a slight motion of his head towards a peculiar looking man in thick-lensed spectacles approaching them, in company with Mrs. Penrose.

"Here you are, Lord Exeter," she twittered. "I believe you are already acquainted with Mr. Westmacott." Those two men acknowledged one another with a slight dip of the head.

Lord Exeter, after introducing Colonel Fitzwilliam and Major Ashton, whom the newcomer eyed with open curiosity, asked Mrs. Penrose, "Might we make use of your library?"

"Of course. I trust you know the way?" She smiled at Georgiana and Mary. "And you need not be concerned about the young ladies. I will take care of them." She waited until after the men had taken their leave to say, "Come with me, my girls. There is someone I would like you to meet." She waved her fan. "Amongst my guests is another recently published authoress. Her name is Miss Hutton."

Neither Mary nor Georgiana could hide their astonishment. "Why, I have just begun to read her novel!" admitted the latter, but whether Mrs. Penrose heard was questionable, for she was already paces ahead.

Across the room, on the opposite side of a large potted palm, they found a woman with permanent frown lines and streaks of grey in her hair. "Miss Hutton! Why do you hide so, and why do you not have a glass of punch?" Mrs. Penrose raised a hand to catch the attention of a passing servant, who came forward with a tray of filled glasses. "Do take one," she suggested. "It is not every day I introduce two budding authors to one another."

"So, you too are a writer," said Miss Hutton to Mary after Mrs. Penrose had made the introductions.

Georgiana answered for her. "Mrs. Ashton has written three novels, and her publisher is anxiously awaiting the completion of a fourth."

"I see." Miss Hutton looked suitably impressed. "And are your novels instructive, Mrs. Ashton?"

Mary took a moment to form an answer. "When I commenced writing the fourth, I was determined to include something of social significance, but my publisher does not care for the idea. He says my readers will feel betrayed." She made a wry face. "I have always attempted instruction of sorts in my novels—in one I suggested the practical application of pugilism, as a means for ladies to defend themselves."

Miss Hutton shook her head vehemently. "Your publisher is thinking only of profit, I daresay. You must find another, and continue to search for ways to *teach* with your novels. I speak from years of experience and close association with learned, scientific men. My father, a historian of some renown, made it possible for me to meet the great Joseph Priestley, whose experiments in chemistry are of inestimable value. I assume you have heard of him?"

The two younger ladies before her were obliged to admit they were not familiar with the name.

Mrs. Penrose, who was momentarily distracted by a nearby group, turned back with a faint look of confusion. "You writers understand one another so well." She clapped her hands in delight. "I have just had a brilliant idea! At my next literary meeting, each of you will read a selection from your novel!"

Mary took a quick sip of punch, whereas Miss Hutton was almost smiling as she said, "I would very much enjoy hearing how you incorporated the unusual subject of pugilism in your work, Mrs. Ashton."

Georgiana's chin tilted slightly. "We have recently begun to read your book, *The Miser Married*, Miss Hutton. Is it entirely written in epistolary form, like Samuel Richardson's *Pamela* and Madame d'Arblay's *Evelina*?"

Miss Hutton gave her a look of approval. "You are well-read, I see, Miss Darcy. Letter writing is one of the great arts, and one of the few outlets for the minds of women who are wise enough to understand the importance of daily practice. I hope my works will encourage readers to take the composition of letters, which are of intrinsic historical value, more seriously. If so, I have done what I set out to do in *The Miser*." She turned her face slightly towards Mary. "I abhor frivolity, especially in such times as these, when our leaders are influenced by a selfish, unreliable, and irresponsible monarch."

This remark was met with shocked silence, and in a somewhat desperate attempt to prevent their hostess from being charged with treason, or at the very least for hosting guests whose words could be interpreted in such a way, Mary motioned discreetly towards a pair of young ladies standing against the opposite wall. "Those two appear to have studied the art of fan language, though I have not the faintest idea what they are trying to say."

Georgiana, with the use of her own fan, observed them discreetly. "Either they are working on their technique, or their studies have been haphazard. The young lady in the diadem is indicating *follow me*, but no one—save us—appears to be looking. The one in pale blue, by running her fan across her midsection is attempting to relay *I wish to speak with you.*" She turned mischievous eyes on Miss Hutton. "Are you a student of the art?"

"Certainly not!"

At this point Mary searched the room for her husband. However, it was not he, but Lord Exeter, she saw approaching.

Mrs. Penrose laughed a bit nervously. "Oh, look! His lordship could not stay away!" Her teasing eyes were on Georgiana, who quickly turned her attention back to the young ladies and their fans.

Their hostess waved to catch his attention, and when he joined them she introduced Miss Hutton. "Have you read her novel?"

"I have not had the pleasure. But having learned that Mrs. Ashton and Miss Darcy were doing so, I am determined to purchase a copy." He smiled graciously. "It is one of life's great pleasures to discuss a new novel with one's friends."

"It has long been my habit to discuss what I am reading with others—as long as they are worthy." The lace of Miss Hutton's bonnet bounced with her nodding head. "I would be happy to inscribe your copy, and will enjoy hearing how well you liked my work."

"I look forward to it, Miss Hutton." He turned to Mrs. Penrose. "I fear I must apologize for taking these two charming young ladies from you. Major Ashton wishes to depart."

Their withdrawal was clearly of no consequence to Miss Hutton, but Mrs. Penrose did her best to delay them. "We are to begin cards soon. Can you not convince him to stay?"

Her subsequent pleas and promised introduction to the musicians were to no avail and she desisted, but not before extracting a promise from Mary to attend her next literary meeting, and to prepare a 'short section' from one of her novels to read aloud to those assembled.

As they followed Lord Exeter from the room, Georgiana whispered to Mary, "I enjoyed the music immensely, but at what cost?"

"Socializing with authoresses can be arduous." Mary's smile dimmed as they approached Christopher and Colonel Fitzwilliam, who appeared to be engaged in serious conversation. When they saw the others approaching, however, their dialogue ended abruptly and they met the ladies halfway, thanking their escort for his assistance.

Lord Exeter gave the other men an inquisitive look. "I hope you found the meeting worthwhile."

"We did, I can assure you," said the colonel.

"Will we see you at the literary meeting?" asked Mary, but Lord Exeter shook his head.

"Sadly, I cannot attend. I have an engagement in the country and may not be in town for some weeks." He made a handsome bow to the ladies, then wished them all a good evening before returning to the salon.

"He shows remarkable discretion for a man reputed to be an inveterate gossip," said Christopher quietly to the colonel as they stepped outside. "Would you care to ride with us?"

"It is not far to my rooms at the Albany, and a walk will help clear my mind. I'll see you in the morning." The colonel bowed, then strode down the pavement.

In the carriage, Christopher forestalled Mary and Georgiana's questions by asking how they spent their time while he and the colonel were meeting with Mr. Westmacott.

"We met Miss Hutton," said Mary.

"The one who wrote the book about the miser?" At their unanimous nods, he asked, "How did you find her?"

"Just as one might expect," replied his wife.

Georgiana laughed. "Miss Hutton is not hesitant to offer opinions."

"She does have a sharp tongue, but has apparently enjoyed long friendships with learned men—one whose name she was shocked we did not know." She frowned in thought. "Priestley, was it not?"

It was too dark inside the carriage to see Georgiana's nod. "I recall she described him as a scientist of great renown."

"Priestley?" inquired Christopher, suddenly alert.

"You recognize the name?" asked Mary.

"I recall a scientific man whose radical views were so strongly opposed that his house was burned down as a result, and he was forced to flee the country many years ago. He was a great supporter of the French Revolution." Christopher paused. "Just how old do you think this lady might be?"

"It would be a guess only," answered Mary, "but quite old. Forty, perhaps."

At this he laughed openly. "Perhaps the Priestley I referred to had a son."

Neither of his companions could say yay or nay, and they moved on to other subjects, including the musical performance, the freedom with which Mrs. Penrose introduced Mary as an authoress, and the invitation to the literary evening.

Mary shuddered. "I am to read something from one of my novels. Miss Hutton suggested I choose a selection with pugilism."

"Then it must be *The Turret Room*,"[34] said Georgiana. "I benefited much from your tutelage, if you recall."

"I was witness to something of those benefits on one particularly memorable occasion," said Mary's husband.[35]

Back at Aunt Hermione's house, Mary waited until they were alone in their bedchamber to broach a more pressing topic. "Did you learn anything about the disappearance of the courier from your blackguard?"

Christopher punched his pillow and laid back with a sigh. "I would not care to meet the man again—Richard said he felt in need of a wash after being in his company. But ultimately, yes. He told us about a house where we might meet with French exiles, some of whom may secretly support their former emperor. Then he very subtly suggested it would make an ideal meeting place for spies."

---

34 Georgiana refers to Mary's first novel, based on events in *Mary, Mary, Not So Ordinary*.

35 Regarding events in *Mary, Mary, Oh So Contrary*.

"In some novels, this Mr. W would not offer information without a price," said Mary, turning her head on the pillow to face him.

"Not only in novels." Christopher smiled softly and reached for her hand. "He was willing to help us now without a fee, no doubt as it may lead to some benefit in future, but I hope neither of us will have dealings with the man again."

At this, Mary frowned. "You think there might be some danger in having done so?"

"Until this mystery is solved, I would not care to have you and Georgiana leave the house without escort, certainly."

"We always take John and William with us. Molly and Lucy too, of course." She moved closer. "I suppose I must be patient until tomorrow if I wish to hear more?"

"Yes, my dearest Mary."

CHAPTER SEVEN
London

~ I ~

Georgiana squeezed lemon into her breakfast tea. "As there are no houses to see today and you are caught up with my aunt's suggestions for your book, we can please ourselves. Where shall we go?"

"It is a shame Montague House is not open to the public in September." Mary spooned quince marmalade onto her plate. "There is so much to see and ponder."[36]

Taking a sip of her tea, Georgiana said idly, "Mr. Hartleton mentioned the importance of the Rosetta Stone, to which we paid little attention on our first visit, if I recall correctly." She looked up. "We could walk to Hatchards later–you did promise Molly and Lucy an atlas."

Mary nodded. "I would like to know the location of Tunisia. While we're walking, they can tell us more about the beautiful Elvira and her handsome general."

"He is a colonel." Georgiana grinned.

---

[36] Montague House, Great Russell-street, Bloomsbury, was the first home of the British Museum.

"Ah, yes. A *handsome* colonel. The tale is predictable and romantic, yet I want to know the fate of the unfortunate young lady."

"The *beautiful* young lady." Georgiana took a bite of her crumpet.

A quarter of an hour later they were in the garden room, where Georgiana was paging through the second volume of Miss Hutton's novel. "Miss Mereval is not so virtuous as the reader is led to believe."

"A flawed heroine?" Mary patted the cushion of the settee for Bonnie to come next to her.

At that moment there was a knock at the door, followed by one of Aunt Hermione's footmen. He was there to inform them that a large item had just been delivered, and would Mrs. Ashton, as the intended recipient, care to see it?

"It is presently in the hall, madam, but I can have it moved elsewhere if you prefer."

"There is no need." She was on her feet in an instant. "We can see it now."

The young ladies and Bonnie followed him to the entrance hall, where the moving men were waiting. "We were instructed to unveil it in your presence if possible, madam," said the elder of the two before pulling aside the drapery with a flourish to reveal the desk from the library at the third house.

Mary gasped with surprise, and while her attention was diverted the footman escorted the deliverymen outside.

"Is this your doing?" asked Mary.

Georgiana was all smiles. "It was Christopher's plan. I only mentioned how much you liked it."

"And described it in such detail he couldn't possibly choose the wrong one." Mary's eyes were dancing.

Just then Molly appeared with a lead in hand and Bonnie, tail wagging, went directly to her side and sat. "Shall I take her now, madame?"

"Please." Mary turned to the footman, who had returned and was waiting for instructions. "Would you have this taken to my study?"

"Certainly, madam." The footman held out two small keys with intricate bows. "Major Ashton asked me to give you these."

Back in the garden room, Georgiana again took up the second volume of Miss Hutton's novel but did not open it. "I've been thinking about the boots boy Lucy and Molly met at the cobbler's." She drummed her fingers on the book cover. "He said he knew about a vacant house on Lower Grosvenor-street, and claimed he could recognize any servant engaged there. Was he referring to the house we viewed, which Lord Exeter also knew was available? And if so, wouldn't it be helpful if someone spoke further with the boots?"

Mary, who had turned to the final page in volume three of the same novel, looked up. "And who would you recommend?"

"Molly and Lucy could take a basket from the kitchen by way of saying thank you to him for his help. After all, it would be reasonable to assume we saw the house only because he mentioned it."

Mary thought for a few moments. "It could not be called an adventure...just two maids bringing a gift to say thank you. They might be offered tea, which could lead to a bit of friendly gossip about the inhabitants on the street." She closed the book with a snap. "They could say we would like to know more about the area before offering on the house, and would be perfectly safe because they would have the footmen with them."

"It is a good plan," said Georgiana with a twinkle.

They found Molly in Mary's study, instructing the footmen to place the desk at a back-facing window. "I did not expect you so soon, madam." She stood back to allow the two ladies to consider the latest location.

"You've chosen the ideal place." Mary excused the footmen and turned to Molly. "There is something we would like to ask of you." She outlined their scheme concerning the boots, adding at the end, "You could say how much we liked the house, and how interested we are to know more of its history."

"We would also like to know about the previous owners and

the parties they hosted, if possible," said Georgiana. "Would you care to do this for us?"

Molly's eyes had lit up at the onset of the request. "Lucy and I would enjoy it very much, just like we did when visiting below-stairs at those houses in York."[37]

"We thought it best for the two of you to go, since you were together when you met the boots." Georgiana went to the bellpull and rang for Lucy. "Would this afternoon suit?"

Molly nodded vehemently. "We could arrive just before the time servants usually take their tea."

"You must not seem overly curious," warned Mary.

"I understand, madam. We won't disappoint you."

"It should seem only natural for you to have questions, but if the other servants are reluctant to talk, perhaps you could mention the story about Elvira to win them over." Mary waited for Molly to understand her meaning. "Did you finish reading it?"

"We read all the way to the end in the magazine we have, but at the bottom of the last page it said 'to be continued' and we haven't been able to find the next edition." She shook her head. "It's two years old."

"How disappointing. Miss Darcy and I would also like to know what happens to the unfortunate couple." Mary frowned. "Mrs. Chadwick might know if any issues have been stored somewhere other than the attic."

Lucy stepped into the room then and was quickly informed about the proposed errand.

"Remember, this is no adventure," said Georgiana in a motherly way.

Within an hour the excited maids had donned their new walking dresses made from the fabric given them by Mrs. Chandler. They were helped into the carriage by one of the Pemberley footmen, the other wielding the basket of treats from the kitchen.

After speaking to their maids Mary and Georgiana had turned their attention to the desk, quite pleased with how quickly they

---

[37] Molly is referring to visits described in *Mayhem at the Minster*.

found the disguised escutcheon plate covering the lock. The top rolled back easily, revealing several small drawers, also with locks, separated by a fixed panel in the center.

As if the desk were a puzzle, they proceeded to remove each drawer and saw they were of varying lengths, which led to the discovery of hidden cavities. Behind one of these, stuffed so far back it was invisible to the eye, they found a folded packet.

Gingerly, Mary pulled it out and held it up to the window. The address was written in French and there was a vermillion seal. She handed it to Georgiana who pushed against the wax with a fingernail.

"It has been opened already." She unfolded the foolscap and looked up with evident disappointment. "The page is blank."

Frowning, Mary looked over her friend's shoulder. "Maybe there was once a token of some sort placed inside."

"It is large enough, but why keep it?" She refolded the paper and gave it to Mary, who, after a moment's thought, put it back where it had been found.

Together they replaced the drawers, after which Mary gave an experimental tap on the center panel. Nothing happened and she began to feel around the edges, but it remained in place.

Showing her tenacious side, Georgiana knelt to look underneath the desk. A few seconds later there was a clicking sound and the panel moved forward enough for them to open it. Inside were two removable shelves, and behind them was a book.

Georgiana read the title. "It is a French novel. I came across a wide selection of them in that library."

Mary was about to flip through the pages when the butler appeared. "Pardon me, madam. There is a visitor."

"What a pleasant surprise." Mary put the book down, glancing at Georgiana. "It must be Lord Exeter or Mr. Hartleton."

"No, madam. It is not a gentleman caller, but a—" Fletcher coughed delicately "—lady. She insists upon speaking only with Mrs. Ashton."

Mary's brows rose as she read the name on the visitor's card, which was handwritten as opposed to the customary printed cards used by members of society. "I am not familiar with the name," she said. "I will see her, but please have a footman standing nearby."

"Certainly madam. I have put her in the anteroom at the front entrance."

"Then let us see what she wants."

"I am going with you," said Georgiana firmly. "No matter what this guest prefers."

Upon entering the smallest and least comfortable receiving room, Mary took a moment to observe their visitor, who was standing at the window facing the street. Notably, there was no waiting carriage in sight. She cleared her throat. "Good day, Mrs.—"

"Miss Carlyle," corrected the visitor sharply as she turned to face them.

Mary, with Georgiana beside her, remained standing within sight of the discreetly placed footman. "You wish to see me, Miss Carlyle?"

"Are you Mrs. Ashton?" The other woman's appearance and manner of speaking did not indicate a lower station in life, yet there was something about her that made Mary lift her chin and move slightly in front of Georgiana.

"I am Mrs. Ashton. What is it you wish to say?"

"You have a piece of property that belongs to me." Miss Carlyle launched into a detailed description of the locket and chain they found.

Mary shook her head firmly. "I am not in possession of the item—"

"You claim you do not have it?" interrupted their disbelieving guest.

Mary let a few seconds pass before she responded with deliberate calm. "I believe inquiries are being made at various jewelers to discover the rightful owner of the necklace you have described." She paused. "May I ask where you misplaced it?"

For a few seconds it appeared Miss Carlyle would refuse to answer. "It was in the house you saw on Lower Grosvenor-street, as you well know."

Mary did not respond to the challenge. "If you will tell me where to have it sent, I am certain it can be returned to you without much delay."

"I am in the process of changing houses," said Miss Carlyle in clipped tones. "I will return here to retrieve it, as I would not care to have it go missing again."

"As I said, it is not here, nor do I expect it to be in the future, as it is in the hands of the authorities. However, you may leave the direction, so it can be sent to you." Mary had her hand on the bell but did not ring it. "I am curious. How did you know my name, and where to find me?"

Miss Carlyle tightened the band attached to the reticule on her wrist. "I was refused entrance to the house on Lower Grosvenor-street, where I last remembered wearing the locket, and was directed to a house agent."

"Mr. Nolan?" Mary sounded surprised and a little displeased.

"Not him. He wasn't in. His assistant found the information and I came here directly."

Mary dipped her head in the manner of Georgiana's Aunt Catherine. "As I said, please leave instructions on where to send it. I doubt we shall meet again. Good day to you."

Georgiana had observed the exchange silently, and only one who knew her well would have recognized the wonder in her eyes as she followed the former Miss Mary Bennet from the room.

The visitor was thus left alone, and Mary stopped for a brief exchange with the waiting footman before proceeding along the corridor to the garden room.

Once inside, with the door closed, Georgiana asked, "You have something planned?"

Mary was about to explain when a discreet knock sounded and another of Aunt Hermione's footmen appeared. "Thank you for coming so quickly, Jimmy. If you would please close the door, I have an unusual errand for you." She waited only until he had done so. "Thomas is at this moment doing what he can to delay the departure of our visitor, a Miss Carlyle. I would like you to follow her and make note of everywhere she goes, and where she resides if possible. It is an important errand that requires discretion." At his sharp nod, she removed several coins from a box placed near the door. "You'll want to change into street clothes and be out on the pavement as soon as may be."

"You can rely on me, ma'am." Jimmy pocketed the coins and hurried out.

Mary caught Georgiana's eye. "I asked Thomas to delay the

return of Miss Carlyle's gloves and parasol. Upon her departure he will do his best to keep her in sight until Jimmy is able to follow."

"Do you not think the locket is hers?"

"I am uncertain, and suspect you are as well. She described it perfectly and knew it was left at the Lower Grosvenor-street house, but it is not proof of ownership. In fact, everything about her makes me suspicious." Mary, who had begun to pace, stopped suddenly. "She was wearing brown shoes, like those I saw from the kitchen window!"

To fill the time before Molly and Lucy returned from their errand, Georgiana suggested playing through some duets.

"This morning's visitor has me questioning the wisdom of sending our maids to speak with the boots," admitted Mary. "The distraction would be most welcome."

"Fitzwilliam's footmen will watch over them," said Georgiana with full confidence before leading the way to the music room.

They were halfway through the seventh duet by the time their abigails returned.[38] The two had been directed to the music room and waited by the door, smiling as they listened, until the end of the movement.

Molly knocked lightly, and they were soon describing what had occurred to their relieved mistresses.

"At first the cook didn't want to talk to us because she was too busy making little tarts for a card party," said Molly.

Lucy, eyes wide, nodded. "She said none of the servants in that house had time for gossiping."

"But after she looked inside the basket we brought," continued Molly, "suddenly we were sitting at the table with a cup of tea, chatting with her and the kitchen maids!"

"And the boots?" inquired Mary.

"We did not see him, madam," said Molly. "He's not allowed to take his tea with them—just a quick sip between duties, so they

---

[38] Georgiana and Mary were playing the first movement of the Duet in E-flat Major, Opus 3 No. 2 for Pianoforte by Muzio Clementi, who, as well as being a virtuoso keyboardist, composer, pedagogue, conductor, and music publisher, was also a manufacturer of pianofortes.

said. But the others got to talking, and complained a lot about the mistress asking for hot water at all times of day, and the master and mistress coming in late for dinner so the cook had to keep things hot, and the two young ladies of the house acting like princesses instead of the daughters of a merchant."

"Merchant?" Mary was frowning. "Did they say what kind of dealings he had?"

Molly shook her head. "Not exactly, madam, but one of the maids gave the impression that the things he sells are hard to get."

"They called him a pro-something, Moll," Lucy reminded her.

Georgiana looked up sharply. "Was the word procurer?"

"That sounds right," said Molly. "One of the maids was about to say more, but the cook suddenly decided she wanted to hear about Elvira—we mentioned it earlier—so we told them the story, up until she was sold as a slave."

Mary nodded approvingly. "And did they invite you to return?"

"Just as soon as we can," said Molly. "So they can hear the ending."

Mary thought for a moment. "You'll want to ask Mrs. Chadwick about old issues; the rest of the story might still be here." She eyed the two maids. "How do you feel about going back there?"

"We said we couldn't promise when, madam," said Molly.

Georgiana, who had been listening closely, asked, "Did any of the servants talk about the house where the necklace was found?"

"No other house was mentioned, Miss Darcy," answered Lucy. "And we were not given the chance to ask about it, because right when Molly got to the slave market part, bells started ringing from above-stairs and they all had to rush back to work...the cook almost shoved us out the door!"

"Could your visit possibly bring trouble upon them?" asked Mary.

Molly glanced at Lucy before shaking her head decidedly. "I think they're used to finding ways to do certain things. If they were afraid of being caught, we wouldn't have been invited to tea. The thing I'm most worried about is what to tell them about the ending if we can't find the rest of the story."

Here, Mary smiled. "Might they have access to old issues of the same magazine?"

"I don't think any of them can read or write," replied Molly. "And, even if they could, the way they talk about their mistress they couldn't admit to it because she would not allow servants who can read and write in her house." She paused before adding, "You and Miss Darcy are different than most."

"Some servants are dismissed for even *trying* to read," added Lucy.

Molly was nodding. "We didn't say we read the story ourselves, only that we knew about it."

"And what is the reaction to your ability to read below-stairs in *this* house?" asked Mary with a slight look of alarm.

"Lucy and I read stories to the others at tea-time, and sometimes before bed. So far Cook likes the one about Snow White best."

"I am relieved to hear it," said Mary firmly.

~ II ~

Christopher returned home frustrated, for there was still no news about the courier despite the combined efforts of Bow-street and the colonel's regiment.

When Mary came to his dressing room to tell him about Miss Carlyle's visit, he admitted that anything out of the ordinary might be of use. And, much to her surprise, he thought her decision to send the footman to follow the woman was a wise one.

"Jimmy knows this city as well as anyone and has run errands of a sensitive nature for me in the past." Her husband was not at all censorious, as she might have expected, and was smiling as he asked, "Shall we go down? You can tell Richard all about it."

"I nearly forgot!" Mary rested her hand on his arm. "Thank you for the beautiful desk."

He leaned down to say softly, "You are most welcome, my lovely bride."

They soon found Georgiana and Colonel Fitzwilliam outside in the garden, the former with a novel and the latter with a newspaper. It was only moments after the colonel had been told about Miss Carlyle's visit that Jimmy appeared, cheeks flushed, cap in hand.

Thanking the major for the offer of a chair but saying he

preferred to stand, the footman launched into his part of the story. "First, the lady went to a house on Saint Martin's Lane—the upper section—where she stayed for about an hour."

"Did you see the number?" asked the colonel, taking out a small notebook and pencil.

"Yes, sir. It was twenty-three. After that, she walked to St. James's Park, where she met a gentleman who was watching those strange birds with the long beaks."

"The pelicans?" suggested the colonel.

"Yes, sir. The two stood talking for a bit, then walked together out of the park towards the square, where he hailed a hackney for her." Jimmy twisted the cap in his hands. "Up to then it was easy for me to keep an eye on her from a distance, but had I tried to follow her right then he might have seen me so I slipped inside a pub where I could look out the front window. Luckily, he waved down another hackney going the same direction as hers. Traffic was slow so I could follow them on foot, only stopping a few times to pretend to look at a shop window. It was by the reflection from one of them that I saw her get out of the hackney and hurry to the next corner. A group of ladies blocked my way, and I almost lost sight of her, but I was just in time to see her taking the steps down to the servants' entrance of a house."

"What kind of house?" inquired Christopher.

Jimmy thought for a second. "Respectable, like one with lodgers. I found a place to hide and waited for her to come out, but after two hours I thought it best to come back here."

"You have the gift of patience," said Colonel Fitzwilliam. "When this lady and gentleman first met, did they embrace, such as a courting couple might do?"

Jimmy shook his head firmly. "Nothing like that. But it was clear they knew each other."

"And did you hear what was said?"

"I'm sorry, sir, but I wasn't close enough."

Christopher, who had also remained standing, clapped the footman on the shoulder. "You did very well today."

"Thank you, sir." Jimmy reached into his pocket to retrieve the coins left from the day's expenses, but the major shook his head when he held it out.

"You've earned it. Now, go enjoy your dinner."

"Thank you." Jimmy dipped his head and left with a discernible skip in his step.

"Perhaps we should have asked him to keep what occurred to himself," said the colonel.

"You needn't worry, Richard. The servants in this house were chosen with great care."

The colonel raised his brows. "A young recruit?"

"He does have a knack." Christopher turned his attention on Mary. "How did you happen to choose him?"

"Thomas said he was the best choice."

Georgiana spoke up then. "I was not fully convinced that Miss Carlyle was who she purported to be...but a servant?"

"Perhaps she comes from a good family of straitened means, forced to take a position as lady's maid or hired companion," suggested Mary half seriously.

Just then the butler came to say dinner was served, at which point the colonel opened his pocket watch. "I'm pleased to see this household runs on a strict schedule. It seems like ages since I've had a decent meal."

Over the cucumber and lovage soup, each of the four at the table offered a theory regarding Miss Carlyle's singular way of going about retrieving the necklace.

"You do realize that few men would solicit the opinion of ladies in this matter." Georgiana smiled at her cousin. "I can only imagine what Aunt Catherine would say if she could hear us."

With the hint of a smile, the colonel shook his head. "If our aunt were with us now, none of us would have the chance to say a word. Nor the time to enjoy this meal."

He departed after the dessert, a trifle with peaches, and Christopher suggested a walk, taking hold of Bonnie's lead himself.

"She is heeling properly," he remarked with surprise as they entered Hyde Park.

"That is Molly's doing," said Mary. "Although I believe our puppy still behaves better for you than she does for me."

As they followed the path at a relaxed pace, Christopher asked Georgiana if anything interesting had happened in Miss Hutton's book.

Pleased at the inquiry, she began an animated summary of the plights of the heroine, who had expectations of a great fortune. "A distant relative is disputing the will and Miss Mereval may be disappointed. Worse yet—" her tone grew dramatic "—she and her mother had in the past knowingly incurred debts, which they planned to dispense by way of the inheritance. But once their creditors learned the will was contested, the bailiffs began knocking at their door and the mother—perhaps the more guilty of the two in overspending—managed to avoid them by taking a cottage in the country under an assumed name."

"Spending funds in anticipation of receiving them is an act of folly," said Christopher, hiding a yawn, and Mary suggested they turn back.

"But please continue," she said to Georgiana, who happily obliged.

"Miss Hutton has given the mother and the miser an equal measure of faults, and I look forward to reading more, but for now I can give you a hint at what is to come. The presumptive heir has a son, who has become acquainted with Miss Mereval. She has discovered who *he* is, and knows his father considers them mortal enemies, but the son is unaware of her identity." Georgiana paused deliberately. "So she decides to make him fall in love with her."

Christopher whistled, and Mary turned her face to him. "I suppose you have never fallen victim to a scheme such as this?"

"Not to my knowledge."

~ III ~

The next morning, Colonel Fitzwilliam had just told Christopher which inhabitants of the houses in proximity to Lower Grosvenor-street had been eliminated from the investigation, when in came a runner, dressed in the signature uniform with prominent brass buttons.

"I am sorry to intrude, sirs, but your presence is wanted at Bow-street, to view a body." He pulled off his tall hat. "It is the case of an unusual death."

"What is unusual about it?" asked the colonel, taking his jacket from a peg on the wall.

"It won't be long before you can see for yourselves—I've a

hackney waiting outside." The runner replaced his hat. "I was told not to say too much."

Once at the Bow-street station, they were led down to the basement and along a narrow corridor. On either side were thick wood doors with bars covering a small aperture.

The runner knocked on the fourth door, which was opened by a man who introduced himself as Dr. Sutton. "I'm surgeon and undertaker here, though in the case of the former my abilities are not often required." He moved aside to allow the two men room to enter, motioning to the linen-covered form laid out on a table. "I've been told to report anything unusual, and at first glance this wouldn't have applied. Given the state of the dress and what looks like near starvation, I would have assumed this was an elderly pauper. That said, there are bruises and lacerations that are rather unusual on someone who jumped off a bridge into the Thames."

"The victim is a woman?" asked the colonel a trifle impatiently.

"If you don't mind looking, I'd like you to see for yourselves what we have here. It isn't pretty, mind," warned Sutton and pulled back the cover, displaying the torso of a male, small in stature, who could have been a boy but for the stubble on his cheeks and some other identifiers. The doctor was watching the other two men carefully. "I was quite surprised when I began my examination. Have you seen enough?"

"Please," said the colonel, whose face was flushed.

Dr. Sutton covered the body before moving to the door. "I can tell you what I've learned but would prefer a room with comparatively fresh air. As you can see, the body is in a terrible state and will need to be interred as soon as possible."

As they followed him down the corridor, Christopher whispered, "Is it Matthew Baker?"

"Yes," responded the colonel grimly.

Once inside a room on the upper floor, windows opened wide, Dr. Sutton shared his findings. "Given the level of bloating, he's been in the water a couple days at most. In addition to the injuries one expects with this type of suicide, there is a head wound that could have been caused by a piling, or something similar, when jumping from the bridge. However, with little or no water ingested, my professional opinion is that the head wound was inflicted prior to his entering the river, which probably would have killed him first." He took out a handkerchief and wiped his forehead. "The body was in a weakened state prior to death. Undernourished, certainly." He wiped his hands with the handkerchief and looked candidly at the two sitting across from him. "Is that enough?"

"It is. Thank you, Dr. Sutton." Colonel Fitzwilliam was first to the door. "If you would please send a messenger with a report of your findings and information in regard to the burial."

"Of course." The doctor did not follow them out.

Immediately after stepping outside the station, the colonel began to walk very fast and Christopher had to lengthen his stride to reach him.

"Where are we going?"

"To the house where Westmacott claims we will find our answers." The colonel did not slow his pace.

"Richard, if you don't mind, the heat is so oppressive I'm having difficulty breathing." Christopher stopped, put his hands on his knees, and bent over.

The colonel sighed and retraced his steps. "I can see your face. You are not out of breath."

Christopher straightened up. "Maybe so, but I am intolerably warm. Can we not take a moment to hail a hackney?"

"It might be wise. By the look of those clouds, we're in for a downpour."

~ IV ~

An hour or so before the Bow-street runner had fetched Colonel Fitzwilliam and Major Ashton, Lucy woke with a headache she could not ignore. By late morning, Georgiana insisted she return to her bed.

"It is only the change in weather, Miss Darcy," said Lucy in a near-whisper.

"It makes no difference how it came about. If your condition does not improve by afternoon, I will summon the physician."

The threat was effective, for Lucy did as she was told.

Molly, however, suffered no ailment and was determined to

visit the boots' house. "I'll be fine if William and John are with me, madam."

"Very well," said Mary, encouraged by her husband's faith in her judgement. "But have the carriage stop beyond the house and stay out of sight. Remember, we only want to know a little more about the house and its prior owners before we consider the purchase."

"Very good, madam." Molly was almost able to hide her pleasure.

Annie, one of the kitchen maids, opened the door to Molly. She immediately placed a finger against her lips, using her head to indicate a bench placed against the wall. "Wait here," she whispered, and hurried away.

Not a minute had passed before Molly overheard a woman's stern voice, her icy tone slicing through the walls. "Your master and I are extremely displeased! Should this occur again, there will be consequences!"

Sitting on the little bench, Molly tried to shrink into the shadows when a door slammed shut and the sound of sharply clicking heels came her way. She was about to slip out by the servants' entrance when the footsteps began to fade.

She exhaled, then sat straighter at the sound of a man's voice. "Your mistress has spoken. Return to your duties and be mindful, or you will find yourselves out on the street before dark!"

Moments later Annie returned, with angry red splotches on her cheeks. Again, she held a finger to her lips, leading Molly to the door and stepping outside with her. "This is a bad time." Her eyes went to the basket from Hertford-street, which Molly quickly offered to her.

Annie accepted it gratefully. "I must take madam's nasty pug on a walk before the rain starts...meet me at the green?" She motioned to the left. "I won't be long."

Molly nodded and hurried up the stone steps, continuing at a good pace along the pavement. The 'green' was a small park, as yet unfenced, meant for the street's inhabitants. William and John were waiting alongside the carriage a bit farther down, but she motioned sharply with her hands when they began to walk towards her. With no sign of recognition, they turned and casually retraced their steps. She then sat on a bench beneath a large shade tree and soon Annie appeared, an over-indulged pug pulling at the lead.

"I'm so sorry we couldn't hear the end of your story today. The master is in one of his terrible moods." Annie shot a look of malice behind her as they walked onto the green. "Just as soon as I can find another position, I'm leaving. My sister's a lady's maid, like you, in a house with *real* quality. She thinks there might be a place for me there one day."

Molly looked down at the unpleasant pug sniffing her shoes. "My mum always says to go somewhere else if you're not happy where you are."

"I think so too. Those above-stairs—" again she looked behind her "—are no better than common smugglers, except they pay others to get their hands dirty."

"Smugglers?"

Annie snorted. "*Procuring* and *conveyancing* he calls it, but those are smuggled goods being carried in and out of that house." She lowered her voice. "We're not supposed to know about it, but there are French words on the bottles and on the crates, and they're always delivered after dark. I know what's going on, because my uncle was a smuggler and plenty good at it too—until he got caught."

Molly was genuinely shocked. "What happened to him?"

Annie pulled at the lead, but the pug resisted until she took a treat from her apron pocket. "He was trapped by the water guard in one of the caves where they hid the crates. You'd be amazed at how far back some of them go, and how big they are. I went along with my brother once when he was exploring, but when he saw the crates inside he got us out fast."

"My mistress went to see the empty house down the street, with an eye towards buying it, and Lucy and I discovered a secret passage." Molly paused, then asked quietly, "Do you think smugglers lived there too?"

Annie shrugged. "The master and mistress were very friendly with the gentleman who used to live there, always going to big parties and never coming back until after dawn. We couldn't do our work at the usual time for fear of waking them." She rolled her eyes. "Her temper is worse than his."

"Did you ever see the gentleman who owned the other house?"

"Not so I would know him in the street, and he's been gone for well-nigh a year now I'd say. He was a lord, and handsome as they come, so it was said, but not one you should stand too close to." Annie lifted her brows suggestively.

"This lord had a reputation, then."

"And well-deserved, no doubt. The guests all came in fine carriages and in fine clothes but weren't such gentlefolk when the doors closed behind them. I used to meet one of the maids in that house on my half-day. She left her position here after being offered a better one there, and had a lot to say about the goings-on. Then one day she up and left without a word. She was well-liked when she worked in our house, but we never heard from her." Annie glanced at the watch pinned to her dress and made a face. "I have to get back. Thanks again for the basket. We don't often get such treats."

Molly frowned. "If you like, I can walk back with you a bit and tell how the story ends, so you can share it with the others."

"Would you?" Annie stopped for a second and the pug snorted.

"Now, where did I leave off?" Molly hurried to match the other maid's steps. "Oh yes...Elvira's husband, the colonel, was luckier than she was. His master was kind and helped rescue Elvira from the palace. After the escape, the colonel and Elvira stayed with him—he was getting on in years, you see, and the colonel reminded him of the son he lost in one of the wars. They lived happily for years, and when the master died he left them his house, where they continued happy and safe for the rest of their lives." She paused for a moment before adding, "And they were always very kind to their servants."

At that moment there was a flash of lightning and Annie glared at the sky. "Thanks, Molly. I'll tell them." She picked up the pug and rushed to the steps leading down to the servants' entrance.

Molly turned and was hurrying to meet the footmen when she saw them motioning to something behind her. She turned round and saw two men in regimental uniform approaching, and in the next instant recognized Major Ashton and Colonel Fitzwilliam. By their stride and posture, it was clear the reason for being there was not a social one.

She watched as they started up the steps to the front door of the house Annie had just entered, then made a frantic motion to the footmen, who came to meet her.

"Major Ashton and Colonel Fitzwilliam are about to enter that house—" she pointed. "Annie, the maid I was talking to, says her master is a smuggler. They may not know this, and it could be important." Rain began to fall in large drops.

"Take the carriage home, Molly—we'll find our way back," said William.

Moments later she saw the footmen speaking with the two men, and she ran to the carriage.

~ V ~

Seated at a table in the garden room, where the French doors had been closed against the rain, Mary was pressing a stamp into hot wax to seal a letter. She held it up with a look of triumph. "I have written to your aunt to say I am satisfied with the manuscript and am sending it to Mr. Egerton."

"How brave of you." Georgiana's lips twitched as she looked up from the book she was reading.

"I daresay she will not like it, but when I was about to change the ending per her orders, I realized it would be against my own wishes. So, given that she and Anne are once more on good terms, any further revisions shall come from the publisher." She sounded resolute.

"He is certain to approve it," insisted Georgiana. "You do realize you are your worst critic?"

"We cannot forget Miss Paige." Mary referred to one of Mr. Egerton's assistants, who had in the past plagued the young authoress with long lists of revisions. "And, I may have good reason to add another critic soon: Miss Hutton."

Georgiana was about to reply but further discourse was interrupted by Molly, who knocked at the door before entering the room, loosening the ribbons of her bonnet as she did so. "Pardon me, madam, but Mr. Fletcher said you wanted to see me straightaway."

"You seem quite out of breath." Mary motioned to a nearby chair. "Please sit and tell us what has happened."

Molly did so, perching on the edge as she described her strange reception at the boots' house. "When Annie and I met in the park, she told me her master is a smuggler of French goods."

"Has Annie seen those goods?" asked Georgiana.

Molly nodded. "Yes, Miss Darcy. She said there are crates and bottles with French writing. But more important is that I saw Major Ashton and Colonel Fitzwilliam heading to the boots' house, so I told John and William about the smuggling, and how Annie said her master has a terrible temper, and I asked them to hurry over and tell the major and the colonel about it." She looked up with a worried frown.

"You did well," said Georgiana calmly.

Mary had taken to pacing. "I wonder if they finally discovered a connection to the courier's disappearance." She stopped in front of her maid. "Did Annie say anything about the house we saw, the one with the secret passage?"

"She said she was friendly with one of the maids there, who didn't care for the goings-on."

"Did she say anything about the previous owner?"

Molly nodded. "She said he was a handsome lord who held parties where the guests didn't always behave nicely." She hesitated.

"Is there more?" prompted Georgiana.

"There was a maid who used to work in the smuggler's house, but was offered a better position in the house with the secret passage. According to Annie, she was there for a good while but left without a word one day and hasn't been heard from or seen since."

Mary finally sat down. "You probably learned more by talking to Annie alone than had you taken tea with the others." She smiled kindly. "Why don't you see if Lucy is feeling better—she has been asleep since you left. I'll have a tray sent up for you to share."

"Thank you, madam."

"And when the major returns, he may want to hear what you've told us."

Georgiana waited until they were alone again before saying, "I wonder about the maid who left without telling the others—could it be Miss Carlyle? Maybe the handsome lord did something to make her change her mind about him. Famous people are always misquoted, so I may as well risk doing the same: *I took to him very well at first, but he won't do upon a nearer examination*."[39] At that moment, anyone hearing her would assume she was far older than her (nearly) nineteen years.

The butler's knock prevented Mary from trying to think of an appropriate response. "Excuse me, madam, Miss Darcy...the, er, lady who visited recently has returned."

"Miss Carlyle?" asked Mary with a look of disbelief.

"Yes, madam." Fletcher's tone was disapproving. "Once more, she insists upon speaking with the mistress of the house."

"There is nothing for her here." Just then there was an enormous crack of thunder, causing all three to start.

"Yes, madam," said Fletcher, quickly recovering his equanimity. "Shall I see her out?"

Georgiana lifted her hand to stay Mary's next words. "Perhaps, given what Molly learned, it might be wise to speak with her."

Mary looked about to argue, then sighed. "Very well. Where is she this time?"

"In the same anteroom, madam."

"We might prefer to meet with her in comfort," suggested Georgiana gently.

During all their experiences together, Mary had never questioned her friend's reasoning powers. "We will see her in the front room with the painted walls, but delay a bit, if you please."

Once Fletcher had gone, she said, "Venturing out in a thunderstorm suggests urgency on our visitor's part." As she spoke a great flash of lightning made her wince.

"Just so." A smile played about Georgiana's lips. "If you and I are more welcoming, we may learn something of use." At Mary's doubtful look she added, "We can but try."

Mary huffed, Georgiana grinned, and they left the room together. They had just chosen to stand rather than sit when Fletcher knocked at the door of the painted room to announce gravely, "Miss Carlyle, madam."

---

[39] Dr. Samuel Johnson's original statement apparently reflected upon the character of a young woman he called Poll. Since those words were spoken, it is difficult to prove whether what was later quoted in written form by his contemporaries, such as Frances (Fanny) Burney and Hester Lynch Piozzi, was accurate.

Standing at the empty hearth, farthest from the door, Mary greeted their unwelcome visitor. "Miss Carlyle. Please do sit down and be comfortable."

"No, thank you." She remained near the door. "This is not a social call. I have little time and came only to ask if you know who has possession of my locket."

"I am sorry you troubled yourself by coming here, for I have no new knowledge of its current holder or whereabouts." Despite the truth of her statement, Mary managed a look of contrition. "Would it not be simpler if the locket was brought to your home?"

"It would not. I must have the necklace before I leave town and will continue to come here until I recover it. Good day."

When Miss Carlyle stomped out of the room Fletcher silently but firmly escorted her to the door.

Mary clenched her fists. "We will *not* be 'at home' to her in future. The woman is intolerably rude."

"Her manner and actions are certainly confusing." Georgiana thought for a moment. "Perhaps she stole the necklace from her mistress and discovery is imminent."

The two were surprised by Fletcher, who had come to inquire if they were 'at home' to Mr. Hartleton.

Mary's features softened. "We would be happy to see him."

When that gentleman entered the room he apologized for coming unannounced and refused to sit. "My clothes are a bit damp, I'm afraid. I meant only to leave a note to say I must go to Derbyshire on Monday." He glanced at the door. "Interestingly, I came across a lady departing just as I arrived. Having recognized her, I lifted my hat and greeted her by name, but she claimed I was mistaken." He frowned, shaking his head. "The resemblance is remarkable."

"Our visitor was a Miss Carlyle," said Georgiana. "She claims ownership of the locket found at the house on Lower Grosvenor-street, and came here to retrieve it."

"I saw the necklace only briefly, but it was a work of exquisite artistry." Mr. Hartleton was clearly perplexed. "Miss Carlyle, you say? It is not the same name, but I would have bet money I knew her, and the strangest thing, when she first saw me I think she deliberately turned the other way."

"Who did you think she was?" asked Mary.

"A Miss LeBlanc, whom I have spoken to on several occasions. She is something of a companion to Mrs. Farringdale, a widowed lady who hosts card parties and so forth, and whose invitations I often regret accepting as late nights have a deleterious effect on my research."

"LeBlanc sounds French." Mary was tapping her lip. "Mr. Hartleton, would you join us for dinner?" When he looked about to refuse, she added, "Christopher and Richard are investigating a mystery, and the lady we know as Miss Carlyle may be involved. I believe they would be very interested to hear what you know of this Miss LeBlanc." She paused. "But I should say no more."

"If there is any way I can help, I will gladly accept your kind invitation."

"Excellent. If you will excuse me a moment, I must speak with our housekeeper." Mary left without further ado, allowing for no objection, although she did leave the door open.

Georgiana immediately took upon herself the role of hostess. "Mr. Hartleton, are you chilled from the rain?"

"Not at all, but I appreciate your concern." He touched the sleeve of his jacket. "It is not a cold rain, given the heat of the day."

She nodded. "It will be pleasant to have cooler weather."

"Yes, it has been unusually warm, even for London." He paused, as if searching for something more to say. "Miss Darcy, the last time we met you spoke of a book you were reading—about a miser, I believe. Were you able to finish it?"

"I was, though it was not the easiest to read at first." She smiled. "Mrs. Ashton and I are to attend a literary meeting soon, to which Miss Hutton, the author, is also invited. Our hostess has asked her and Mary to read a selection from their work."

"I have yet to read any of Mrs. Ashton's novels, but I was able to find all three at the Temple of the Muses."

"I have never been to the Temple, though I have heard much about its unusual architecture and the almost incomprehensible number of volumes on the shelves, which allegedly reach to the sky." Georgiana plucked an imaginary piece of lint from her sleeve. "We have been going to Hatchards, as it is a short walk from here."

"This house is perfectly located, in my opinion." Mr. Hartleton looked about the room with approval. "There is a sense of peace here, and it seems quite comfortable."

"I think Mary would prefer one like this to the others we have seen."

"As would I." Mr. Hartleton cleared his throat. "In a recent letter Charles Bingley mentioned there is to be a ball at your home in Derbyshire soon. Included in his letter was a kind invitation from your sister-in-law, Mrs. Darcy, who apologized for not yet having set the date."

Georgiana's face lit up. "The ball is to celebrate the wedding of my cousin, formerly Miss Anne de Bourgh, to Mr. James Chandler—a poet who enjoys conversation about books. Elizabeth wants it to be both a wedding and a harvest ball, which will include the servants and my brother's tenants. Among the other guests will be Jane and Charles, Mr. and Mrs. Bennet, the Burnabys, whose property abuts Pemberley, and perhaps Caroline Bingley and the Hursts—unless his gout prevents their coming." She eyed her guest to confirm his familiarity with Charles Bingley's relations. "And my aunt, Lady Catherine de Bourgh of Rosings Park, the bride's mother."

Georgiana smiled at Mary, who had returned from a short conference with Mrs. Chadwick about dinner. "I've been telling Mr. Hartleton who will attend Elizabeth's ball."

"I understand from Charles Bingley that your father is something of a scholar," said Mr. Hartleton, his eyes on Mary.

"He is certainly a great reader and a formidable opponent at chess and backgammon as well, who will suggest a game at the slightest sign of interest, so be warned. Also, he does not care to discuss the plots of novels, though he is pleased enough to listen when one is read aloud. As a family, we read to one another in the evenings quite frequently, and he often quizzed us about the viability of the plot and such when we were finished."

"A custom of my own father's," said Mr. Hartleton. "Perhaps history is more to his taste? A gentleman from Surrey recently asked me to look over the writings of an ancestor, Mr. John Evelyn, a prolific diarist, whose entries and letters encompass the time of Charles the First, the Interregnum as it is called, and well beyond the reign of Charles the Second. The family is considering publication and would like my opinion." He glanced at the two ladies to make certain they were interested before continuing. "I have only read a small percentage, but there is no doubt of the historical value. Amongst Evelyn's papers I have found copies of letters he wrote to Mr. Samuel Pepys, who, I believe, was of the same era, and about whom I am quite interested to learn more. Personal letters and diary entries offer the most accurate record of events, far more unbiased than a history written decades later, when few are alive to say whether it is a fair representation or no." He broke off. "Forgive me. I tend to go on."

"Not at all," replied Mary. "Christopher said much the same thing to me only the other day when I asked his opinion regarding a history I considered purchasing for my father. You say the diary of this gentleman is not yet published, but are there others available you would recommend?"

"I will set my mind to it and prepare a list." He made a handsome bow. "But I must go now, for I have already taken too much of your time."

Three hours later Mr. Hartleton returned, but things did not go as Mary planned. Upon hearing what their guest had to say about the alleged owner of the necklace, Christopher asked if he would mind forgoing dinner. "It seems the woman you know as Miss LeBlanc may be important to our investigation, and you might be able to help us."

Mr. Hartleton readily agreed and they were soon away, taking Jimmy, the footman, with them.

~ VI ~

Despite her conviction that she would not sleep at all, Mary was in the middle of a dream in which Georgiana was presiding at Miss Bingley's wedding when Molly drew the window curtains aside, bringing light and fresh cool air into the room.

Mary sat up, rubbing her eyes. "Has the major returned?"

"No, madam. Shall I bring a tray?"

Mary threw back the covers and reached for her dressing gown. "Not this morning, thank you. I will have my coffee in the breakfast room in the event he comes back."

"Then I'll have you ready in no time." Molly was as good as her word, choosing a particularly becoming morning dress and arranging Mary's hair in a single plait.

Georgiana had also chosen to come down before breakfast and the two had just been served coffee and tea when Christopher appeared.

Mary did not hide her relief. "Dare I ask if your work is completed?"

"You may dare," he answered with some satisfaction. "Is the coffee hot?"

"Very."

"In which case, may I join you as I am?" He motioned at his evening clothes, which were not in a state his valet would approve.

"Please do, for we are impatient to hear what happened," answered his wife.

He sat down with a sigh. "First, I must tell you that the courier was found." At their hopeful looks, he shook his head. "I wish it were not the case, but once his body was discovered our task quickly turned to finding those responsible for his death—thank you," he said, taking the coffee Mary had poured for him. "And it is due in great part to Mr. Hartleton's assistance that we were successful last night." He took an experimental sip before continuing. "The name LeBlanc was given to us by that fellow Westmacott at Mrs. Penrose's house, who would only say, 'Find her and the rest will fall into place.' The only other information he offered was the number for the house Molly visited yesterday, and where Richard and I went to speak with the alleged smuggler who is master there. We had already made plans to return with more men to search the place." He gave Mary a long look. "As we were approaching it last night, who do you think came out but the woman Hartleton recognized in an instant as Miss LeBlanc, whilst Jimmy recognized her as the Miss Carlyle you had him follow. She was in the company of a well-dressed man we later discovered was a French officer—in fact an escaped prisoner of war. The house was being used to keep such escapees hidden, who would remain there until papers and travel across the channel could be arranged, most often aboard smugglers' boats."

"Molly was told by one of the maids there that the master of the house was a smuggler of French goods," said Mary. "It seems this included more than brandy."

"We did find many interesting items in the wine cellar but let me go back a bit. The so-called mistress of the house, Mrs.

Farringdale, hosted frequent, large parties, allowing these Frenchmen to slip in and out unnoticed. It was the duty of Miss Carlyle—who is in fact Miss LeBlanc—to partner them in turn, helping to maintain the illusion of an Englishman enjoying an evening out." He reached into his pocket and retrieved a jeweler's box, which he opened and placed upon the table.

"Is it truly Miss Carlyle's?" asked Georgiana.

"It is." Christopher removed the necklace and pressed the side of the locket, revealing a head-and-shoulder portrait of a man and woman wearing pre-revolution pouf wigs, as made popular by Marie Antoinette. "This was allegedly the only item of value her mother managed to keep when narrowly escaping the guillotine. Miss LeBlanc came to England as a young girl and as soon as she came of age married a French émigré against her mother's wishes. Her mother died soon afterwards, and her husband was killed during the battle of Grand Port.[40] Penniless, Miss LeBlanc was soon recruited by Mrs. Farringdale."

Georgiana was frowning. "But how did the necklace come to be in the other house?"

"If you can wait for the answer, Richard should be here soon. He can tell the rest of the tale better than I." He set his cup down. "In the meantime, I should dearly like to change out of these clothes before breakfast."

"I will make certain cook knows to prepare something substantial," said Mary with a smile.

After Christopher left the room, Georgiana asked, "Do you recall that conversation we overheard—in French—between two people in the maze at Devonham?"

"It has been a long time since then, but yes, I do."

"At the time, we were convinced Harry was one of them."

Aunt Hermione's cook was not one to balk at a challenge, and a full breakfast was prepared and laid out upon the sideboard in covered dishes by the time the colonel arrived.

It was not until he was nearly finished with the meal that he began at the point where Christopher had left off.

---

[40] Major Ashton refers to a naval battle between French and British frigates, August 1810.

"We met at the house supposedly owned by Mrs. Farringdale. Our hackney, driven by a man from my regiment, stopped a few houses away and we had just stepped down when we spied Miss LeBlanc—identified by Hartleton—coming out the front door in company with a man, each of them formally dressed. As it happened, it was our hackney she hailed, apparently unaware of us, and we gave our driver instructions to take them directly to Bow-street for questioning." He looked quite pleased with himself as he dropped a chunk of sugar into his tea, then motioned for Christopher to continue.

"As soon as the carriage was away, we went inside the house. It didn't take long to sort things out, and we soon had four French prisoners, the good lady of the house, and her husband in hand." He pointed towards the colonel's right eye. "Though it was not without a scuffle or two."

Mary, who had avoided looking at the swollen part of his face, asked, "Is there anything to prevent further, er...traces?"

"Arnica," suggested Georgiana, to their surprise. "Mrs. Annesley was quick to apply it if I suffered an abrasion, which I often did as a child, especially when playing with my cousin." Her eyes went to the colonel. "Do you know why Miss Carlyle was so intent upon retrieving the necklace?"

"Ah—" the colonel spooned plum jam onto his plate "—that took a while to draw out of her. She can be quite unpleasant, but eventually admitted to using it to identify herself as a friend to the French officers. She would hold it just so, revealing the portraits inside."

Mary leaned back with a pleased sigh. "Then we need not suffer another of her visits."

"For that, we have Mr. Hartleton to thank," said Georgiana stoutly.

"Indeed you do, and I am very pleased to say our part in this investigation is nearly over." The colonel set his napkin aside. "Thank you for this, but it's time we were back."

Mary could not hide her dismay. "So soon?"

"It is but a matter of handing over the reins to people better suited to the work to come," said Christopher. "I can say, without fear of breaking my promise, that I will be free to escort the two of you to the theatre tomorrow, should you care to go, and that we should turn our thoughts to returning to Pemberley."

With a look of happy anticipation, Georgiana turned to her cousin. "Will you join us tomorrow?"

"Thank you, no. I have an engagement."

"Hartleton has postponed his departure due to our late night," said Christopher. "He might enjoy the play."

Mary looked to Georgiana for approval, who only smiled softly in response.

An hour or so later Mary waited until the strains of music faded away before entering the room. "What a pretty tune."

Georgiana twisted round on the bench seat. "It is called *Les Roseaux,* or in English, *The Reeds*."

"Is it new?"

"I found it in Aunt Hermione's collection. It was written by Couperin, a French composer, more than a hundred years ago so my playing it should in no way offend British sensibilities, though some may object to one performing it on other than harpsichord."

"I'd like to hear the difference." Mary waved the letter in her hand. "This is the latest from Lydia. She wants me to send several inscribed copies of my books to the West Indies so she can give them to her friends." Mary waved another sheet. "Here is the list of names. She also wants me to increase the amount I send to her, but I cannot read the rest, given all the crossing and re-crossing. I hoped you might have better luck."

Georgiana took the letter to the window, frowning as she rotated the page. "Lydia would not have needed to re-cross had she refrained from describing the costumes ladies of the West Indies are currently wearing." She retraced her steps, a finger marking her place as she held the letter so Mary could see. "What I gather from this is she plans to gain passage on a ship to England—and do you see that word? Could it be 'ball'?"

Mary took the letter and studied the passage. "It seems Lydia intends to go to Pemberley." She turned anguished eyes on her friend, who once believed she had feelings for the infamous George Wickham, now Lydia's husband. "The date is smudged, so who can tell when she will arrive? We must warn Elizabeth."

After the brief, carefully worded note was written and added to the post, Georgiana suggested they plan the rest of their time in London.

"I would like to read the history of music written by Charles Burney, Fanny Burney's—rather Mrs. d'Arblay's—father, as mentioned by Mrs. Penrose. Which means a visit to Hatchards, or perhaps The Muses. There is also our list of items to purchase on behalf of others, the upcoming literary meeting, and I'd like to hear the performance by a string quartet in the Argyll Rooms, which is said to have superior acoustics. They are to perform works by Herr Haydn, as well as a piece by Herr Beethoven commissioned by a Russian prince. After the music there will be a lecture given by a member of the Philharmonic Society."[41]

"It all sounds wonderful. Christopher recently said he has missed going to hear music, especially the opera, since being in town."

"If only we could hear certain works played over and over, whenever we chose." Georgiana sighed dreamily.

"You said something similar after Mrs. Penrose's soirée and need only a group of musicians at your disposal, such as Herr Haydn's orchestra, who were reportedly required to perform at the whim of their patron, Prince Esterhazy."

Georgiana laughed. "Or we could be less extravagant with a single musician—one who plays piano and harpsichord."

"We may not have an orchestra or a virtuoso harpsichordist at our disposal," said Mary, "but I enjoy hearing Molly sing, especially when she is unaware of being overheard. I also like to hear Christopher play, though he does not like anyone to listen when he is working on a piece." She eyed her friend. "You play so well. If it were an acceptable occupation for a lady, you could earn your living."

Georgiana's cheeks grew rosy. "Can you imagine what Aunt Catherine would say?"

---

[41] The Philharmonic Society of London was only recently formed at the time (in early 1813).

~ VII ~

Early the next evening, the Ashton party left Hertford-street for the theatre in high spirits. Their carriage joined the other equipages vying for space on the London streets, and all was well as they approached their destination until suddenly there was a warning shout followed by the cracking of wood and high-pitched neighs.

The Ashton coachman pulled hard on the reins of the two horses and those inside the carriage were suddenly unseated. Seconds later the slightly disheveled but unhurt passengers rearranged themselves, and in the next moment Christopher was talking to his coachman through the window.

Assured that it was safe to do so, he stepped out onto the street to assess the situation and returned shortly to report to Mary and Georgiana. "There has been an accident. Not serious, but it will take some time to untangle. We're not far from the theatre and the pavements have been swept. Are you able to walk?" He looked doubtfully at their delicate slippers.

Mary and Georgiana, their eyes wider than normal, nodded silently, straightened their elegant bonnets, and with his help were out on the pavement in little time.

Walking away from the scene, they turned down Drury Lane where they soon came across Mr. Hartleton and proceeded together.

The pavements being narrow, he and Georgiana were ahead of the Ashtons. After assuring him that they suffered no ill effects from the street accident, she asked about his experience at the smuggler's house. "It must have been frightening."

"Given my companions, there was little to fear but I will admit to an unusually fast heartbeat."

They had reached the theatre by then and once seated in the box the two continued talking amiably until the bells rang to announce the start of Mrs. Inchbald's play, *The Child of Nature.*

Afterwards, they crossed over to the next street in hopes of finding an unengaged hackney coach, for Christopher had instructed his coachman to return home as soon as the accident was cleared.

The ladies were walking together, arms linked, and were naturally talking about the play. "Miss Foote may be the most beautiful woman I have ever seen," said Georgiana.

"I agree, and her portrayal of Amanthis was captivating."

Behind them, Mr. Hartleton was frowning. "I was expecting a comedy."

"It was billed as one," said Christopher. "But I think satire would be more accurate." He stopped to hail an approaching coachman. "Would you care to join us at the house for refreshment?"

"It has been a delightful evening, and I thank you for the invitation," responded Mr. Hartleton, "but I must leave early in the morning."

"Then perhaps we can discuss the play further when we meet at Pemberley," said Mary.

"I would enjoy that." Mr. Hartleton tipped his hat and waited until they stepped into the coach before walking away.

Inside the hackney, which moved at a halting pace due to so many other vehicles, Georgiana peeked through the window covering. "Why do I feel I should know the playwright's name?"

"Elizabeth Inchbald is an actress, author, and playwright who also translates foreign works, adapting them to the English taste," said Christopher, evidently surprising the other two. He added with a grin, "I read it in the playbill."

"Any one of those occupations would be a remarkable accomplishment for a woman," said Mary with a slight frown. "But I remember something unpleasant regarding Mrs. Inchbald's association with Mary Wollstonecraft. I learned something about it when I was reading her work, *A Vindication of the Rights of Woman*. There was an unfortunate, public argument between them, but I must be wrong because it seems unlikely with those two forward-thinking women."

"Maybe it had to do with the subject of Mrs. Inchbald's play, *Lover's Vows*," suggested Georgiana only half-seriously. "Deidre Burnaby described it in a whisper as 'shocking'—although I don't believe she ever saw or read it."[42]

"I've seen the play," admitted Christopher, raising his hands in defense at their shocked expressions. "It was extremely

---

[42] It is not surprising that both Mary and Georgiana were incorrect in their assumptions about the feud between the two women, for the issue was complicated. (See citation in Selected Sources.)

popular, but she wasn't the original author. It was one of her adaptations, written by a German playwright who had an interesting perspective about how we live in this time."

Mary's lips twitched. "Have you been studying in preparation for discussions with my father when he comes to Pemberley?"

Christopher was saved from replying for they had reached home, and a few minutes later they were saying goodnight to one another after Georgiana claimed she could not keep her eyes open any longer.

In their chamber, Mary stood still while Christopher assisted with the buttons at the back of her dress. "You are frowning," she noted, having caught sight of his expression in the long mirror.

"Forgive me. My mind has gone back to recent events and some disturbing news." He paused. "I don't wish to worry you or to blacken Harry's name any further, but the house on Lower Grosvenor-street was his. That is, until his uncle disinherited him and the rights to the property were revoked."

"Do you think Harry used his house to help smuggle prisoners out of England and perhaps to learn secrets he then shared with the French?" She looked disbelieving.

Christopher shook his head. "There is no proof, but suspicions are aroused."

Mary went behind the screen to change into her night dress before joining him in their bed. "Have any of those taken prisoner mentioned his name?"

"No, but they have said very little so far." Christopher leaned back into the pillows with a sigh. "I fear I must tell you...we believe the courier was kept prisoner at Harry's house."

"How awful," she whispered.

They were silent for some time, until Mary asked quietly, "Are you awake?"

"Yes, just thinking how fortunate I am that you agreed to marry me."

"It is I who should be grateful." She snuggled against him. "I had already decided against that house, you know."

"I was hoping so. What do you think of *this* one?"

"It is ideal, except—"

"No library."

"Yes, but I feel very much at home here and will be sorry to go."

"Then we must do all we can to find something that suits you just as well."

~ VIII ~

At the breakfast table, Christopher took a letter from the salver. "My father has written from Vienna." He broke the seal and began to read, then looked up. "My mother finds the suite of rooms they were assigned to be extremely confining and my father fears it will be difficult to get anything better, given the influx of visitors from all over the continent." His forehead creased as he read on. "He insists it is time I resign my commission, and unsubtly inquires if we are expecting an heir." There was a sudden rosiness to her cheeks and he changed the subject. "How do you like your new desk?"

"I love it. What a wonderful gift."

"Have you discovered any hidden recesses?"

Mary set her crumpet down, eyes wide. "We did!" She told him about finding the blank paper and the French novel. "You may think me silly, but I felt sentimental and replaced both items as they were."

He tossed his napkin aside and slid back his chair. "Will you show me?"

In the study Mary was quick to open the secret cavity, and Christopher held the sheet against the window. "There are faint indentations here."

Without needing to ask, she went to her other desk to take out pen, ink, and paper so he could write a message to Colonel Fitzwilliam.

In seemingly little time, Georgiana, Mary, and the two gentlemen were standing round a table with an oil lantern directly in front of them.

Colonel Fitzwilliam explained, "To reveal what is written in invisible ink, heat, or some form of acid is most often used. Now, please focus on the page and memorize anything you see—there may only be a second or two before it disappears. I'll try heat on a small section but can't risk burning the paper. If that fails we'll rub it with soft lead, and finally milk or lemon juice." He slowly lowered the sheet.

"L, L, G!" cried Georgiana.

The colonel instantly moved it away from the flame, holding it so they could all see the three letters written there before they disappeared.

Christopher looked up. "There could be more."

"I hope so." The colonel again warned them to be vigilant and slid a clean piece of paper towards Georgiana. "If you would transcribe it exactly as it appears—and quickly."

This time, Georgiana furiously copied all the letters. Reading through them at the end, she shook her head regretfully. "If the language is French, these are nonsense words."

"You think it's a cipher?" asked Christopher quietly.

The colonel nodded. "With any luck, a simple one." He glanced at Mary. "We could all have a go at deciphering it. Would you ring for more paper and pens?"

"I will be right back," she said, and returned promptly with a hurriedly gathered supply of writing materials.

The colonel arranged quill pens, paper, and ink in four sets and motioned for the others to sit down before he did as well. "The simplest would be a message hidden in the third or first letter of every third word, or something of the kind."

"You show great confidence in our ability." Mary was already copying the letters as Georgiana had written them.

For a long while they worked quietly, each of them extracting different letters of the alphabet based on the simple system suggested by the colonel.

Suddenly, Georgiana leaned closer to the page, writing a series of letters at the bottom before drawing vertical lines to separate them. She reviewed her work and pushed the paper to the middle of the table.

Messenger Bogner's Singerstrasse Princesse de Clèves

"Can we assume Singerstrasse is the name of a street in Vienna? I'm not familiar with the city," said Christopher.

"Nor am I," admitted the colonel. "But it should be easy enough to verify."

Georgiana surprised them all when she suddenly rose from her chair. "I will be back directly—please say nothing of importance while I am gone!" She rushed out in a very un-Georgiana-like manner.

Christopher read the message once more. "It could be years old."

"Still, it might be of interest." The colonel was reviewing Georgiana's work. "Perhaps agents used to meet—or continue to do so—in the Singerstrasse. Bogner's could be the name of the place."

"Or a person." As he spoke, Christopher was already shaking his head. "That would risk exposure."

"And the princess?" asked Mary.

The colonel frowned at the transcription. "It looks like a French surname, but we need more information."

The door opened and Georgiana re-appeared, a bit flushed, holding a book. With something of a flourish she placed it on the table in view of the others.

"*La Princesse de Cleves*!" Mary looked up in wonder. "Is this the book we found hidden in the cylinder desk?"

Georgiana nodded vehemently.

Something caught the colonel's eye as he flipped through the pages. "I'll need to take this with me." He retrieved his jacket before addressing Georgiana and Mary. "I wish all young ladies could be as sensible as you two have been. Walk me out, won't you, Ashton?"

After the two men left, Mary gently told her dear friend about Lord Harold's connection to the house on Lower Grosvenor-street.

For a few moments Georgiana did not speak, but then smiled softly. "I see what you're thinking, but I assure you I no longer fear knowing the truth about Harry." She sighed. "Why is my judgement of men so poor, given the very good examples with which I was raised?"

"None of this is proof of his disloyalty to England."

"Yet the desk, the message, and the French novel named on the paper were in his house."

"Any of it could have been placed there without his knowledge when he was hosting those parties. Or, it was all put there after he was forced to leave." Mary rose with a determined smile. "If this were a work of fiction, I would cast Lord Harold as the misunderstood gentleman who sacrifices his reputation for the better of his country."

Georgiana took her by the arm as they walked out. "You are a terrible romantic."

"I never used to think so." Mary smiled as she saw her husband approaching.

"It is time we saw something of London together." Christopher rubbed his hands together. "Where shall we go?"

~ IX ~

On the following evening the three members of the Ashton party entered the salon adjoining the Penrose library, where their hostess regularly held her meetings of the literati. She greeted them effusively, at the same time motioning to another of the guests. "Here is Lord Exeter, who has been looking for you!" She then hurried off to greet a newcomer.

His lordship made a handsome bow. "My engagement was cancelled, so I was free to accept Mrs. Penrose's invitation." His glance went to Christopher. "I hope your meeting with Mr. W proved fruitful."

"It has, thank you."

"My pleasure. It is not often I have such an opportunity." His lordship eyed Georgiana. "Having decided to postpone the tiresome journey to Vienna, I have accepted Mrs. Darcy's kind invitation to the ball at Pemberley."

"I am happy to hear it, as will be others of your acquaintance."

He turned his attention to Mary. "Will you be viewing other houses, Mrs. Ashton? Or have you decided upon one?"

Mary shook her head. "The search must be suspended as we will return to Derbyshire soon."

At that moment Mrs. Penrose reappeared, with Miss Hutton close behind. "Nearly all the guests are here." Her searching glance went to the first volume of *The Turret Room* Mary held in her hand—Georgiana's copy in fact. "We will start by hearing a selection from each of your books, after which we will retire for refreshments and free discourse."

At her words, Mary had grown a trifle pale.

"Will you be the first to read, Mrs. Ashton?" asked Miss Hutton, apparently unbidden by Mrs. Penrose.

Mary looked directly at their hostess. "If you wish, I would be pleased to do so."

Mrs. Penrose clapped lightly. "Delightful! Come with me, ladies." She led Mary and Miss Hutton away to show them where they would be seated and where they would stand for the reading.

When Mary returned to Christopher's side she said quietly, "I rather wish I had not agreed to do this."

"I can make our excuses, if you like." A teasing smile appeared. "I feel a sudden ache coming on."

She held his arm. "When it is over, and we are home again, perhaps we could have a glass of sherry."

There was no time for further discussion, as Mrs. Penrose was clapping her hands to gain the attention of the dozen or so guests.

"This evening I am happy to say we have amongst us two authoresses, fairly new to the literary world, who have kindly consented to read an excerpt from one of their works." She swept her arm towards Mary. "First, we will hear Mrs. Ashton, whose works are published anonymously, and who kindly steps from the shadows...if only for this evening."

Accompanied by polite applause, Mary made her way to the portable lectern, placed at the end of the long oval table where the guests were seated.

Mary opened her book, took a deep breath, and began to read the chapter in which ruffians forced to a stop the carriage of the beautiful and wealthy Miss White, who was travelling to a relative's estate in company with her dear friend Miss Sweetling. Their servants had been left on the wayside, leaving the two young ladies to endure a harrowing ride to an unknown destination.

Miss Sweetling took her dear friend firmly by the shoulders. 'We must rely upon one another, for no one knows where we are, or where we are going. We must sustain ourselves until rescue comes or we manage to escape our captors.'

'But what can we do?' whimpered Miss White.

Miss Sweetling thought for a moment, then pulled a handkerchief, delicately embroidered by her younger sister, from her reticule. Without hesitation she began to tear the cloth into small pieces.

"'Whatever are you doing?' asked Miss White.

'Do you recall the story you read to me, about the two children who were lost in the wood? They left a path of crumbs so they could be found.' She tore the last of the cloth and held the pieces in her open palm. 'These are our crumbs.'

'Oh, I see!' Miss White immediately pulled a similar item from her reticule and began to tear.

Miss Sweetling bravely peeked through a gap in the shade to make certain her next action would not be observed. She then placed her closed fist on the edge of the window and released a piece of handkerchief at short intervals. When she had used all her own, she took the pieces Miss White had torn and did the same until there were no more.

'Will it be enough?' whispered Miss White.

'It must be.' Miss Sweetling's countenance reflected her determination. 'Meanwhile, we must prepare for the worst.' She saw the tears forming in her dear friend's eyes. 'You must not give way, dearest. I promise we will prevail.' After a moment's thought, her eyes grew bright. 'There is a way we can defend ourselves! If you hold out your hands I can demonstrate what I learned from a book on pugilism, borrowed from your uncle's library.'

Miss White, trusting her friend without reservation, held out her hands and an intense lesson in the art commenced.

Mary looked up from the volume in her hands, surprised to see her audience not only politely attentive, but apparently interested to hear more. However, it was her foresaid opinion that leaving them in that state rather than the opposite was advantageous, and so she closed the book and smiled, bowing her head slightly before returning to her seat between Christopher and Georgiana.

The applause she received was no doubt both gratifying and unnerving, but she had little time to reflect upon it before Miss Hutton proceeded to the lectern, clearly waiting for the applause to end before she would speak.

"My work cannot promise to entertain you with tales of

imperiled young ladies who feel it necessary to protect themselves. It is a true-to-life tale in the epistolary style, designed to bring attention to the absurd actions of those ruled by the acquisition of wealth, as well as the maintenance of it."

She opened her book, removed the marker, and took a steady breath. "I wrote the following as a forward to my novel more than a twelvemonth past, having no thoughts of reading it to a discerning audience such as is assembled here...like-minded enthusiasts for higher culture, who would demand in our writers a certain responsibility in what they offer to a world teeming with impressionable minds. What I wrote before the publication of my first novel, *The Miser Married*, from which I will be reading to you, continues to reflect my feelings about the unfortunate state of affairs in some corners of the literary world, and rather than re-phrase what I so carefully wrote, I will simply read it to you now."

She began:

> *To step forth at once, from the most impenetrable solitude, and present myself before the awful tribunal of the Public, is an effort so great, a transition so violent, that it agitates all my nerves, and, for the present, 'murders sleep.'*
>
> *My skill in the composition of various sorts of puddings has never been questioned: my epistolary talents have been commended by my few correspondents, and not denied by myself...*

Mary and Georgiana dared not look at one another as she read in entirety the familiar words of the preface.

Upon finishing that section, Miss Hutton chose not to read from the first letter, but a later one from the miser, his primary topics being money and the latest lawsuit in which he was involved. She then removed another marker from farther into the book to read a letter written by her female protagonist, Miss Mereval, who confessed to her dearest friend the shameful debt she and her mother had accrued, which was the reason they were residing in a cottage in the countryside, and under assumed names.

Miss Hutton interrupted her reading to say, "If only all young people could feel as does Miss Mereval, I would have more confidence in future generations."

She read on:

> *One word more, and I have done with this hateful subject, owing what I cannot pay: more hateful, far, than the loss of fortune, were it certain; for, of all feelings, that of having done wrong is the most insupportable. Concealment implies guilt. We have, indeed, been guilty. I must beg you to address your letters, not to your old friend, Charlotte Montgomery, but to your new acquaintance, though no less affectionate Charlotte Mereval.*

Miss Hutton closed the volume softly and inclined her head to acknowledge the applause.

"Thank you, ladies!" Mrs. Penrose approached the lectern. "And now, let us adjourn to the next room, where I hope you will enjoy the refreshments. I expect there will be many interesting conversations about the works, and the writers, to which you have just been introduced."

The guests dutifully rose and walked from the room, Mary hearing two women talking excitedly about Miss Hutton's story as they went.

Georgiana held Mary back a little. "I cannot like her allusion to your work."

Mary exhaled. "I am not concerned with what she said, but what will be said during the free discussion." She looked up at the ceiling. "I would so much rather remain anonymous."

Christopher held tight to his wife's arm. "If you feel faint, I will send for the carriage." He was not wholly teasing.

There was no need for Mary to faint, however, for when they stepped into the room a turbaned lady immediately invited them to join her group. "I read *The Turret Room* when it was first published, my dear, and enjoyed every minute. Are you at work on another?"

"Mrs. Ashton has just completed her fourth novel," said Georgiana proudly.

"What is it to be called?" asked one of the gentlemen politely.

"It is yet to be approved by my publisher, but I had thought to call it *The Bell Tower*," replied Mary.[43]

The others in the circle made kind remarks about her work before turning the conversation to the latest three-volume novel on offer. "*Waverly*, as it is called," remarked a man in spectacles. "Written by another author who prefers to be nameless—" his teasing eyes rested momentarily upon Mary "—though as the book was initially published in Scotland, might we understandably suppose him—or her—to be from that country?"

"Scott, perhaps?" suggested the turbaned lady.

"He is a poet!" exclaimed the spectacled man. "Those who write in that genre generally have no taste or talent for prose. Additionally, I have heard the book is one of adventure." He sipped his punch. "But, being a Scot himself, he *may* be acquainted with the author." He elbowed the man standing next to him. "Whoever wrote it must be a gentleman of some importance, for the three volumes together cost a guinea!"

This led to discussion about the rising cost of paper and the myriad consequences of it, until Mrs. Penrose appeared, the feather in her diadem waving.

"I am sorry, but I fear I must take Mrs. Ashton away from you for a few moments. Miss Hutton would like to speak with her before leaving us—she does not care for late nights."

Mary, who also did not care for late nights, swallowed her trepidation and followed her hostess.

Her fears regarding what Miss Hutton wished to say to her were proved unfounded, however, for after their initial greeting that lady said, "I congratulate you, Mrs. Ashton, on the clever introduction of pugilism into a novel, the treatment of which may serve as a lesson to impressionable readers. In this case, they can see that athletic prowess is not only practical, but admirable in a female. I have thoughts of incorporating like lessons in my next work and would enjoy meeting with you to compare ideas."

Mary was taken aback, but managed to inform the austere authoress of their imminent departure. "Though I would be pleased to meet with you when we are once more in town." Given her countenance, one could assume it was a true reflection of her feelings.

---

[43] Mary based the tale on experiences chronicled in *Mayhem at the Minster*.

Upon their return to Hertford-street, Georgiana declined the Ashtons' invitation to join them for a celebratory libation. "It has been a long day." She eyed Mary. "I enjoyed your reading immensely, and heard many compliments about your book this evening."

They wished each other a good night and the Ashtons went out to the back garden, with Bonnie at their heels.

"When you went to speak with Miss Hutton, many people told me how much they enjoyed your selection," said Christopher. "Some of whom had already read the novel."

"They were very kind. But still, I would not care to repeat the experience." Mary sipped her sherry. "By-the-bye, Lord Exeter offered to view more houses with us—" she looked up "—but I would prefer to continue the search with you."

"I'm pleased you recognize my value." He set his glass down. "My dear, there is something I wish to tell you."

His attitude had so changed that Mary unconsciously held her breath as she looked upon him with concern. "What is it?"

"When we first came to London, I wanted you to make the decision about our new home without prejudice."

"Christopher, have I been looking at houses that are too grand? You know I would be content with a cottage."

His lips twitched. "That will not be necessary. And no, the houses Mr. Nolan showed you are not too grand." He motioned with his hand. "It is about *this* house I wish to speak."

Had Mary described his expression in one of her books, she might have chosen the word sheepish. "This house?"

"Yes. I have a confession. It is not Aunt Hermione's, but ours."

Mary's brows rose. "Ours?"

"Yes. It was a gift from my father upon reaching my majority. I asked my aunt to take charge of it because I wanted to keep my situation private—secret if you will—especially from those in the regiment. My aunt agreed, but after our wedding she wrote to say it was time for her to reside elsewhere, and for me to give my bride a proper home. She plans to travel to exotic lands once she grows tired of Vienna."

Mary was frowning. "But what of her things?"

"The attics offer plenty of space, but most of the furnishings are attached to the house." He reached for her hand, which she willingly gave him. "We need not remain here, but you will have as much time as you need to find the perfect place." He paused. "Had I told you from the first, you might have felt obliged to settle here permanently."

"I must admit your strategy worked," said Mary, bemused. "Because I had the opportunity to compare this house with others, without prejudice as you say, I realize that not one of them suits us better than this."

"Mr. Nolan is happy to continue the search on our behalf, just to be sure."

"There is no need, Christopher. I do not care to search for something better." She smiled down at Bonnie. "This garden is perfect for her, and she has been playing with other dogs at the park lately. Also, Molly is quite content and frequently states how enjoyable she finds the company below-stairs." Suddenly, her eyes narrowed. "I suppose Aunt Hermione's servants have long been aware of your situation?"

"They are remarkably discreet, are they not?" He waited for an answering smile before lifting her hand to his lips. "You are a treasure."

She pulled back slightly. "There is *one* thing I would like."

"Anything."

"Before we leave for Pemberley, might we speak with someone about modifying the large room on the first floor, the one we rarely set foot in—"

"To make a library?"

"Yes, please. And when it is finished, may we go together to a shop called The Temple of the Muses?"

"It would be a great pleasure. But I must warn you, they claim to have over a million volumes."

"It sounds like a dream. But what of you? Is there something you would like changed in the house?"

"Well, I might like to have one or two of those bathing machines installed—one cannot allow Darcy and Bingley to get too far ahead of us in regard to innovation."

~ X ~

Sitting down at her new desk, Mary was absently humming a strain from the Couperin tune she heard Georgiana playing earlier. She opened each of the small drawers and doors in turn, half-heartedly searching for another hidden recess. Finding none, she arranged paper, pen, and ink and began to work.

Within the hour Georgiana came to join her. “I’ve never seen you write so fast.”

Mary finished with a flourish, set her pen in the stand, then applied the blotter. “It was easy, given you and I had already worked it out.”

“Before we continue, you might want Molly to see to that.” Georgiana pointed to the right side of Mary’s face. “It could become permanent.”

Mary touched the offending area and frowned at the ink now on her fingertip as well. “I’ve done it again, and I forgot to put on my writing sleeves.”

“Is something wrong, madam?” Since learning they were to reside in the house on Hertford-street, Molly had begun a systematic reorganization of the adjoining dressing room and was standing in the doorway.

“Miss Darcy thought you might like to see to this sooner than later,” said Mary, pointing to her cheek.

Molly went directly to the cupboard where she kept the special cream she made for the single purpose of removing such stains. “If you wouldn’t mind sitting at the dressing table, madam.”

Just as soon as Mary did so, her maid liberally applied the cream, counted twenty silently, wiped the cream away with a clean cloth, then surveyed the two affected areas. “I’m sorry, madam, but I’ll need to apply more to your cheek and will have to rub it in a bit harder than usual.”

Mary grasped both sides of the bench.

Georgiana, meanwhile, had finished reading what Mary had written and came to join them. “It is perfect.”

Without moving a muscle Mary returned her glance through the mirror.

“There.” Molly stood back, hands on hips. “The cream should sit for a while.”

“I will not touch it,” promised her mistress. “In the meantime, perhaps you would find Lucy and ask if she would go with you on a short walk with Bonnie." She eyed Georgiana. "And please bring Lucy with you to my study afterwards."

"Yes, madam." Molly, who admittedly looked forward to such walks, smiled and walked briskly out.

After she left, the two young mistresses slipped back to the study. "If we work quickly," said Mary, "each starting from a different end, we might have it bound before they return."

In the next few minutes the pages were sewn together, though not as perfectly as they might have imagined, at least on Mary's part. On the cover sheet was an evocative rendering of the heroine and hero, drawn and painted by Georgiana.

They had barely put away their needles when the two maids entered, and Mary was once more forced to grip the edges of the bench.

"The area will be red for only a short while, madam," said Molly. "I think if we had waited much longer to apply the cream, far stronger measures would have been needed."

Mary turned to look in the mirror, her eyes widening. "Thank you, Molly." She rose with dignity and led the other three back into the study where she and Georgiana stood in front of the desk, thereby hiding the surface from the maids.

"As a thank you for all you have done for us in recent weeks, Miss Darcy and I have prepared a surprise for you." Mary took the manuscript from the desk and held it out for them. "Miss Darcy did the artwork, and we worked on the ending to Elvira's story together."

"Truly?" Lucy's eyes were wide with wonder.

Molly blinked rapidly as she thanked them.

Later in the day, Christopher suggested a walk. "I would like to stop at Hatchards to see if they have the novel the literati were so excited about. *Waverley*, wasn't it?"

"It was, and very dear, so I understand," said Mary with a twinkle.

She and Georgiana required little time to prepare for the outing and presently the three were walking past the other houses on Hertford-street, their pace leisurely as they described Molly and Lucy's reaction to their gift.

"A colonel should always be brave," said Christopher with mock severity after Georgiana told him how they had decided to end the story. "Two lovers torn apart, sold into slavery to one kind and one evil master, and a daring rescue. I wonder what Miss Hutton would have to say?"

"I can well imagine," said Mary. "It brings to mind a fantastical novel we read together at Longbourn, about a young lady of good family, much prone to fainting, who refuses to marry the man she adores because he had a love affair with another woman at the same time he was wooing her. Why she bothered with him I cannot imagine, for there was no need for her to marry at the time." She paused as they politely acknowledged a couple passing in the opposite direction. "Despite his, er, transgressions, she still cared for him, and made him promise to behave, for two full years, exactly as a gentleman should—"

"—to demonstrate restraint!" Georgiana's eyes were bright. "Hence the title: *Self-Control.* I remember the book well. Self-control was something the man wooing her did *not* exhibit. The ending was so fantastical I was tempted to throw the book across the room."

"I am heartily sorry for recommending it to you," said Mary.

Georgiana adjusted her parasol. "You only said your family found it entertaining, though I can well imagine what your father had to say."

"He was critical, yet the first to suggest we continue to read it each evening." Mary described how her family members—save Lydia, who was by then married to Wickham and living in Newcastle—had read by turn. "When we finished the book, my father promised to disown any of us should we behave in the smallest way like the heroine." She paused. "Mamma found the story very romantic."

"As I recall," said Georgiana, "the heroine's father, on his deathbed, promised her to another man she had learned to fear and abhor, and who, in a final act of desperation and betrayal, abducted her."

"Oh my," said Christopher.

They had reached Piccadilly-street by then and a few minutes later were inside the bookshop, where an apologetic assistant informed them that all copies of the book had been sold.

On their return home, Christopher voiced his disappointment, explaining that he had planned to purchase the three-volume set for Mr. Bennet as well as a set for himself.

In the days following, Molly and Lucy were sent to numerous shops with a list of items to purchase for their mistresses and for Mrs. Bennet, Jane, Elizabeth, Miss Bingley, and several others.

The architect and the designer came nearly every day with plans for the new library, given that the work was to commence as soon as the Ashtons departed.

Christopher was less often with his regiment and was therefore able to drive Mary and Georgiana through Hyde Park in an open carriage, and on two different evenings Colonel Fitzwilliam rode with them along Pall Mall to see the dazzling gaslights, as well as those along Westminster Bridge.

Mary was frequently closeted with Mrs. Chadwick, who had gently suggested that any changes her mistress desired regarding curtains, furniture, paint, wallpaper, and the like, could be made during their absence. For this, Mary frequently asked Georgiana's opinion and the pleasurable days went by quickly.

On the departure morning, Christopher joined Mary and Georgiana inside the carriage at their insistence, for rain seemed likely.

Riding along the streets, they passed hawkers selling every kind of vegetable, strolling players calling out their lines, and street musicians playing violins and barrel organs. It was not until they reached the outskirts of the city that the cacophony subsided, and Christopher rubbed his hands together in pleased anticipation. "What shall we talk about first?"

Mary's eyes were bright, as if she had been hoping for the opportunity to share something new. "There was a fascinating article in one of the editions of *La Belle Assemblée* about the powerful effect music can have on animals."

Her companions both relaxed into the seat cushions, smiling as they listened to her summary.

— THE THIRD PART —

CHAPTER EIGHT

Pemberley

25 September 1814

~ I ~

When Elizabeth came to Pemberley as Mrs. Fitzwilliam Darcy, Mr. and Mrs. Burnaby had been the first to call upon the new, much talked of mistress to give her a warm welcome. It was a deeply appreciated gesture, especially given Lady Catherine's reaction to hearing about Darcy's intention to propose marriage to a presumptuous young miss from Longbourn.[44]

Hence, on the same day the Ashtons were having their first meeting with the designer and architect in London, the Burnabys were to be the guests at Pemberley for an informal gathering. They had recently returned home after spending the season in London with their daughter Deidre, and Darcy was keen to present his son to them.

---

[44] This was to be his second proposal, unknown to Lady Catherine, whose words spoken directly to Elizabeth were: *...Do not expect to be noticed by his family or friends, if you willfully act against the inclinations of all. You will be censured, slighted, and despised, by everyone connected with him. Your alliance will be a disgrace; your name will never even be mentioned by any of us.* (As recorded by Jane Austen in *Pride and Prejudice*.)

Sadly, the arrival of Miss Bingley, her 'French' maid, and copious baggage was to disrupt the carefully made plans. She marched inside the house, demanded to know the whereabouts of Mr. and Mrs. Darcy, ordered a passing maid to prepare a bath for her, then followed a footman to the family sitting room to greet her hosts as if she were expected.

"Caroline, what a surprise." Darcy set aside his newspaper and rose somewhat hurriedly from his chair. "Where are Charles and Jane?" (The Bingleys had recently gone home to Beechwood, but would return for the ball.)

"I have come on my own." Miss Bingley's tone was slightly clipped. "I noticed a tent near the cascade. Is there to be another celebration of the Chandlers' nuptials, aside from the ball?"

"The Chandlers have gone on a short wedding trip." Elizabeth had reluctantly risen from her own comfortable chair and handed Gregory to the nursemaid. "The tent is for the Burnabys, who should arrive any moment." She went to ring the bell for Mrs. Reynolds who, with her usual efficiency, managed to have Miss Bingley's apartment ready before she reached it.

Shortly thereafter, the expected guests arrived and Miss Bingley was down in time to meet them in the grand hall. She was freshly adorned in a charming dress of cream lace with complementing gloves, shoes, hat, and parasol. After an effusive greeting to 'Darcy's dear friends,' she took Deidre's arm and the two stepped outside, strolling towards the cascade as they discussed how to dress correctly for an outdoor ball.

Lady Catherine, habitually opposed to walking on grass and to taking a single bite between meals, had at first said she would not join the party at the cascade, but upon learning from her maid Dawson that Miss Bingley had arrived (without invitation), she changed her mind. Upon entering the hall her cough alerted the others, and Darcy made the proper introductions.

As they proceeded outdoors, Mrs. Burnaby asked Lady Catherine if she were acquainted with Lord Exeter, whom they had met during the season. She lowered her voice. "My daughter insists there is an understanding between him and Miss Bingley."

Lady Catherine looked down her nose at the other woman. "I have heard something about it, but, if true, I doubt she will succeed in the end."

Undaunted, Mrs. Burnaby turned to Elizabeth and winked. "The Miss Leighs will be with us in time to come to your ball, and I have ordered a new gown for each of them!"

Lady Catherine's eyes narrowed. "Who are these Miss Leighs you speak of?"

As they stepped out onto the lawn, Mrs. Burnaby explained that the young ladies were the daughters of the gentleman whose estate Mr. Bingley had purchased. "The two are gently bred, and delightful company, I assure you."

"Where is their mother?" demanded the great lady.

Elizabeth was first to respond. "Mrs. Leigh is a widow, and as she does not care for London Mrs. Burnaby kindly acted as chaperone to her girls during the season."

"Ah! I recall the name now." Lady Catherine expertly flipped open her fan. "I believe it was my dear friend Lady Metcalfe who told me of the reprehensible habits of the father, who lost his estate to gambling." She stopped walking to say directly to Mrs. Burnaby, "It never does to spoil those whose fortunes have changed for the worse. It would be far better to advise them to take a position as governess with some kind family. Without fortune they cannot hope to marry well, and should not stand in the way of others who are better endowed."

Elizabeth and Mrs. Burnaby kept their thoughts to themselves as they stepped inside the Ottoman-style tent placed near the cascade, where a soft breeze wafted across the water and into the covered area.

Caroline and Deidre were already seated at a small table, leaning towards one another in whispered conversation. Unfortunately for them, the proximity of water made their voices carry.

Lady Catherine marched past Elizabeth and Mrs. Burnaby. "What have the two of you been saying about Princess Caroline?"

Deidre was on her feet in an instant, her whimpered response to the question unintelligible.

"Stop sniveling, girl! Repeat exactly what was said between you!" Lady Catherine took one step closer.

The sharp tone had the desired effect. Unfortunately, Deidre had not the wit to anticipate the level of impertinence she was reaching (at least in Lady Catherine's mind) when she claimed that the princess was involved in a scandalous relationship with a servant, living openly with him in the city of Rome. "I learned this from a dear friend who knows everything about everybody."

"Your friend knows nothing!" Lady Catherine's walking stick struck somewhat ineffectively on the canvas-covered grass. "No one connected to the Royal Family would behave so!" She glared at the two impudent females before her. "It is a spurious falsehood, which should never have been repeated!" She stepped out into the open and said to Darcy, who had just engaged Mr. Burnaby in a discussion about fishing, "Nephew, you will please escort me back to the house." She sent one last chilling glance to the offenders.

Deidre Burnaby waited only until they were no longer in danger of being overheard to say breathlessly to Elizabeth, "Did you know the princess was excluded from all festivities celebrating the defeat of the French Monster?" She paused dramatically before tasting the ice in her dish. "Oh, this is delicious, Mamma. Our cook must have the receipt."

"Yes, dearest," replied Mrs. Burnaby with something like confusion.

Elizabeth stepped outside the tent when she caught sight of the approaching nursemaid. "I see young master Darcy is finally ready to join us!" She hurried to meet them.

When she returned with her son in her arms, Mrs. Burnaby held out her own to take hold of the baby. "He is adorable!"

Elizabeth's hesitation was barely noticeable. "He does still need his head supported."

"Of course he does, my dear." Mrs. Burnaby gently cradled the child and made cooing sounds. "Never fear, I will take great care with your treasure."

Miss Bingley, meanwhile, had sauntered out to join them. "I have not held young Master Darcy for such a long while." She stood next to Mrs. Burnaby, who, despite the broad hint, did not relinquish the baby.

"How did you leave Jane and Charles?" asked Elizabeth brightly, despite having received a cheerful note from Jane that very morning with no mention of Miss Bingley's plan to make a solitary journey to Pemberley.

"They are fine and Louisa is well, but Mr. Hurst's infirmity has the unfortunate consequence of a foul temper." Miss Bingley formed her most charming smile. "It struck me that I had done you a disservice by my absence, given my experience planning formal events, especially with the seating of guests and so forth—precedence can be so difficult for those unfamiliar with the intricacies of society. I can also help with details often overlooked, such as the calling of too many country dances, which might be frowned upon by the more auspicious of your guests."

"You would not dare to suggest the waltz?" Mrs. Burnaby sounded disapproving.

"Certainly not in the countryside. But in town, society is growing more comfortable with its integration." Miss Bingley took Elizabeth's arm to lead her a few steps away from the other woman, seeming to have forgotten all about little Gregory. "I can review the guest list, to make certain those of higher rank are treated appropriately."

Elizabeth stopped abruptly. "We have invited the whole of the countryside to this ball, by Mrs. Chandler's special request. She wishes it to be a celebration not only of the wedding, but also of the harvest."

Miss Bingley had begun turning her head back and forth halfway through Elizabeth's outburst. "I make reference only to the important guests. We certainly need not concern ourselves with the lower classes—the housekeeper can do that well enough."

Elizabeth kept her countenance. "I appreciate your offer of help, but Mrs. Reynolds and I, along with Lady Catherine—the mother of the bride—have the project well in hand. You need only concern yourself with looking your very best, for there will be more than one eligible gentleman—with sophisticated tastes—amongst our guests."

"I see." The smile did not reach Miss Bingley's eyes. "Then I can only wish you well in your efforts." She began to move away, but stopped, a vision in lace. "To which gentlemen do you refer?"

"Lord Exeter is one," responded Elizabeth, turning her head as she heard a little cry from the baby. "Please excuse me. I must get back to Gregory." Her hands did not unclench until she was near her giggling child, perfectly safe in the arms of Mrs. Burnaby.

The remainder of the afternoon and evening passed pleasantly enough, with the help of backgammon, archery, and chilled wine—and the fact that Lady Catherine claimed a headache and did not come down for dinner.

It was not until Elizabeth and Darcy retired to their own chamber that the mystery of Miss Bingley's sudden reappearance was unveiled in another letter from Jane.

Dearest Lizzy,

Rest assured, we are all well, but as there is little time before the next post I must get directly to the point.

No doubt you were surprised by Caroline's sudden appearance. It stems from an exchange she had with Charles regarding our servants—some of whom have threatened to give notice if we did not check her interference. This includes our excellent cook, the only one in the county able to re-create the Italian dishes we cannot do without.

Needless to say, Caroline did not react well to his gentle remonstrance, but still, we were quite surprised to learn she instructed her maid to prepare for immediate departure. The trunks were already taken down when she asked Charles (quite coldly) if she might have use of one of the carriages. Of course he agreed, but only after she would state her destination (she insisted you are in need of her expertise for the ball).

After she left, Charles surprised me by claiming he did not regret anything he said to her and even ventured to say it was late in coming.

Caroline also threatened to go to town on her own, but when she heard Mary and Georgiana would soon be on their way to Pemberley there was no further mention of it. I am certain she was too angry with Charles to suggest she stay at his house in town, for which I must be grateful, otherwise the servants there might have acted upon their threat to give notice should she ever enter without us. She could go to Louisa and Mr. Hurst's house, but she claims to be uncomfortable there.

Do not think ill of me for wishing Lord E would come

to the ball and whisk her away!

Your loving sister,

Jane

n.b. In Lydia's latest letter to me, written weeks ago and only just arrived because the direction is almost unreadable, she claims to miss England terribly but Wickham refuses to pay her passage. She is therefore asking us to do so.

Also, I believe Lady Catherine was wise to insist Charlotte join Mr. Collins at Hunsford.

"Oh my!"

Mr. Darcy looked up from the third volume of *Waverly*, which he intended to finish prior to Mr. Bennet's arrival. "Has something upset you, my dear?"

"Not me." She waved the sheet. "Apparently, Charles was obliged to speak with Caroline about how she ill-treats his servants, which is why she left Beechwood in a huff and is now *our* guest."

"Elbows and servants appear to be her weak points."

"Yes, they do." Elizabeth sighed and wandered over to an open window. "The rainbirds are singing." She rested her head against the frame to listen for a time before looking back at Darcy. "Do you suppose anything will happen between Caroline and Lord Exeter, or is it only me who sees his promise to attend the ball as encouraging?"

Darcy shrugged. "If not, there is always Hartleton. Charles claims his friend is so absent-minded that he needs someone to prevent him walking into the path of fast-moving carriages. He may not notice anything amiss with her."

The ormolu clock she had given Darcy chimed. "Fitzwilliam, if we wait any longer, Gregory will be sound asleep and will not take well to being moved into our little nursery." She glanced at the open door of the adjoining room.

Darcy set his book aside. "He *has* grown accustomed to my goodnight stories." Prior to leaving their chamber, he took his wife's hand and lifted it to his lips. "I do so love our private time, my dear."

~ II ~

The morning following Miss Bingley's arrival, Mrs. Reynolds entered the kitchen filled with the usual trepidation when having to ask something of the Darcys' prized cook. "I apologize for disturbing you, but I am obliged to pass on a special request from one of the guests."

Monsieur Renault deftly applied his heavy rolling pin to the extremely thin pastry dough. "Forgive me—I must continue or the butter will grow too warm."

"Please do." Mrs. Reynolds remained at a distance, hands clasped in front of her.

Monsieur Renault rolled the dough to near transparency, then placed a thin layer of pre-flattened butter atop it, folded it deftly and began to roll again. "You appear nervous. As Mrs. Ashton is not currently at Pemberley, I cannot assume you are here to say she wishes to observe me while I am creating my prized croissants."

"I believe Mrs. Ashton has forsaken cookery—at least for the present."

"I imagine the major is much pleased."

Mrs. Reynolds dipped her head in response and continued boldly, "It is on behalf of Miss Bingley I have come."

The roller went suddenly still. "Again, that dictatrix demands something from me?"

"Yes, I am extremely sorry for the inconvenience, but she wishes her meals to be prepared without any butter."

"Inconvenience! How she tasks me!" He sprinkled a trace of flour over the dough. "One of the under-cooks will prepare her meals." He grunted. "No butter! See how she endures." Had he set aside the rolling pin and crossed his arms, his decree could not have been more final.

"Mrs. Matthews, perhaps?" Mrs. Reynolds referred to a kindly assistant who had recently developed painful shins and did much of her work while seated, refusing to take leave even on full wages.

Monsieur Renault vigorously applied his rolling pin. "She has not the skills for such an undertaking."

Awaiting his decision, Mrs. Reynolds subtly put her fan to use.

After a few quiet moments he said, "I will see to it. But first, tell me why she asks this—how did you put it—*special request*?"

"I believe it has something to do with the fit of her ball dress."

"Aha! You see? Vanity!" He folded the dough precisely before wrapping it in cloth, motioning to an eager apprentice. "Put this in the cooling room and return to me at once; I have special instructions for you."

Much relieved, Mrs. Reynolds left the kitchen to report her success to Mrs. Darcy.

"You managed the situation particularly well," said Elizabeth after the good housekeeper described the scene below-stairs. "One day I fear we will try Monsieur Renault's patience too far." She released a sigh. "I have finally decided upon the arrangements for my parents. In the south wing is a lovely apartment with gilded ceilings, which my mother will enjoy. And it is also near the library, which would please my father."

Mrs. Reynolds scribbled a few notes, then looked up. "But Lady Catherine is in the east wing."

Elizabeth smiled. "Exactly."

The two then discussed final arrangements for the ball. "I believe Miss Darcy, the Ashtons, and the Chandlers may all be arriving on the same day." Elizabeth absently chewed her lip. "In fact, I would not be at all surprised to see the carriages for the three parties come down the lime drive simultaneously!"

As soon as the housekeeper bustled away to give orders regarding the south wing, Elizabeth began to write a letter.

Dearest Jane,

With Papa and Mamma on their way, along with everyone else, it is time you returned. Mrs. Reynolds assures me the geese are ready, and the blackberries are growing in abundance.

You must know what I am going to say next—please come as soon as you are able. Or sooner.

Your loving sister, E

n.b. Caroline arrived yesterday.

The afternoon letters brought news from her sister Kitty in York.

Dear Lizzy,

I have never been so disappointed in all my life, except when Papa would not allow me to go with Lydia to Brighton! My entire family will be at Pemberley for a wonderful ball, but I must be content with Mrs. White and her pug! I tried my best to convince Edward that all would be well on the journey to Derbyshire, and that you would be more than happy to have us at Pemberley until after the birth, but he was very stubborn and refused to think of it.

If Mr. Darcy will not allow you to come to York to be with me, when I am so lonely and grow more fearful each day, you must convince Papa and Mamma to do so directly after your ball.

To the wonder of some of those concerned in the matter, Mrs. Bennet had truly been a comfort to her two eldest daughters during their confinements. In retrospect, Elizabeth and Jane agreed their mother had demonstrated unsuspected practicality of a maternal nature.

The next paragraph in the letter brought a furrow to Elizabeth's brow.

I do have something to comfort me at least, for Lydia is already aboard a ship sailing to England, and she has promised to stay with me long after the child is born.

The next second, the heels of Elizabeth's mules could be heard clicking down the corridor.

She entered Darcy's study after a light knock and came quietly to his side. The master of Pemberley, a first-time father who had been awakened several times during the night, was relaxing in an oversized chair near an open window.

"Fitzwilliam?"

Darcy's eyes opened. "Yes, my dear?"

"I have news." She paused as he rubbed his eyes. "But perhaps it would be better to wait. Aunt Catherine will be down soon."

He took her hand. "Nonsense."

Elizabeth smiled and settled next to him in the oversized chair, her head on his shoulder. After a few quiet moments she murmured, "This is pleasant."

"Indeed, and it can continue to be so after you tell me your news—no matter how upsetting it may be."

"Then I shall begin with Mrs. Reynolds, who assures me that everything is in place for the ball."

"This is good news, but not surprising...and?"

"Kitty wants me to convince Papa to bring Mamma to York directly after the ball."

"A perfectly reasonable request. If I recall, you also wanted your mother when the time came near." He looked into her eyes. "Do I sense you are saving the worst for last?"

"You do. Lydia is reportedly aboard a ship sailing for England as we speak."

There was a brief silence.

"And where will she be stopping?"

"Kitty says she will come to York, but gave no indication of the seaport or stops along the way." Elizabeth turned her gaze to the outdoors. "She might intend to come here."

"Did Kitty mention if Lydia travels with Wickham, or when the ship departed the West Indies?" Darcy was frowning. "Even with the westerlies, the voyage should take several weeks."

Elizabeth was shaking her head. "I would give a great deal to answer your questions." She reached over to brush a stray lock from his forehead. "York is quite far from here, is it not?"

"Nearly one hundred miles. Why do you ask?"

"Assuming Lydia's ship lands near York, my parents might already be in residence and could discourage her from travelling to Derbyshire, or at the very least postpone a visit."

Darcy's look was sheepish. "It would be best to do so until my aunt has returned to Rosings. Wickham, if he is foolish enough to risk returning to England, is prohibited from setting foot near Pemberley, as he is well aware."

Elizabeth's dimples appeared. "After the ball, perhaps we should consider a visit to the seaside. Aunt and Uncle Gardiner are constantly asking us to join them."

Darcy's fingers intertwined with hers. "Sanditon is not so very far away."

~ III ~

Relations between Lady Catherine and Miss Bingley were excessively cool, one barely acknowledging the other's presence when in the same room.

Without the distraction of other guests, it was becoming difficult for Darcy and Elizabeth to overlook the situation, which was nearly intolerable, so when the gatekeeper's son alerted the house to the Bingleys' imminent arrival, the couple nearly applauded.

Lady Catherine chose not to join those waiting in the courtyard to greet the newcomers, but to Elizabeth and Darcy's surprise Miss Bingley did. Interestingly, she was dressed in a flattering travel costume, with a handsome satchel in hand.

"Caroline, are you planning to leave us again?" asked Darcy, shading his eyes against the sun.

Miss Bingley's chin went up. "Louisa has written. Mr. Hurst has decided to take the waters in Bath and wishes to leave just as soon as I can return to Beechwood."

"I had no idea he was so very bad," said Elizabeth. "But if you go now, you will miss the ball."

Further converse was forestalled by the sound of carriage wheels against the stone drive, and soon the Bingleys were standing in the courtyard with wide, happy smiles. That is, until Charles became aware of his sister standing at the door of his empty carriage, her eyes directed at him.

He leaned over to whisper to Darcy, "Has something happened again?"

"Louisa has apparently summoned her," responded Darcy softly. "The Hursts wish to go to Bath immediately."

"Indeed?" Mr. Bingley frowned and approached the carriage, not to help his sister inside as she expected, but to speak with the groom. Following a brief exchange, he said to her, "You will need to wait, Caroline. The horses must be changed."

"No, Charles. I need to leave now!" Miss Bingley stamped one delicately shod foot.

"You must be patient; I will not have my horses abused. I daresay Louisa will not begrudge the little time it takes." He eyed her with suspicion. "They made no mention of this plan when I last saw them—not two hours ago."

A slight cough from Jane recalled the presence of others.

"Very well." Miss Bingley sniffed. "But I insist you oversee the exchange, Charles, for it is imperative we leave without delay."

"Are you expecting me to attend you?" Her brother placed his hands on his hips. "Jane and I have only just arrived. Tell me what has occurred to bring about this sudden flight."

"I will not speak of it openly." Miss Bingley was growing ever more cross. "I had thought you would be happy to escort me back to Beechwood, rather than let me travel alone, but I see I must beg Mr. Darcy for the use of one of *his* carriages!"

"My dear—" Jane had moved closer "—might we wait inside?"

"Please do." Elizabeth included all those standing there. "I am quite sure we would be more comfortable."

Miss Bingley did not object to this reasonable request, though it was perhaps because she had neglected to bring her parasol against the bright sun and she was extremely careful of her complexion.

Darcy and Bingley walked in the direction of the stable, and the ladies went inside, relieved to be in the relative coolness of the grand hall.

Once the nursemaid had taken little Eliza and was enroute to the nursery, Elizabeth led them to the nearest sitting room. "It was good of you to come earlier than planned," she said to Jane. "Now that the day of the ball is nearly upon us, there is much to see to." She directed her gaze at Caroline. "Were you not compelled to attend to Mr. Hurst and his gout, I would have been grateful for your assistance." She sighed somewhat dramatically. "One *must* try to anticipate the needs of our guests...only yesterday I received a kind note from Lord Exeter, who asked particularly after you."

Miss Bingley did not respond, but after a few minutes of hearing various arrangements discussed, especially for the dancing platforms, she could remain quiet no longer.

"Given that I am the only one of us who has taken charge of an event of this magnitude, I cannot, with good conscience, allow you to fail. I will write to Louisa and ask her to postpone the journey."

"Mr. Hurst will not object?" asked Elizabeth.

"Once I impress upon them the dire need for my continued presence here, he must be content to wait." She tapped her lip.

"Perhaps they can come here for the ball, after which we could depart for Bath."

"It is an ideal plan, thank you." Elizabeth sounded appreciative. "I will ask one of the servants to inform Fitzwilliam and Charles." She did not say she would also stop briefly to speak with her housekeeper about the scheme.

A short while later, having left Miss Bingley and Mrs. Reynolds in conference, the two sisters were in the nursery.

Rocking her chair back and forth, her sleeping child in her arms, Jane asked quietly, "Did Lord Exeter really inquire after Caroline?"

"No. But he *did* write, so we may consider it a half-truth."

"Oh Lizzy." Jane's lips turned up slightly at the corners as she resumed rocking.

~ IV ~

Two days before the ball, Mrs. Bennet was greeting her eldest daughters effusively in the Pemberley courtyard. "My dears! What a trying journey! On the very first day, not an hour had gone by before I insisted we raise the top. The sun was torturous!" She pulled back to examine their charming countenances. "But we should go inside this very moment. Well-married or no, you *must* protect your complexions!"

Within moments they were inside, and Mrs. Bennet raised her gloved hands to her cheeks. "I nearly forgot! My sister Philips is so disappointed that they could not come with us! Mr. Philips had a sudden case to prepare—something to do with a trespass between two gentlemen with large properties who should know better than to fight over hedgerow boundaries...or was it the number of deer in their parks? No matter—Mr. Philips cannot be spared and my sister refuses to come without him." She took a fan from her reticule and began to wave it. "I must write to tell her she was lucky not to be riding with us. It would have been intolerable!"

Meanwhile, Mr. Bennet greeted his sons-in-law with quiet affection. Darcy, after hearing him say he would like to stretch his legs a bit, suggested a visit to the stables. "If you choose your mount straightaway we can go riding on a whim."

Mr. Bennet, who had not stopped smiling since he stepped down from his carriage, clapped him on the shoulder. "This is a fine idea, young man. Of late, Mrs. Bennet does not like me to ride alone, and I miss the exercise."

His wife might have felt a tickle on her nose when expressing her wish to visit the nursery as soon as she could change out of her travelling costume. "I long to see my grandchildren!"

Presently, alerted by Mrs. Bennet's excited voice coming from the top of the stairs, the nursemaids stepped into the corridor. They were holding their fingers to their lips, having managed to calm the excited infants only a short time ago.

Frequent visits between Pemberley and Beechwood had resulted in an undeniable bond between the two children and they were resting peacefully alongside one another in a single cradle. Little Gregory's nursemaid whispered, "Young Master Darcy would not be separated from his cousin."

Mrs. Bennet tiptoed to the cradle and peeked inside, waiting until her daughters led her away from the nursery before remarking upon her grandchildren's plump, rosy cheeks. "Those two are like little angels."

Elizabeth laughed. "Because they are sleeping, Mamma." She led the way to the apartment in the south wing, where Mrs. Bennet was delighted with the gilded ceilings, the rich, striped fabrics, the comfortable furnishings, and an unimpeded view of the lake. "All this *and* my own private sitting room! You are a dear, Lizzy!" She perched upon the edge of a softly upholstered chair. "And with these long windows, I can watch the geese even when seated!"

"This bell will summon your abigail," said Elizabeth just before that young woman entered, a trifle flustered, for she had never been in a house the size of Pemberley.[45]

Mrs. Bennet went with her to the dressing room to issue instructions before returning to the same chair. She sighed with pleasure as she sunk into it. "When do you expect Lydia?"

"Lydia?" Elizabeth's fingers rose to her temples.

---

45 Mrs. Bennet was forced to find a new abigail because her former maid had recently married the Meryton butcher's son.

"Isn't it wonderful? She will be here for the ball!" Mrs. Bennet was blissfully unaware of the sudden twitch under her second-eldest daughter's left eye.

Jane asked, quite calmly, "Do you know where her ship was to land, and when? In her most recent communication to me, she gave no indication."

"I cannot say exactly where or when she was arriving," responded Mrs. Bennet with a fluttering of hands. "But I do know that she wished more than anything to surprise you by arriving in time for the ball." She gasped. "Now I've ruined it!"

"We will wait to see what happens." Elizabeth unclenched her hands. "But I should speak with Mrs. Reynolds about accommodation, in case she does arrive without proper notice. Would you like to take a bath now, Mamma?"

"Indeed, I would," replied her mother. "Once refreshed, I can tell you the latest news from Meryton: Maria Lucas is engaged to marry the vicar's son! Just think, had I not intervened, Mary could well be married to *him* instead of to Major Ashton!"

~ V ~

Later that same day, the first to exit the Ashtons' carriage was their puppy, after which Darcy's prized spaniel, Samson, raced forward with a wildly wagging tale. In the next second the two were running towards the nearest pond.

Next to step out was Georgiana, whom Miss Bingley greeted like a long-lost friend. "You must tell me everything! How many of my dear friends did you see whilst in town?"

Georgiana, who had fallen asleep during the final leg of the journey, blinked as she looked round the courtyard. "Where are Louisa and Mr. Hurst?"

"They are not here." Miss Bingley waved a hand dismissively. "Mr. Hurst is comfortable at Beechwood and does not care to be moved, and I daresay Louisa does not mind missing the ball as it is to be something of a country dance."

By then the Ashtons had been greeted affectionately by their hosts and by Mr. and Mrs. Bennet, so Elizabeth suggested they go inside. "We can re-assemble in the family drawing room once you are refreshed. But no dallying; we expect Anne and James any moment."

As soon as the entire company (except Lady Catherine) was settled in the designated meeting place, Mrs. Bennet took Mary to task. "I have not had a letter from you in many days and am eager to know if you have found a house!"

"We did, Mamma," answered Mary, who then told the assembled company about her husband's singular strategy regarding the house on Hertford-street.

Mrs. Bennet nodded sagely. "It was wise of him not to tell you it was in his possession at first, for you may have set your mind against it."

"Or chosen it because of the fact," suggested Jane gently. "How typical of you to be so mindful of her feelings," she said to Christopher before turning back to Mary. "I imagine there are small changes you wish to make."

It was Christopher who answered. "One of the larger rooms on the first floor is to be a library—" he glanced at Darcy "—like yours here, but on a smaller scale."

Georgiana, meanwhile, wore a slight frown. "I had thought Mr. Hartleton would be here before us. And where is my aunt?"

"She has a slight indisposition and has been keeping to her rooms." Elizabeth did not mention the friction between that lady and Miss Bingley, turning to Jane. "I also thought Mr. Hartleton would be here by now."

Jane smiled at her husband. "He came to us at Beechwood yesterday after little notice, because he discovered that the Evelyn family—who have requested his aid with an ancestor's diary—were frequent visitors at Netherfield when Charles' elderly butler was first engaged there. Mr. Hartleton wished to interview him."

Bingley was nodding. "The two were closeted in my study when we left—I've asked one of the footmen to make certain the scholar is on his way here in the morning."

"We thought Richard might have accompanied you," said Darcy, his eyes on Christopher.

"There were a few things he needed to address, following our investigation. He said to expect him early tomorrow afternoon."

"He wrote to me about the courier," said Darcy quietly, his eyes on Bingley and Mr. Bennet, who were coming to join them.

Just then, through the open windows, they heard another

carriage coming up the drive and within minutes were outside once more, welcoming Anne and James Chandler back to Pemberley.

~ VI ~

By early morning on the day of the ball, the kitchen safes were brimming with blackberry pies and the ovens fired for roasting. Tents had been raised on the sweeping lawn, one with tables for cards.

Each of the ladies at Pemberley attended the hair-dressing party in the early afternoon, save Lady Catherine, who said she would have her coiffure done in private, as was proper.

The abigails involved had met to compare magazine plates showing the latest styles, and even Miss Bingley's maid (who claimed to be French, though Molly had learned she was born in Hampshire) shared two of her own images.

They assembled in a sizeable sitting room connected to the Darcys' apartment where individual dressing tables had been arranged. Upon each could be found bejeweled combs, ribbon, lace, and many other pretty things, alongside practical items such as plain hairpins and hand mirrors.

Prior to the commencement of the activity, Mrs. Chandler asked Molly and Lucy to twirl round so the ladies could admire the dresses they had made from her gifted fabric. "It seems you cannot help but make magic with your needles." She indicated her marriage dress, which she had chosen to wear a second time (thus unveiling a practical side to her nature).[46]

Mrs. Bennet, who had been conspicuously silent when in company with Lady Catherine or her daughter—about which some were amazed, but grateful—could not resist asking Mary's maid if all the gowns in the room were by her design.

"Not all of them, madam." Molly made a slight gesture towards Miss Bingley across the room, who was adorned in a deceptively simple gown designed to enhance specific attributes. "And, I had help from Miss Darcy's abigail."

---

[46] Lady Catherine had predictably objected to this seeming economy, but to no avail.

"My daughter is fortunate to have you with her still." Mrs. Bennet turned to Mary, eyebrows raised, before sitting down at the dressing table where her own maid was nervously realigning combs and hairpins.

Soon it was time for the maids to begin their work. With brushes in hand, they waited for Mrs. Darcy's signal before applying them with perhaps more zeal than was usual.

Mrs. Bennet turned suddenly to face her second eldest, nearly causing her abigail to drop the brush. "Lizzy, you never said whether you expected Major Ashton's parents to come for the ball. They seem to be forever on one journey or another." She turned back to face the looking glass. "It does make one wonder."

A flush covered Mary's cheeks. "They travel extensively, Mamma. In fact, Christopher's father was recently summoned to Vienna."

Elizabeth was quick to recognize her sister's discomfort. "There will be so many guests here, Mamma. We expect all the tenants, and it seems all of Lambton as well. It is too bad Aunt and Uncle Gardiner will not be here."

Meanwhile, Colonel Fitzwilliam rode directly to the stable without fanfare, shortly afterwards grinning widely at Darcy's surprise when he appeared, formally dressed, in the sitting room where they were all to meet. Lord Exeter and Mr. Hartleton had also arrived, but when they joined the others it was time to proceed outdoors.

Lady Catherine, in company with her daughter and son-in-law, was first to step out to the front courtyard, where buggies, carts, chaises, and grand barouches were approaching along the lane.

The guests were directed to the substantial open lawn, where the more active could play or observe archery, lawn tennis, and nine pins. Those who preferred a quieter pastime took pleasure in finding their place markers at the banquet tables (done at Miss Bingley's insistence, who surprisingly had Lady Catherine's support) before taking part in table games or simply in conversation. Wherever her guests went, it was Elizabeth's design to have light refreshments and beverages at the ready, with musicians playing works appropriate to each setting.

Freed momentarily from his duties as host, Darcy took his cousin Richard aside to ask if the mystery involving the courier was solved.

The colonel shook his head. "The primary suspect is our smuggler of escaped French officers, but so far he has admitted nothing useful to that investigation. There is also the question about Harry's involvement, but currently no way to prove his innocence or guilt. Yesterday I assisted in the composition of a sensitive message to Lord Castlereagh, fully aware that anything we send may be deciphered by Harry since there is no reason for the foreign secretary to doubt his allegiance." As he looked round at the guests near them, something caught his eye. "Speaking of Harry, is it possible our charge is no longer interested in him, but in a scholar?"

Darcy followed his gaze to see Georgiana in animated conversation with Mr. Hartleton. "Truly?"

"He was several times with her in town, in the company of the Ashtons. They seemed quite companionable." The colonel grinned. "Though I would have thought him better suited to Mary."

"Then I will speak with Charles about him." Darcy finished his glass of chilled Italian wine, brought from Beechwood for the occasion. "Let's join them, shall we?"

Bingley too had his eyes on their subject, and, in company with Mr. Bennet, came to where Mr. Hartleton and Georgiana were standing together so he could introduce his father-in-law to his long-time friend.

Darcy and the colonel joined them, followed by Christopher, who had observed his two brothers-in-law heading that way. They were just in time to hear Hartleton telling the ever-expanding group what he had gleaned from Bingley's butler.

"This diary you speak of—" Mr. Bennet reached inside a pocket for his pipe "—whose was it?"

"Mr. John Evelyn, but it was Sir Hugh Evelyn who visited Netherfield, according to Charles' butler." Mr. Hartleton also took out his pipe, with a quick glance at Georgiana, who did not object. "The diary is of great historical interest, though at first I feared that would not be the case, for the early entries consisted primarily of long descriptions of buildings and statues—Evelyn began writing as a young man when travelling extensively on the continent."

"What have you found of interest?" asked Lord Exeter, who had quietly joined them.

Mr. Hartleton frowned. "There was something I read late last night, which has me perplexed. Evelyn described a shining cloud high up in the sky, shaped like a sword—the point reaching to the north—and as bright as the moon. The sky was otherwise clear, and this phenomenon lasted from eleven o'clock at night until after one in the morning. He claimed it could be seen by the entire south of England."[47]

"Sword-shaped, you say?" Mr. Bennet accepted a lit taper from a passing servant. "How very intriguing."

"I thought so. Also of historical interest are his experiences during Cromwell's era." Mr. Hartleton watched as another servant held a box of peninsular cigars open for the gentlemen's perusal. "Oftentimes, there are significant entries interspersed with the mundane; I need to read carefully."

Georgiana, her attention on the conversation, was completely unaware of Elizabeth, Jane, and Mary's considering eyes upon her. They looked at one another in silence, eyebrows raised, before attending to Mrs. Bennet, who was describing the seaside house Mr. Gardiner planned to purchase. "And Mr. Bennet has agreed to visit them!"

What they did not see was Miss Bingley approach those standing in a circle with Mr. Hartleton, nor did they hear her say to him, "I so look forward to hearing all you learned from my brother's aged butler—one wonders why he keeps him—and how it pertains to your research." Her smile was its most charming, bringing a slight frown to Miss Darcy's otherwise placid countenance.

Seemingly unaware, Lord Exeter puffed on his cigar.

---

[47] Mr. Hartleton refers to John Evelyn's diary entry of 11 March 1643.

At the designated time a gong sounded, and the guests began to take their seats in the largest tent.

Harriet slid into the place next to Molly at the servants' table.

"Where have you been?" whispered her older sister.

"In the kitchen. But don't worry, Moll. I remembered to wear an apron this time."

"You have a bit of flour—" Lucy was pointing at the spot.

Harriet grinned and rubbed the tip of her nose. "It was very busy in the kitchen, so I helped Dora with the bread baskets." She smiled. "We were trying to remember the old saying about geese and Michaelmas, and I told her you would know it."

"Eat a goose on Michaelmas Day, want not for money all the year," said Molly.

"Even though it is a day late, I hope to have my fill tonight." Harriet laughed and took a manchet from the basket passed to her by Mrs. Chandler's abigail.

Before the blackberry pies were served, Mr. Darcy stood and asked the entire company to raise their glasses. He thanked all those who made the successful harvest possible, praising their persistence and industry, much to the satisfaction of most of the people assembled there.

Shortly after the dessert course, during which the blackberries were proclaimed the plumpest in years, the ball commenced.

The Chandlers were the lead couple for the first formal dance, and all was going just as Elizabeth had hoped until the middle of the third set when an urgent message was brought to Mr. Darcy by a breathless young man who had ridden all the way from Lambton by the light of the moon.

Darcy took advantage of the light from a nearby torch to read it, looking up with a far more serious countenance than moments before. "I need to speak with your father, Lizzy."

"What is it, Fitzwilliam?"

Darcy held the message for her to read.

"Lydia." She breathed the name.

"Will you come with me?"

"Of course." She held tightly to her husband's hand as he led her through a multitude of guests, stopping frequently to say a few words before moving on, as if they were without a care in the world.

Upon reaching Mr. Bennet, they took him aside and he read the note quickly, his countenance suddenly grave. "I think we should keep this to ourselves, my son." He was quite calm, considering the news he had just read about his youngest daughter. "We gain nothing by sharing this news tonight."

Darcy and Elizabeth agreed and the three rejoined the unsuspecting guests with determination, appearing to fully enjoy the dancing, the bonfire, and finally the supper, until they waved a cheery goodbye to those returning to their own homes, or wished a pleasant goodnight to the guests remaining at Pemberley.

CHAPTER NINE

~ I ~

(A Letter from Mrs. Bennet to Mrs. Long)

Pemberley
1 October 1814

My dear Mrs. Long,

I write in haste because there is little time to report many things. First of all, Mr. Bennet and I will not be returning to Longbourn as planned, but will instead leave this beautiful house to begin the long journey to York where we can watch over our dear Kitty during her final weeks of confinement.

Secondly, you cannot imagine what has happened to my dear, dear Lydia! She was on a ship, sailing to England—I believe I spoke with you about her plan to do so—when it was taken by an American warship and all the passengers were declared prisoners! (Why must they persist in this idea of separating from our great country, I ask you?) As you can imagine, I suffered from nerves so badly that sal volatile was necessary.

Luckily, on the very next day we were sent word of dear Lydia's safe arrival on English soil. We were further comforted by a note from Lydia herself, currently under the protection of a kind family with whom she is travelling to York (instead of Derbyshire). She is to reside with Kitty and Mr. Darnell, whilst we will stay in Major Ashton and Mary's house, remaining there until Kitty is safely delivered of her first child. I will write again when we are settled, by which time I hope to know more details about Lydia's horrifying experience.

Now that we no longer fear the worst, all is felicity here. I must admit to looking back on the past with wonder, for my Lizzy and Mr. Darcy are perfectly matched, just as are my dear Jane and Mr. Bingley. Even Mary has been fortunate in her choice of husband. Only yesterday, Mr. Bennet remarked upon how we hear laughter in this house so often that we cannot doubt the wisdom of our daughters in accepting these gentlemen.

There is another young married couple here: Miss Anne de Bourgh of Rosings Park, as she was, is now Mrs. James Chandler. She is perfectly charming and amiable (nothing like her mother). Mr. Chandler is perhaps the quietest of all the gentlemen here—except for Mr. Hartleton, a studious friend of Mr. Bingley's. Mr. Bennet spends a good deal of time in conversation with those two, mainly about books it seems.

I must dress now for the special outing Elizabeth has planned for our final day on this grand estate. Please send word to me in York should either Mr. Collins or Charlotte return to Hertfordshire in our absence. I cannot abide them upsetting the Hills.

Speaking of Mr. and Mrs. Collins, Mr. Darcy's aunt, Lady Catherine de Bourgh, sent them back to Hunsford with a flea in their ears, from what I understand. I hope the experience teaches them to remain where their duty lies.

Yours affly,
Cassandra Bennet

~ II ~

(A Letter from Molly Turner to Mrs. Turner)

Pemberley
3 October 1814

Dear Mum,

The outside ball was not at all like what we read about in the ladies' magazines. Even Harriet had fun during the country dances.

Did you know she has taken to cookery? The French chef here has been teaching her. She says she will not leave her post with Mrs. Bingley, but sometimes I wonder. Mrs. Ashton likes to remind me that if I choose to start a shop of my own, she will help with the business, as I told you, but with all the adventures Lucy and I have had, and all the freedom she gives me, why would I leave?

The servants here are happy, except when a certain Miss B visits. I would never have thought one person could make so many others miserable, but they say she has a different complaint or another demand every day. She left for a while and came back and now seems happy to stay. Lucy says it's because there are two unmarried gentlemen guests remaining.

There was shocking news the other day. Mrs. Ashton's youngest sister was on a ship heading to England when it was taken by the Americans. Don't worry, because it ended well, with an exchange of prisoners, just like in a story.

Mrs. Ashton suggested I should come to you for a visit this week, along with Lucy and Harriet, because we will be leaving soon. Major Ashton had planned to return to London after the ball, but the Darcys now want everyone to go with them to the seaside.

Your loving daughter,
Molly

~ III ~

(An Entry in Mary Ashton's Journal)

Pemberley
5 October 1814

The last time I took up this journal was in late August, which is neglectful, for when reading it I am reminded of certain events I have apparently forgotten, about which Christopher likes to tease me. The physician who attends Lizzy spoke with me a bit about my little memory losses and assures me it is perfectly normal after having suffered a head injury.[48] *It was he who suggested I read my old entries regularly in an attempt to stimulate the memory.*

As it happens, the message regarding the fate of Lydia's ship was received several days after the actual occurrence, for it was first sent to my father at Longbourn and taken to my Uncle Philips in Meryton before being forwarded to Pemberley. It is not surprising that negotiations were in place by the time we heard anything about it, and we had only to wait a single day before receiving the news about Lydia's safe return. Following an apparently amicable exchange of prisoners, she and the other passengers were taken to a northern port. During the process, Lydia became familiar with a family from York, who have undertaken to see her safely there. (This was clearly a relief to Elizabeth, who was justifiably dreading an incursion.)

Papa and Mamma will journey to York, and though she admired the model of our little house in York, she seemed a bit taken aback by how small the original must be. Christopher and I were very happy there, and I have written to the kindly housekeeper who I know will make them comfortable.

The Miss Leighs are remaining with the Burnabys and we are frequently included in planned outings—Mrs. Burnaby being a firm believer in distraction. The most memorable excursion was to the ruin of an ancient abbey on their property, something Mr. Hartleton wished to see. On that day I became convinced that my dear Georgiana's affection is once more engaged, for I saw her purposely lead him away from Miss Bingley when she was

---

[48] Mary refers to an incident in *Mary, Mary, How Extraordinary.*

clearly intent upon joining them in the examination of the scattered segments of a statue. Since then, Miss Bingley has turned her attention back to Lord Exeter, who has remained at Pemberley longer than any one of us expected. Between me and this journal, it is a good thing she has a fortune to offer.

Mrs. Burnaby rivals Mamma as a matchmaker and it is becoming quite clear that she has chosen Richard for Deidre, who seems perfectly amenable. However, Jane, Lizzy, Georgiana, and I are certain it is Diana Leigh he wants.

This morning there was surprising news: Anne and James have invited Lady Catherine to their home in Scotland, and she has accepted. Interestingly, Anne sent for her own solicitor, who has come and gone, but for what purpose we do not know. There is much speculation, but without fact it is a useless pastime. Therefore, I will avoid conjecture but wonder if it has something to do with the Miss Leighs, of whom she has grown quite fond, and whom she has invited to her new home in Scotland.

Mamma believes I had better prepare myself, for how could Molly, who shows such great ability in dressmaking, wish to remain a lady's maid? At present I see no immediate need to fear, for each time I suggest she has a shop of her own, which Christopher and I have agreed to support monetarily, she claims to enjoy her current way of life too much. However, she did blush a bit whilst admitting that should she ever wish to marry she might consider a change. She and Lucy are close to marriageable age now and would make charming partners for someone worthy of them. They are each far too pretty and were engaged for every dance at the ball.

Christopher has just put down his book to remind me how soon we must leave for another outing. We are to go to a place called Dovedale, where the River Dove is highly praised for fine fishing. Coincidentally, Christopher found an enticing description of the area in The Compleat Angler, *a book he hopes to discuss with Papa. Apparently, there is much nature to admire, including great limestone formations.*

~ IV ~

(A Letter from Georgiana Darcy to Mrs. Annesley)

Pemberley
6 October 1814

My Dear Mrs. Annesley,

Since I last wrote there has been another adventure, the result of which has shown me once more how little I can trust my own judgement. Choosing the very worst of men is a pattern I thought to have broken, and the only solution I see now is to remain a spinster. I would be free to do so many things, including taking a larger role in the charitable works Mary and I have begun to support. Truly, the picture is not at all an unpleasant one.

There is a dear friend of Charles Bingley's who is staying with us at present with whom I enjoy conversing. Even though I have no thoughts of romance, it is still vexing to watch Miss B's manipulations. Was it not you who first pointed out her propensity for stealing the attention of certain gentlemen away from me? This one is of a scholarly bent and a bit absent-minded—not her usual prey. If flirting with him is her way of making Lord E jealous, it does not seem to be effective for other than dancing one set together at the ball they have had little contact or conversation. More notably, Lord E left us yesterday. Poor Jane and Mr. Bingley!

Recently, Elizabeth's youngest sister was aboard a ship that was overtaken by an American frigate. After an exchange of prisoners, she has gone to York but has written nothing of substance in her letters, so we still do not know if Mr. W is with her!

By-the-bye, my cousin Anne and her husband came across Lord Wickford on their wedding-trip, and though his manner was quite cool he did introduce his companion, who by all accounts he hopes to marry. Lord Exeter knows of her family, and says her fortune is substantial. I wonder if you have met, or heard of her—she is called Miss Dunbar.

Another point of interest is regarding my cousin Richard. You no doubt recall my writing about the Miss Leighs, especially Miss Diana, who was so good to Mary following that terrible accident. During the ball he spoke with Diana at length, all the while looking as I have never seen him look before, and danced two sets with her (I have mentioned his dislike of the activity). Anne noticed this as well and asked me particularly about his feelings for Diana, surprised to hear my opinion that due to his lack of fortune he would not propose to her.

Elizabeth and Fitzwilliam send their best wishes to you and your sister, and have asked me to make a special point of inviting you both to Pemberley in December, for having experienced the success of the harvest ball they now desire to hold one at Christmas.

I must add that what my sister-in-law referred to as a 'parley' was highly successful. My aunt is at this very moment travelling with Anne and Mr. Chandler to his ancestral home in Scotland.

In a few days we are to go to the seaside, where Mary's Aunt and Uncle Gardiner are residing. Fitzwilliam has found us a house and I must admit to being quite excited about the prospect, though I will miss the conversation of my new friend, Mr. H, who plans to remain in Derbyshire to continue his research.

Yours most affectionately,

G. Darcy

The tale continues in

Villainy in Vienna
~ or ~
Scul-duggery in Sanditon

by S.M. Klassen

(sample chapter in following pages)

ACKNOWLEDGEMENTS

Without Jane Austen's six novels, the two she did not complete, her juvenilia, and her remaining letters, there would be a great void in this world. Wishing that she had written many more, I began to write my first continuation, *Mary, Mary, Not So Ordinary*, choosing the much-abused Mary Bennet as a protagonist, who, it seems, was hiding behind a pedantic manner and a pair of spectacles. Since then I have written several more adventures, hoping to keep the characters from *Pride and Prejudice* (and from some of Miss Austen's other works) alive.

Thank you to all those who read and enjoy these books, and to my friends and family for being so supportive.

Sample Chapter

Villainy in Vienna

– or –

Scul-duggery in Sanditon

by S.M. Klassen

2nd edition, published by Hobbins & Donavon Press

Chapter 1

~a letter from Georgiana Darcy to her former companion~
Sanditon House, October 1814

Dear Mrs. Annesley,

As you are aware, my cousin Anne de Bourgh left Lord Wickford at the alter last June and eloped to Scotland with Mr. James Chandler. At the time, Lady Catherine refused to acknowledge the union and arranged to disinherit her daughter irrevocably.

Despite little reason to do so, Mrs. Darcy held fast to the hope of a reconciliation and devised a parlance of sorts at Pemberley, her scheme being to reunite mother and daughter by holding a second wedding in our chapel. It was some time before Lady Catherine agreed to the plan, but only under certain conditions—one being that Mr. Collins would perform the ceremony. He obliged, of course, and, despite a bit of drama, Anne was eventually well and truly married.

After the wedding, Aunt Catherine agreed to travel with her daughter and son-in-law to his ancestral home in Scotland. Considering the length and difficulty of the journey, this must be considered an excellent sign of improved relations.

Almost as soon as the carriages were out of sight, Fitzwilliam suggested a visit to the seaside. Specifically to Sanditon, where Mr. and Mrs. Gardiner have recently taken to residing during the summer months.

Given the fine weather we were soon on our way, in company with the Ashtons and the Bingleys. We stopped frequently, and after several nights at coaching inns we are now settled at Sanditon House, the grand home of Lady Denham. It is a fine place, to be sure, but set in the countryside. The Gardiners live in town and can walk along the seashore on a whim. (Fitzwilliam says we were lucky to find a house with so little notice and we are determined to be content.)

Miss Bingley and the Hursts claimed Sanditon is not fashionable enough, despite handsome assembly rooms and a long promenade beside the strand. They have gone to Bath instead, where they believe Mr. Hurst's gout will benefit from the healing powers of the water there. The distance from Pemberley is considerable, so they will probably not be returning to Derbyshire for some time.

The residents of Sanditon say the weather is unusually warm for so late in the year, which allows us to experience sea-bathing. Mrs. Ashton does not care for the shock of cold water (or changing out of a wet swimming costume in the bathing-machines) and therefore observes us from under cover of a tent on the sandy beach.

This is a place where nature is yet unspoiled and we take great pleasure in walking. As for society, the Gardiners introduced us to Mr. Thomas Parker and his family (it was he who convinced Aunt and Uncle Gardiner to purchase a house here). There is to be a gathering this evening at the Parkers' home, including his sisters, Susan and Diana Parker, and one of his brothers, Mr. Arthur Parker, a gentleman obsessed with his health. He consults physicians frequently but without fail acts contrarily to their advice, instead relying on his sisters' recommendations for treating what may in fact be imaginary ills.

In your last letter you asked after Lord Harold, who has been ordered to Vienna for the congress. You know I once entertained feelings for him but that has all come to an end. It is not only due to persistent rumours regarding his disinheritance, but recently Mrs. Ashton and I viewed his former home in London, which is for sale, and what we saw there has unfortunately led to further speculation.

Mrs. Darcy asked Mr. Bingley's school friend, Mr. Hartleton, to join us here. In the past weeks he has been using the Pemberley library for his research and chose to remain in Derbyshire to continue his work. He has with him his English Mastiff, a sweet, but fierce-looking animal. Recently, certain residents at the Albany complained about the size of the dog and as a result the two are quite homeless. He plans to return to London soon, for he is considering the purchase of one of the houses Mrs. Ashton and I viewed in his company, along with Lord Exeter. It is a beautiful place, though perhaps too large for an unmarried gentleman.

After viewing several houses, the Ashtons decided to remain in the house on Hertford-street. Christopher let us believe the house was owned by his Aunt Hermione, not by him, so Mary would not feel obliged to stay there, but she truly prefers it to all others. It is ideally situated and perfect in every way for them, especially now one of the larger rooms is to be converted into a library.

We are so pleased you and your sister will be with us for Christmas. My little nephew is an affectionate, cheerful infant, who has just begun to laugh and to grab his toes.[49]

Yours affectionately,
Georgiana

~a letter from Molly Turner to Mrs. Turner, October 1814~

Dear Mrs. Perkins,

Thank you for kindly reading my letters to my mother. I hope you and your family are well and that you enjoy hearing our news.

Dear Mum,

Harriet and Lucy asked me to send their greetings, as have Mrs. Ashton and Miss Darcy, who still help us with our letter writing.

Did the mustard paste help your cold? I copied the receipt

[49] Mrs. Annesley's sister is Mrs. Halifax, a midwife, who presided at Gregory Darcy's birth in June.

from a book in the stillroom at Pemberley. There is a little footnote saying it can also take away the pain of a bee sting.

The grand lady whose house we are in has gone to visit cousins and left only a shy maid and an unhappy cook behind. It's a big house, and if Mr. and Mrs. Darcy hadn't brought some of their own servants from Pemberley the work would never get done.

On the way here the road was often little more than a narrow path. At times it was very rocky and on one of the days a carriage wheel got stuck on top of a boulder. Lucy and I were leaning so far to the side we thought it would topple over and be the end of us. After that, the road (you would call it a path) was covered by grass and the coachman could hardly make it out. We were so near the edge of a steep cliff that we held on to each other for dear life.

This house is not far from the town, which is right next to the water, and Mrs. Ashton and Miss Darcy said we should try sea-bathing. Yesterday, Lucy and I walked across the sand to what looked like a gypsy vardo (Mrs. Ashton says they call it a caravan). It was like those we've seen at the fair, but smaller. Inside there were plain benches and hooks for our clothes, with a door on either end. After we changed into our bathing-dresses, the horse pulled the whole thing into the water, and we had to sit down fast or we would have fallen. The dipper, as the bathing helpers are called, was strong as a man. She helped me down the steps into the waves and tied a rope round my waist before pulling me away from the shore (you can be sure I held tight to her rope). She stopped when the water was just below her shoulders and lifted me up and told me to stretch out, flat on my back.

Would you believe I was floating on top of the waves? I was thinking how lucky I was, looking up at the blue sky and puffy clouds, when I saw Lucy standing at the top of the vardo steps. She looked as scared as I've ever seen her, and the other dipper had to force her out.

Lucy says she'll never go again. If I do, I will alter the bathing costume. The one I wore blew up like a balloon in the water.

I must tell you about poor Harriet. The cook here complained about having to serve so many, being used to only the grand lady and her young companion, and never any guests for dinner. Harriet, being the kind person she is, offered to help and she's been in the kitchen ever since. Yesterday the cook gave her full charge of the apple butter, which she calls black butter because there's licorice in the receipt, which she said comes from Jersey Island, where she was raised.

Lucy and I helped peel and cut the apples, but later Harriet had to tend the fire and stir the mixture constantly, so we took on her regular duties. When I went to arrange Mrs. Bingley's hair, she said to do it in any style I liked. She is the oldest of the three sisters who have much in common but are still very different. One thing for certain is they are all kind mistresses.

The cook doesn't like talking at mealtimes and gives us fierce looks if we so much as whisper to each other, very different from Pemberley, where we are encouraged to talk during meals. I thought about offering to read some stories to them but don't think I will. There are some, I've found, who won't be pleased no matter what.

Bonnie, the Ashtons' spaniel puppy, has just come in to tell me it's time for her walk. I'll write with more news next week, and Harriet says she'll send a letter just as soon as she gets the black butter jars sealed with wax.

Your daughter,
Molly

End of Sample Chapter

Villainy in Vienna

-or-

Scul-duggery in Sanditon

by S.M. Klassen

2nd edition published by Hobbins & Donavon Press

www.ingramcontent.com/pod-product-compliance
Lightning Source LLC
LaVergne TN
LVHW091129080826
845145LV00008B/2099